In The Stars

Elizabeth Jayne

IN THE STARS
Author: © Elizabeth Jayne, 2012

ISBN: 978-0-9873521-3-2

Elizabeth Jayne Books, Australia

Cover design by: Bec Bennett I Firefish Creative Pty Ltd www.firefish.com.au

A catalogue record for this
book is available from the
National Library of Australia

Chapter 1

Not everyone had an understanding of the sciences as she did. Did that make her eccentric? Unladylike? Most definitely not, Millicent thought firmly as she hurried along the footpath, her latest borrowed book clasped secretly to her chest. She determinedly pushed the librarian's disapproving look from her mind.

A carriage rumbled past much too closely, bringing her out of her thoughts. Glaring at it, Millicent brushed her black curls from her face and set forth across the road. Her footsteps quickened as she neared her home.

Careful to keep the title of the book hidden as she entered the house, Millicent hurried up the stairs to her room. If any of her siblings caught sight of it, she would never hear the end of it. They never read anything more exciting than the monthly women's periodicals and could not understand her desire to read anything more in-depth, and her older brother just liked to tease her on any subject he found available. But this latest passion of hers was beyond their understanding. At eighteen, she should have been excited about balls and parties and her poor mother could not understand how a daughter of hers would prefer to bury her nose in an academic tome than shop for gowns.

But astronomy! Her pulse quickened at the mere thought of it. When the choice was between a bland novel about the adventures of a young woman constantly getting herself into trouble or the exciting tomes describing the universe and objects that lay within it then how could anyone possibly pass up the opportunity to read about anything so exciting as stars and planets and galaxies? Millicent exhaled as she sat on her bed and eagerly opened the book.

A knock on the door interrupted her and she hastily slipped the book beneath her pillow.

"Come in."

Her younger sister, Jemima, bounced into the room.

"What are you doing, Milly?" she enquired.

Millicent's lips pressed together at the abbreviation. Despite all efforts, her ten year old sister had never called her anything but Milly.

"I am not doing a thing," Millicent told her. "Is there a reason you are here?" She really wanted to get back to her book.

"Yes. Mother is looking for you. She says you have been gone a very long time and she is despairing of ever seeing your nose out of your books and is going to find a husband for you so he can stop you from reading." Millicent's eyes widened as her sister innocently recited words she had obviously overheard. "She is in her sitting room," Jemima added before skipping out of the room.

Millicent made her way to her mother's sitting room. A husband was definitely not in her future and she would make sure her mother realised this.

"Good afternoon, mother," she greeted. "You wished to see me?"

Mrs Addleton turned on her stool as her daughter entered. Her glance took in Millicent's unfashionably tall figure and Millicent quickly sat down before anything could be said on the subject.

"Yes, I did, my dear. Now, you may have heard that Mrs Everington is throwing a ball next month. It is going to be a very grand occasion and, naturally, we have received an invitation. We must begin making arrangements for a new ball gown right away, dear. I was thinking white would be perfect with rose buds adorning the bodice and perhaps a flounce to your hem with rosebuds dotted around it. I have seen a picture in one of the latest periodicals that has this delightful large bow at the back of the waist. I think that would be most attractive."

Millicent cringed inwardly with each uttered word. She could not, and would not, parade around a ballroom dressed like a flower with frills and buds hanging off her person. She was hesitant to dash the excited gleam in her mother's eye but really this was too much!

"Mother," she began in what she hoped was a coaxing tone. "That does sound interesting but I do have many gowns already. Would it not be just as well to wear one of those?"

"Good heavens, no! Millicent, you cannot possibly attend such a grand occasion in a gown others have already *seen*. Everyone, simply *everyone*, will have a new gown made especially and we will not be the only ones to arrive in second hand clothing."

Millicent was tempted to remind her mother that her ball gowns had rarely been worn more than twice and could hardly be called second hand, but held her tongue. A new gown seemed definite. Now she just had to ensure the flounces, bows and buds were omitted.

They discussed the gown for some time with Millicent making many of, what she assumed were, well-founded suggestions as to the colour and design of her ball gown.

Mrs Addleton held up her hand. "Millicent, enough. We will consult Madame Le Cruz. She will know best what is fashionable."

Millicent resigned herself to a visit with the modiste and the unenviable prospect of a new gown that was sure to make her look like an escapee from the garden.

Millicent was thankful for the book hidden beneath her pillow when she returned to her room. Her meeting with her mother had been quite deflating and she planned to bury herself in the words of astronomy and forget all about the ball. She groaned when a knock on the door interrupted her. She really needed to put a sign on her door. Ideally it would read 'Go Away!' but more than likely a suitable sign would be 'Do Not Disturb'. Somehow, she didn't think her mother would agree to such a thing but a girl could dream. Resignedly, she bid the knocker to enter.

"What you doin' Mill?" Millicent softened as her young brother popped his head around her door.

"Reggie, you must say 'What are you doing, Millicent?'" she gently corrected him.

"I did say that."

"No, dear, you did not complete all of your words, and you called me Mill. We have spoken before about the importance of you calling me by my full name."

He had walked across to her bed, his curly blond locks bouncing on top of his head, and stood looking at her in confusion. "But you call me Reggie."

"Yes, that is your name."

"Uh-uh. Mama calls me Reginald because that is my name and she says that everyone should call me Reginald. But you call me Reggie. So that means I can call you Mill."

Millicent blinked at the logic of her five year old brother. "When you are a young man I will certainly call you Reginald."

He grinned at her eagerly. "Will I be a young man soon, Mill?"

"You have several more years to wait, Reggie, but before we know it you will be fully grown."

"Will I be in the military when I am growed, Mill?" he asked, climbing on to her bed.

"You may do whatever it is you wish, Reggie."

He looked at the ceiling for several minutes. "I think I would like to ride big horses when I am growed."

Millicent smiled affectionately. "When you are grown you shall, my dear." Reggie's eyes glowed at the prospect. "But while you are still growing you must remember to call me Millicent."

"Alright, Mill."

"*Millicent.*"

"Milllllicent," he repeated carefully.

"Well done, Reggie. You are growing up already," she told him and he sat up straighter and grinned.

Scrambling from the bed, he made his way to the door. "I am going to play with Spot."

"Remember not to pull his tail. He almost bit you last time."

As he slipped out of the room, he called "Bye, Mill" and scurried away. Millicent sighed and shook her head. She still had work to do there, she realised.

*

The trip to the modiste the next morning was more disheartening than the meeting with her mother had been. Millicent could only watch in dismay as the two older women discussed her ball gown, completely ignoring her own wishes. She could see herself now, decked out in gauze and satin and whatever material the women could think of with rose buds and greenery hanging from her person. She would be a twirling garland and felt mortified at the thought.

"Mother, stop. Please, please, stop," she blurted.

"Millicent, dear, what is it?" asked Mrs Addleton. "Are you feeling unwell? All this excitement, I expect," she added to Madame Le Cruz. "This is the first grand ball my Millicent has attended."

Madame Le Cruz was sufficiently impressed. "Oh, then certainly we must make the gown as grand as can be to enhance the young lady's natural beauty," she gushed.

"Mother, I don't want rosebuds and gauze and," she waved her hand around her body, "all that fuss."

"Millicent, you just do not understand these things. You must leave it to me to make sure you are suitably attired for such a grand occasion. Oh, I almost forgot!" She turned to Madame Le Cruz. "I saw a picture of a gown with a large bow at the back of the waist. Do you think we could incorporate this into the gown?"

Millicent thought she would die on the spot. There was only one solution. She would not go to the ball. Not that she had particularly wanted to go in the first place but now she would definitely not be going. While her mother and the modiste continued discussing the design and fabric of the gown, Millicent quietly slipped out of the shop.

She hurried away, desperately thinking of ways she could avoid going to the ball. Perhaps she could become ill. That would be easy. She was sure she could manage a cough.

A hard body crashing into hers brought her steps to a halt. She cried out and stumbled. Before she hit the ground, strong hands grabbed onto her arms and brought her back to her feet.

"Please forgive me. I am terribly sorry," a male voice said above her. "I was not looking where I was going. Are you hurt?"

Millicent looked up, ready to tell this clumsy person exactly what she thought of people who raced around barging into innocent pedestrians. Clear, hazel eyes looked back at her. She blinked. The eyes quickly flicked over her, looking for injuries.

"Are you hurt?" he repeated.

Millicent shook her head. "No," she managed to get out.

He let out a sigh of relief and let go of her. "Good. I would have felt dreadful if my clumsiness had caused you harm."

Millicent pulled herself together. What was wrong with her? She had seen a man before. Perhaps not such a devastatingly handsome man, though. She gave herself a mental shake and took a step back.

"I am unharmed, thank you." She turned to continue on her

way.

"May I ask your name?" he asked.

"I beg your pardon?"

He smiled, and she barely heard the words he spoke next. "I cannot apologise properly if I do not know your name."

"Oh." He waited expectantly as she remained silent. "Millicent Addleton," she finally uttered.

"Pleased to meet you, Miss Addleton. My name is Jonathon Westercott." Millicent placed her hand in his and watched as he bent over it. He smiled at her as he released her hand and Millicent felt a tingle all the way up to her neck. "Please accept my sincerest apologies. I am glad you are unhurt."

Millicent nodded in reply. With a quick bow, he continued on his way. She watched his back for a long minute and then turned towards her own home.

Her mind was still in a daze as she entered her bedroom. Sitting by the window, she relived her meeting with the handsome Mr Westercott.

"Millicent? Millicent?" Footsteps hurried up the stairs before her door burst open. "Millicent, there you are! Never, ever, disappear from the shop like that again. I was worried sick not knowing where you were. I swear you gave me the most horrid turn." Mrs Addleton sat down heavily in the chair and fanned herself with her handkerchief.

Millicent stood as her mother entered and felt contrite at the worry she had caused her. "I am sorry, mother, truly sorry. You and Madame were so busy discussing the ball gown I didn't think you needed my presence."

"Of course we needed your presence. After all, it is your ball gown and how can we know what you would like if you are not there?"

Millicent looked at her mother for a surprised moment. "I am able to make a decision on the style of my gown?"

"Of course, dear. And I shall be right by your side to make sure those decisions will ensure you are the belle of the ball."

Millicent's hopes sank a little. "Could we please dispense with the rosebuds?"

"Rosebuds are perfect for a young woman such as yourself. Why, just everyone will be wearing them."

Millicent perked up. "Then surely, mother, you won't want me to be just like everyone else? Would it not be better if I stood out in the crowd by being dressed in a different manner?"

Mrs Addleton sat up straight. "I had not thought of it in that way. Quickly, Millicent. We must return to Madame this instant!"

She hurried out of the room, Millicent following closely behind, her hopes rising. If she must go to the ball, it seemed now she would not be attending dressed as a flower arrangement.

Chapter 2

Millicent sat beneath a shady tree in a quiet section of the park. Finally, she could read her book without interruption. Leaning back against the tree, she was soon completely absorbed in all things astronomy. Occasionally, she turned her eyes to the sky imagining she could see the planets described in the book. Her fingers eagerly flipped the pages as she read about what else lay beyond the world.

She sat back with a contented sigh and looked again to the sky. How wonderful it would be to see these things. There was no doubt about it, she would just have to get her hands on a telescope so she could see for herself. She could barely put into words how exciting that would be. Closing her eyes, she let her imagination flow.

A discreet cough brought her out of her dreams. She looked up to find Mr Westercott looking down at her. With a gasp, she quickly sat up and snapped her book closed, sliding it out of sight behind her.

His glance followed her movement. "Good morning, Miss Addleton. What a nice surprise to see you again."

"Good morning, Mr Westercott," Millicent replied as she tried to scramble to her feet in a dignified manner. It would help if she weren't trying to hide her book at the same time. He reached out his hand and she gratefully accepted his help.

"It's a lovely day, don't you think?" he asked her.

"Yes, very nice." A quick glance showed her that the book was in clear view. A step or two to the left should conceal it.

"Is everything alright?"

"Yes, of course." She stood perfectly still, her book now

hidden by her dress.

"The park is busy this morning, which is why I came across you. I was escaping the crowd," he added at her querying look.

"Yes, I often come to this spot when I don't wish to be disturbed. Very few people come this way." He nodded and stood watching her. Millicent began to feel uncomfortable. "Well. I expect you would like to continue with your stroll. Please don't let me keep you. It was nice to see you again."

He smiled. Not the full devastating smile from their first meeting but it was still enough to make her catch her breath. "Is that your way of telling me to leave you to your reading?"

Millicent blushed. "No, I would never be so rude … that is, you did say you were escaping the crowds."

He continued to smile at her and then his eyes slid to the ground near her feet. "What are you reading?"

"Just a book. Nothing that would be of interest to you, I expect."

"You might be surprised at how well read I am. I read all varieties of books."

"It's just a silly women's novel. Not anything a man would find interesting."

He pulled a rueful face. "My sisters are constantly reading such books and often make me listen while they read some exciting piece. Exciting is their word for it. I am sure I could think of another more appropriate one."

"So, you see my book would be of no interest."

He cocked his head. "It sounds as though you are eager to be rid of me. It must be a very exciting book. May I see it? Perhaps I should recommend it to my sisters."

He stepped towards her and Millicent took an involuntary step back. Unfortunately, it brought her foot down on the book and set her off balance. Before she knew it, she was toppling backwards, her arms flailing in the air.

Once again, Mr Westercott's strong arms saved her from a fall. Millicent was sure she had blushed to the roots of her hair. Then she noticed he was looking down at her book with a very curious expression on his face. She knew that any moment now he would turn and look at her as if she were some freak from the circus. In one swift movement, she scooped up the book, muttered something that sounded like goodbye, and hurried away.

Jonathon Westercott watched her go, a thoughtful smile on his face as she disappeared around a bend.

"Millicent, you must come and see this article. It is most interesting."

She had just entered the drawing room after hiding the book in her room and was trying not to think of her encounter with Mr Westercott at the park. Susan's words came as a pleasing distraction. She walked over to the settee and sat next to her sister.

"What is it about?" she asked.

"I know you are not very much interested in fashion, Millicent, but I think even you will enjoy this article about the fashions worn at the last Royal gala. It is most amusing."

Millicent looked at the article as Susan pointed out the more amusing comments. "Can you imagine anyone turning up to such an occasion with so many large feathers drooping from their hat? I swear I have never heard of such a thing but that is exactly what Mrs Draywood did. Where can she have gotten her fashion sense? And old Mr Nealy had two different stockings on," she laughed. "Perhaps he should employ a new valet." Millicent joined in the laughter as they continued to read the article.

"Oh my goodness, did you read that bit about Lydia Farnsworth?" asked Millicent. "The last I heard, she had managed to snare herself a very rich, and very old, husband. It says here that she was dressed in a flowing orange gown trimmed with purple lace." Millicent screwed up her face as she looked at Susan. "Her new husband must be almost blind to allow her to wear something so horrid."

"Who was wearing something horrid?" Catherine asked as she entered the room at that moment. At fourteen, she was two years younger than Susan and had the same golden blond curls as young Reggie, unlike the dark curls of her two elder sisters. She was a beauty and everyone knew that Mr and Mrs Addleton held out great hopes for a very grand marriage when she was of age. However, for the present she was as eager for gossip as any young girl and plonked herself beside Susan on the settee.

"We were reading the article about the Royal gala. You know, the one you showed me this morning," Susan told her.

Catherine laughed. "Oh yes, I think our parents would lock us away if we dared to turn out dressed like some of those who attended. I do hope these do not become the new fashions," she added worriedly. "If they do, I would have to remain very unfashionable because I could not wear anything so strange."

The three bent their heads over the paper and continued to discuss the apparent lack of fashion present at that particular event.

"Good morning, my dears," greeted Mrs Addleton as she joined the girls. "What has you all so intently peering at that paper?"

"Just the news from the Royal gala, mama," answered Catherine. "It is very amusing this week."

"Anything that brings Millicent away from her dry, academic readings has my full approval," said Mrs Addleton with a sidelong look at her eldest daughter. Before anyone could comment, which was perhaps a good thing, she continued, "Tomorrow we are to receive a visit from my old friend, Mary Farley, and she is to bring her son and daughter with her. I know

I don't need to tell you that I expect you to entertain young Petunia while she is here."

The three girls covered their mouths but it was too much. Laughter burst forth.

Susan was the first to catch her breath and uttered, "Petunia? Is that truly her name?"

Her mother gave her a warning look but said mildly, "Her mother is very fond of flowers."

"I dread to think what the brother is named," commented Catherine.

"Perhaps he is Marigold," suggested a laughing Susan.

"Or merely Petal!"

The three girls collapsed into peals of laughter.

"Girls! You will not make fun of our guests and their names," remonstrated Mrs Addleton. But her words fell on deaf ears and she eventually left them to their laughter. "I will remind you of your manners once you have returned to a more sensible demeaner," she clipped, and left the room.

Chapter 3

The arrival of Mrs Farley and her two children caused great excitement amid the Addleton household. Not merely for the fact they were receiving special visitors, but the girls were eager to see what someone with the unusual name of Petunia looked like, and also an equally strangely named male. Not that they knew his name, their mother had not been very forthcoming during the silent evening meal but the girls had conjured visions of an effeminate, flowery young man.

As the young man in question stepped down from the carriage, all three young women gasped. He was anything but effeminate or flowery. Susan practically swooned at the sight of the handsome young man standing on the footpath. If not for the discreet nudge in the ribs from Millicent, she would have continued to stare in a most ill-mannered way.

A young woman about the same age as Catherine was helped down from the carriage and she immediately spied the girls and made her way towards them.

"I have been so eager to meet the daughters of Mama's best friend. I am Miss Petunia Farley."

"So lovely to meet you, Miss Farley," Catherine greeted warmly.

"Oh, please call me Petunia."

"I am Catherine."

"I am Millicent and this is our sister Susan."

"It is such a pleasure."

They chatted in a friendly fashion while their mothers greeted each other.

"Girls, please come here," Mrs Addleton called.

They descended the few steps and Mrs Addleton turned to the other guests.

"May I introduce my daughters. Millicent Addleton, Miss Susan and Miss Catherine."

"It is such a pleasure to see you all again," Mrs Farley greeted. "You have all grown so much since we last met. A time, I daresay, you were too young to remember." She turned to the young man beside her. "May I introduce my son, Tristan Farley."

It was all Susan could do not to stare open mouthed as Tristan was introduced. He stood stiff and tall, deigning merely to utter a brief greeting to each of them before standing back and allowing his eyes to scan the surroundings in a bored and disinterested manner.

Millicent was not at all impressed by him. His manner was rude and she was glad they were only visiting for the day. She would have to have a word with Susan and steer that girl's mind away from her obvious interest in him. He would not do at all.

At a nod from Mrs Addleton, Millicent climbed the steps to the house and the others followed.

They all entered the drawing room where refreshments had been laid out. Mrs Addleton and Mrs Farley sat to one side catching up on each other's news. The four girls chatted while Tristan sat nearby. Susan kept glancing in his direction until she caught her sister's disapproving eye.

"Tristan, come and join us," Petunia said. "I am about to tell my new friends about our trip to the botanical gardens." She turned back to the girls. "He is very knowledgeable about flowers and shrubs and can explain the things we saw more eloquently that I could possibly hope to."

The four young women looked his way and he reluctantly moved to a chair near his sister. He glanced at each of the Addleton sisters present and couldn't help noticing the way

Susan continued to stare at him. He lifted his chin and looked away from her. Out of the corner of his eye he saw a flash of some emotion cross her face but made certain he didn't look at her again. He encountered an unfriendly look from the elder of the three and decided to focus his attention on the youngest, and obviously friendlier, of the young ladies. Petunia regaled the young women with stories about their recent trip and he added his knowledgeable information when asked but otherwise sat in silence. If he had to join in, he tended to direct most of his conversation to young Catherine whom he could speak to as he did his own young sister. It was either that or receive the unfriendly attitude of the elder Miss Addleton, or the fawning gaze of Miss Susan.

Fresh tea was brought into the room and Millicent poured for the mothers and then for their own group. As she handed Mr Farley a fresh cup of tea, his eyes held hers briefly in a questioning look. She turned away from him and passed tea to Petunia and her sisters. She was not about to let him think she liked anything about his manners, or lack thereof. At least his sister had turned out to be a most charming young woman. She and Catherine were well on their way to becoming the best of friends.

Voices were heard in the hall and the door opened to admit a very elegant young man in his early twenties.

"Harry!" Millicent hurried over to him and hugged him. "We didn't expect to see you for several weeks."

"Careful of the clothes, Mill. You'll make me all wrinkled."

Millicent stepped back and looked over her elder brother. "I must say, Harry, you are looking truly elegant today," she told him quietly so that only he could hear.

He looked around at the occupants of the room. "Please excuse my abrupt entrance," he told them.

His mother stood and walked over to him. "It is so lovely to see you so soon, Harry. Welcome home." She reached up and kissed his cheek. "Harry, let me introduce you to my dear friend, Mrs Farley." After introductions were made, she then turned to the young people in the room and introduced the visitors. "Your father is out for the day," she told him, "but he will be very pleased to see you when he returns. You are home for a while?"

"Yes, mother, for several weeks at this stage."

"Wonderful. We will have a cosy chat later this evening," she added and returned to Mrs Farley.

"Harry, would you like me to pour you a cup of tea?" Millicent asked him.

Harry pulled a face. "No, thank you. I think something stronger than tea would be preferable," he told her and walked to the cabinet against the wall. "Mr Farley, could I interest you in a drink?"

"Much appreciated," Mr Farley replied as he stood and walked over to join Harry.

The two men stayed on that side of the room and, much to Millicent's dismay, seemed to have struck up a friendship quite quickly. Didn't anyone notice his rudeness but her?

The only word Millicent could think of to describe lunch was interesting. Catherine and Petunia were seated next to each other and continued to chat throughout the meal. Harry and Mr Farley were as close as thieves and anyone would have thought they had known each other since birth. And on top of that, Susan sat beside her emitting sighs and throwing longing looks at their guest. Millicent felt if she jabbed her sister one more time in the ribs, Susan would be black and blue for a month. Millicent sat throughout most of the meal in silence, only speaking if she was asked a question directly. She kept half an eye on Mr Farley trying to determine what it was about him that caused her siblings to react to him in such a friendly manner. For herself, she still found him rude and distant and would speak to Harry the first moment she had. When she explained his manners since arriving, Harry would see just how ungentlemanly their visitor truly was and would ensure he was kept at a distance from their family.

Millicent had been mulling over the things she would say when she looked up and found Mr Farley watching her with what she was sure was amusement. She quickly looked away but not before letting him know by a single look just what she thought of him. She was very glad they were only visiting for the day.

"Why don't we all take a stroll through the park after lunch?" Susan suggested. "I'm sure you would enjoy it, Petunia."

"I would, very much," she agreed.

"Harry, you and Tristan can accompany the girls while Mrs Farley and I enjoy a cosy chat," Mrs Addleton added.

"Me? Walk through the park?"

"Please, Harry."

"Very well, mother, we would be pleased to provide them protection." He threw an apologetic glance at Tristan who gave a slight shrug of acceptance.

A short time later they were strolling beneath the shade of the trees. Mr Farley had somehow managed to place himself beside Millicent as the others continued ahead of them.

"Miss Addleton, I sense I have offended you in some way."

Millicent glanced at him in surprise. "Not at all," she told him politely.

They walked along in silence for a long minute. "Do you often stroll in the park?" he asked.

"Yes, I do."

"Perhaps I will see you again one day as you stroll along here."

Millicent couldn't help looking at him, a curious frown between her brows. His distant attitude was at variance with his words of seeing her again. She was not at all inclined to encourage him, though, and merely nodded. With relief, she saw Harry about to join them and took that opportunity to move ahead and join her sisters.

Susan looked at her enviously. "What did you talk about?"

"Nothing of importance." Millicent added no more on the subject. Susan's time would be better spent focused on her new friend and not her friend's brother.

They had turned around and were heading for their home when Susan managed to place herself between Harry and Mr Farley. "Harry, it is wonderful to have you home," she said.

Harry looked at her suspiciously. "Thank you, Susan."

"Mr Farley," she continued, turning to their visitor. "I imagine you are also absent from home for periods just like Harry."

Tristan looked down at the young lady gazing up at him. That women found him attractive was not news to him. They usually knew exactly what they wanted and used all manner of tactics to attract him, but they very rarely looked at him as openly and innocently as Miss Susan Addleton. He relaxed his stiff manner slightly and replied, "My business does take me away from home for short periods of time."

Susan opened her mouth to question him further when Harry jumped in. "Catherine is trying to get your attention, Susan. Perhaps you should see what it is she wants."

Susan gave him a speaking look and turned to Tristan. "If you will excuse me." She marched off to join her sisters.

Millicent took one look at her mutinous expression and knew that Harry had put it there. He had little time for schoolgirl flirting and, even though Susan was sixteen, he had yet to think of her as a young lady.

The remainder of their outing went smoothly and they were soon stepping through the front door of the Addleton home.

"We had the most wonderful outing, mother," Petunia

gushed. "I swear I could spend all day in such a place."

"Perhaps we can return another time. However, it is time for us to take our leave."

"Oh, so soon?" Susan asked.

"I am sure we can arrange another visit with Petunia soon," Mrs Addleton told her.

"Yes, mama. That would be lovely," Susan agreed, trying hard not to glance at Tristan.

"I hope to see you all again soon," Petunia said and hugged each of the girls in turn.

Tristan offered a tight nod. "Ladies." He turned towards the door.

They all followed him outside, finished their goodbyes and the Farleys climbed into the waiting carriage. Moments later, the carriage was rolling down the street. Catherine hoped to see her new friend very soon and Susan hoped very much that Petunia would bring her brother with her.

"What a lovely visit we had," exclaimed Mrs Addleton as they returned to the drawing room. "I am very much looking forward to seeing them at the Everington ball."

Susan's eyes lit up. "They will be at the ball?"

"Yes. At least, Mrs Farley and her son will attend. Petunia is not yet out and so will not be attending."

"I wish I were going to the ball," Susan said wistfully.

"I would gladly allow you to go in my place," muttered her older sister.

"Millicent, how can you even say such a thing? To attend such a grand occasion ... the dances, the gentlemen vying for your hand, the refreshments, the gowns." She sighed as her mind filled with her imaginings.

"The rooms are crowded, it is hot and tiresome. I would much prefer to be at home reading my ..." She stopped abruptly and covered by saying, "reading to my young sisters."

Susan gave her a disbelieving look.

Mrs Addleton frowned at her. "I think, Millicent, it is high time you put your books behind you and concentrated on your social obligations."

"I wasn't aware I had certain obligations, mother."

"You know perfectly well what I am talking about, Millicent. You are the eldest daughter and we expect your season to be successful. It would not do for you to be having another season when your sister comes out next year."

Millicent tried to hide the grimace that sprang to her face. She wished her mother wouldn't speak of these things out loud. It made it so much harder to pretend it was not so. If she were married, how could she possibly sit in the fields and look at the sky through her telescope? No, she would not marry and would have to make sure she did not attract anyone at the ball, or any other social event. So far she had been lucky, having only attended a few occasions and not been interested in any males in attendance. Some had shown interest in her but she had been able to put a damper on their interest without much effort. Nobody so far in the short space of this season had caught her eye. A vision of warm, hazel eyes swam before her. No, nobody held even the smallest amount of interest for her and it would remain that way until her parents gave up trying.

Chapter 4

Millicent browsed the library shelves, sighing in frustration. The selection of scientific books, especially those relating to the planets, was pitiful. Didn't they realise that there were some people who liked to read about this subject? Just because men did not frequent the library did not mean the stock of these items should be minimal. Now, if she wanted to read novels or learn how to keep a house or how to maintain an elegant garden, there were an abundance of books she could borrow. But she was not interested in any of these things. She moved along the shelves of scientific tomes one more time. If this was all the choice there was, she may as well select something.

Jonathon Westercott was waiting impatiently for his sisters to choose a novel so they could leave. He wasn't fond of wandering through the library and it was the last place he wanted to be at that moment. He had planned to wander through the park. Not for any particular reason, he kept telling himself, but you never knew who you might meet. But, instead, here he was escorting his sisters who were taking their own sweet time to make their choices.

He turned away from them and leisurely scanned the room. Books filled the shelves, reaching far above his head in places. A few gentlemen were seen but mainly women browsed the bookshelves. He walked to a section that didn't look like it was frequented much. On closer inspection, he found himself looking at scientific readings. He reached out to pick up a book when a movement caught his eye. A young woman had stepped into the aisle. She stopped suddenly when she caught sight of him and before he could utter a sound she spun on her heel and hurried out of sight.

Jonathon replaced the book and hurried after her but she had disappeared. He walked all around the room looking for her but she was nowhere to be seen. He stepped outside onto the pavement and scanned the street in both directions. She must have had a carriage waiting because there were few people around and none of them were Millicent Addleton. He cursed beneath his breath and slowly returned to the library. He went back to the science section and walked along the aisle, scanning the floor. On the other side of the bookshelf, resting at an awkward angle, was a small book on planets. Jonathon picked it up and turned it over in his hands. Twice now he had found this young woman reading such books. He was thoughtful as he replaced the book on the shelf where it belonged.

Millicent's heart raced as she pressed herself against the shop door. She was fairly certain he hadn't seen her. She swallowed, wondering how long she would have to stay where she was. Her answer came a moment later when the door was pushed open, forcing her forward onto the path. Her panicked gaze turned towards the library but thankfully Mr Westercott was nowhere to be seen.

Hurrying away, she turned into the first street she came to and slipped inside a small tea shop. A cup of tea was what she needed to calm her nerves. It was a quaint little store, the aroma of freshly baked delicacies filling the air. But her stomach was too churned up to eat anything. Instead, Millicent merely ordered tea and was soon pouring herself a cup from the china teapot placed in front of her. She sipped at the warm beverage and let out a sigh. Much better. A few more sips and she began to relax, her heart settling back to a normal, comfortable rhythm. Then her thoughts turned to Mr Westercott and she wondered what had brought him to the library. And the scientific section, to be more accurate. He didn't appear to be a man of science, although, if she thought about it, she really didn't know much at all about him apart from the fact he walked around without watching where he was going and liked to walk through the park. Oh, and he was polite. Nothing there led her to presume he was scientific. Then again, nothing about her would make people suspect it was her passion, either.

The door opened and Millicent almost choked on her tea. Pressing back into her corner, she prayed the new arrivals would not notice her. She groaned as her wish was denied and Mr Westercott murmured to his companions before approaching her.

"Miss Addleton, we meet again."

"Hello, Mr Westercott."

"Miss Addleton, please allow me to introduce my sisters to you," he said and, gesturing to the women by his side, he continued, "Juliette, Edith, and Lilian."

Millicent stood briefly as all young women greeted each other.

"It is very nice to meet you, Miss Addleton," stated Juliette Westercott, whom Millicent judged to be the eldest of the girls.

"It is nice to meet you also, Miss Westercott," she replied.

"Please don't let us interrupt your tea," she continued. "Come, let us find our table," she said to her sisters and, with a smile, they moved away.

Jonathon lingered behind and Millicent sat down, not sure whether to ask him to join her or not.

"Miss Addleton, did I see you not long ago in the library?"

"I don't believe so," she replied quickly.

"Clearly I was mistaken. I was there escorting my sisters while they searched for a novel to read," he told her in explanation.

"I see."

"I should rejoin my sisters. Enjoy your tea, Miss Addleton," he murmured.

Millicent was relieved when he left but watched him covertly for a short time. She had the strongest feeling that he knew she had lied about the library. The sisters glanced her way and she quickly lowered her eyes. They all seemed pleasant enough from the brief encounter but she didn't want them to find her watching them. Hastily finishing her tea, she left the shop.

Jonathon watched her leave. He wasn't sure why she had denied being in the library but he was glad he had met up with her again. There was something about her that intrigued him and he knew he wanted to know more about her.

"Why don't you go after her, Jonathon? Escort her home," Juliette suggested.

"I have no wish to escort anyone but my sisters today," he remarked and sipped at the tea she had poured for him.

All sisters gave him a disbelieving look.

"She is quite lovely," Juliette remarked.

"Who is?" he asked innocently.

"Oh, please, Jonathon, don't play me for a fool. We all saw the way you looked at her and the way you watched her walk away. It is clear to anyone who has eyes that you find her attractive."

"I find many women attractive."

"Suit yourself," Juliette told him airily. "But do not say we kept you from your heart's desire."

"Heart's desire?" he scoffed. "Juliette, you read far too many novels!" Lowering his teacup, he stated, "I believe I have an engagement nearby which I cannot break. I will return in one hour to escort you home." He excused himself and left the shop, his sisters watching him go with amusement.

Millicent returned to the library. With Mr Westercott out of the way, she could borrow the book she had carelessly dropped.

Once that task was completed, a quick trip home would have her in her room avidly reading all the book had to offer, her mind determinedly off Mr Westercott.

As she reached out to open the library door, an arm appeared in front of her and opened the door for her. Looking up, she found herself looking into the eyes of none other than Mr Westercott. Her heart sank. She could not borrow that book now, not with him looking on.

"Allow me," he murmured as he held the door open for her.

Millicent passed through and paused in the foyer. Mr Westercott turned towards the scientific section and looked at her expectantly. She hesitated, undecided which direction to take.

Determinedly, she made her way to the novel section and began perusing the shelves. She randomly picked up a book and read the cover. Boring.

Replacing it, she chose another and screwed up her nose. Unbelievably dull.

Millicent sighed as she walked along the aisle. She really didn't want to borrow any of these books but had little choice under the circumstances. She reached out and selected a novel that stated it involved a romantic heroine who experienced adventure after adventure as she escaped from the clutches of a dastardly fiend. Millicent looked at it in disgust but at least she could give it to Susan who seemed to enjoy such novels. She turned to find that Mr Westercott had disappeared. Her mood lifted. If he had truly left the library – even with the ill manners of not saying farewell – she could borrow the book she truly wished to read. Her spirits dropped when she saw him walking towards her.

Putting on a smile, which she hoped didn't look as false as it felt, she said, "I have made my selection," and held the book up briefly.

Mr Westercott held a book out towards her. "I think you will find this of more interest."

Millicent looked at the book he held in his hand. It was the book she had dropped earlier, the book she had been about to borrow before hurrying away from him. She groaned inwardly as she realised he knew it was the same book, knew she was reading astronomy.

"You are mistaken," she said in a small voice. "I have the book I wish to borrow."

His arm dropped away and she watched the book with longing. He reached out and took the novel from her hands, placing it on the shelf. To her surprise, he then lifted her hand and placed the astronomy book in it. She stared at it for several minutes in silence. Then, slowly, she placed her other hand on it and held the book close. Her eyes rose to his, questioning and anxious at the same time.

Jonathon smiled at her confusion. He led her to the librarian who ran through the borrowing process. A few minutes later, Millicent was standing outside the library, the book clasped in her hands, feeling slightly dazed.

"Shall I signal a hackney for you, Miss Addleton?"

"Thank you but my carriage is nearby," she murmured, gesturing to where her driver sat patiently waiting for her.

Jonathon walked her over to the waiting carriage and took her arm to assist her into it. She turned to him. "Why?"

"Excuse me?"

"The book." She didn't seem to be able to make sensible sentences.

He smiled. "I know it was the one you truly wished to borrow. I couldn't let you leave with one that obviously burned your fingers just to touch."

Millicent couldn't help the short laugh that escaped her. He was far too observant, but so correct in his observation. She looked up at him and was quite surprised to find him smiling down at her in a friendly fashion, her interest in astronomy not seeming to bother him in the least.

With a barely audible, "Oh," she climbed into the carriage and settled back against the seat as it rolled away.

Chapter 5

"Millicent, you look very beautiful." Jemima watched her sister in awe as she paraded in front of them in her new ball gown. It fell softly to the floor and, while Millicent had accepted the fact that it was to be white, she had managed to convince her mother to forgo buds and flounces. Tiny seed pearls adorned the bodice and the puff sleeves showed off her slender arms.

"Don't forget your shawl," Susan reminded her as she draped the silky slip of material across her shoulders.

Millicent gathered the shawl at her elbows, tugging her long, white gloves neatly into place.

"Tell me all about it when you return," Susan whispered as they all followed Millicent to the door.

Mr Addleton helped his wife and daughter into the carriage and they were soon on their way to the Everington ball.

As she alighted from the carriage, Millicent gazed in wide-eyed wonder at the large mansion rising before them. She had never set foot in such a grand building before and for the first time she felt some anxiety about the evening ahead. Mrs Addleton urged her forward and they were soon stepping through the large, carved doors into the magnificent foyer. Millicent dragged her eyes away from the ornate ceiling to exchange greetings with their hosts. Taking a deep breath, she followed her parents into the ballroom.

It was already busy with many guests and she looked around for any friends who might have arrived.

"Oh, I see Amanda. May I go and speak with her?"

"Of course, my dear," said Mrs Addleton.

Millicent made her way through the guests to her friend.

"Millicent, isn't this the most lavish place you have ever beheld?" Amanda gushed. "I swear I have never before in my life attended anything so grand."

"It took my breath away when I arrived," agreed Millicent.

The two young women strolled around the room, arm in arm, admiring the gowns and awe-inspiring aspect of the grand ballroom. Musicians began to warm their instruments and the two women made their way to the refreshment stand. Neither of them wished to stand up for a dance as they each had decided not to become attached to any gentlemen this season.

Amanda was not interested in astronomy like Millicent but she was most interested in drama and the arts. Much to her parents' mortification, as they chose to remind her at every opportunity, she wished to be on the stage. Even Millicent had tried to persuade her that this was not something she should pursue but to no avail. All Millicent could hope was that her friend would soon find another interest that was far more acceptable. In the meantime, she stood by her as a friend should. And it provided them both with the excuse to avoid dancing and provide company for each other.

Millicent was sipping her lemonade when she suddenly turned her back on the gathering.

"What is it?" asked Amanda.

"I don't want him to see me," she whispered.

"Who?" Amanda's gaze roamed around the room, looking for a possible suspect. "I can't see anyone looking our way, Millicent."

"Really?" Millicent slowly turned around, her eyes scanning the nearby guests. She relaxed and gave her friend a small, apologetic smile. "You must think me quite mad but there is a gentleman of my acquaintance whom I would prefer not to meet tonight."

Amanda's eyes opened a little wider. "You have a beau and you have not thought to tell me about it?"

Millicent laughed. "He is not a beau, Amanda. Far from it, in fact. However, he does tend to show up at the most inopportune times and I don't wish to have any encounters with him this evening."

"Of course not." Amanda's tone was clearly disbelieving.

"You know how I feel about these balls. I feel the same way you do and that means I do not wish to dance with anyone or become too familiar with any gentleman."

"Who said I did not wish to dance?"

Millicent looked at her, surprised. "You have often said you do not wish to dance for the same reasons. That you wished to go on the stage and not be deterred by any romantic entanglements. Those were your very words," Millicent reminded her.

Amanda shrugged. "Well, yes. Although, if a certain gentleman were to ask me to dance I may be persuaded."

Amanda's unusual coyness piqued Millicent's curiosity. "You have met someone."

"No, how could I?"

"Amanda Bladestoke, I have known you for several years and can tell when you are keeping something from me. Who is he? Am I acquainted with him?"

Colour swept into Amanda's cheeks as she looked at her friend. "I hardly know him myself. He is a friend of my brother's and paid us a visit a few days ago. I could barely keep my eyes from straying to him because I swear, Millicent, I have never seen such a handsome man before." At her friend's surprised look, she continued, "I know we have both sworn not to become attached to any gentleman but … oh Millicent, I do believe I may have some difficulty keeping to that agreement."

"Amanda, if you have met a gentleman who makes you happy then, of course, I am pleased for you. Just because we swore not to become attached doesn't mean it is a total impossibility. Does this mean you are not planning to go on the stage?" she added hopefully.

"I have not given up on my dream, Millicent. I know I could be a very grand actress but, to be honest, if Richard, I mean Mr Jenson, feels it would be best for me to pursue some other activity then I believe I would do so," she admitted.

"You are in love," Millicent announced.

"How can I be in love after only one meeting? It is laughable. Oh my goodness, Millicent," she gushed in a panic, "he is coming this way! What shall I do? How do I look? What should I say?"

Millicent let out a soft chuckle. She had never seen her friend so confused and self-conscious before. "You will greet the gentleman and if he asks you to dance you will gladly accept."

Two gentlemen walked towards them, one being Amanda's brother, Gerald, and the other obviously being his friend who had caused Amanda to almost swoon on the spot.

"Good evening, Millicent," greeted Gerald. "I have not seen you in quite some time. I trust you are having an enjoyable evening?"

"Good evening, Gerald."

"Allow me to introduce my friend, Mr Jenson. Richard, this is Miss Addleton. And you may remember my sister from your visit earlier in the week."

Richard Jenson bowed politely. "Miss Addleton."

His eyes turned to Amanda and it was clear in his manner of greeting that he felt as much interest in her as she did in him. "Miss Bladestoke, it is a pleasure to see you again."

"Good evening, Mr Jenson," she murmured.

"I wondered, Miss Bladestoke, if you would care to join me

for the next dance?"

"I would be delighted," she said softly and, taking his outstretched hand, Amanda floated towards the dance floor oblivious of the amazed look on her brother's face as they walked away.

Millicent looked at Gerald with amusement. "It seems your friend is quite taken with Amanda."

He made a noise that sounded very much like a grunt then with a very brief farewell he left her standing by the refreshment table alone. Millicent was not offended. She had known him for some time and was used to his unusual ways and knew his rudeness was not meant as such. Still, it was a little disconcerting to find herself standing on her own in this way so, putting down her empty glass, Millicent made her way back into the ballroom. A friend lifted a hand in greeting and as Millicent began walking in her direction, she found her way blocked by Mr Farley.

Her heart sank.

"Good evening, Miss Addleton. It is a pleasure to see you again."

"Mr Farley." Her plan to avoid him failed miserably.

"May I have the next dance?"

She did not wish to dance with Mr Farley at all but could hardly show such rudeness in the midst of such a grand ball.

"Thank you, you may," she agreed, and continued across the room to her friend.

"What has you looking so put out?" Sara asked as she reached her side.

"Mr Farley. He has asked me to dance with him!"

"And that is a problem?" Sara asked, her eyes wandering over the handsome man standing nearby.

"I do not like him at all," Millicent told her. "I had thought to avoid him tonight."

"Every other woman in this room will be exceedingly envious

when they see you in the arms of that man. He is absolutely gorgeous."

Millicent looked at her friend as if she were mad. "Then you may dance with him in my place. Please."

Sara laughed. "I don't think so but please advise him that I am sure to be available should he need a partner in the next set."

The musicians began the strains of the next dance and Millicent reluctantly turned as Mr Farley claimed her for it.

"Please allow me to tell you how lovely you look this evening, Miss Addleton," he said as they began.

"Thank you."

"I was hoping you would be attending this evening."

Millicent said nothing as she moved through the steps of the quadrille, silently praying for the music to end quickly. Her hand brushed his during the movements and he briefly took hold of her fingers, giving them a gentle squeeze. Millicent could be in no doubt that he wished to become better acquainted with her. She, on the other hand, wished to encourage no such familiarity and kept her eyes turned stubbornly away from him.

"You dance divinely," he told her. "There is no need to watch your feet or concentrate so intently," he added, mistaking her reason for being quiet.

"Thank you, Mr Farley, but I have been dancing for several years and do not feel the need to watch my steps."

"Oh. That is good," he replied.

Millicent felt a pang at her rudeness. There was no need for it. It was not as though he had made any untoward advances. Except for the finger squeezing, perhaps, but he was very polite. She could at least be pleasant for the few minutes they were standing so close.

"You dance well yourself, Mr Farley," she remarked.

He bowed his head in acknowledgement. "You are very kind, Miss Addleton."

The music came to an end and with a polite curtsey Millicent turned to move away from him. She found her arm being linked through his as she was led towards the refreshment table, instead.

"Allow me to obtain a cooling glass of lemonade for you, Miss Addleton," he recommended. "Perhaps you would then do me the honour of joining me for a walk around the garden?"

This was something Millicent definitely did not wish to do. "Thank you but my mother has requested my presence following this dance."

"Then you must not disappoint her. Perhaps we will take our stroll later."

Millicent made no comment but sipped the lemonade he handed to her. Placing the empty glass on the table, she said, "Very refreshing, thank you. If you will excuse me, I must take my leave."

"I will find you later for a turn in the garden."

Millicent smiled politely and walked away. Once she was confident she was out of sight of Mr Farley, she turned towards the french doors and slipped outside.

Breathing a sigh of relief, she made her way to one of the garden seats and watched the stars begin their entry into the night sky. With Amanda now spending most of the evening in the vicinity of Mr Jenson, Millicent had a lonely evening to look forward to. Not that she could be lonely. She had many friends in attendance at the ball but they did not want to sit out of the dancing and so Millicent was bound to find herself standing quite on her own for most of the evening. Certainly that was her own choice. She had nothing to complain about. It was how she wished it to be. There was nobody here she wished to dance with.

"Good evening, Miss Addleton," a soft voice murmured from nearby.

Millicent caught her breath. She rose to her feet. "Good

evening, Mr Westercott."

"The evening is quite lovely."

"Yes, it is."

"Would you care to take a stroll through the gardens?"

Millicent felt flustered. A feeling she was not used to experiencing, which made her even more confused. "I should return to the ballroom," she said quickly and began walking in that direction.

She had half expected him to follow her but a quick glance showed her he still stood where she had left him, watching her walk away. She entered the ballroom determined not to think about him.

Millicent stood next to her mother and watched the dancing. Amanda was completely besotted with Richard Jenson and spent most of the evening standing near her brother, who happened to be standing next to the said Mr Jenson. Sara had, thankfully, cornered Mr Farley and had managed to prevent him from seeking out Millicent for a good part of the evening. Mr Westercott appeared to have left the ball because Millicent had not seen him again since the meeting in the garden. She was thankful for that, although now and again found her eyes searching the crowd for the familiar mop of brown hair, at which point she brought herself to task severely and swore not to think of him.

"Mrs Addleton," trilled Mrs Everington as she danced over to them. "Isn't this the most wonderful ball?" It did not occur to her that she was praising her own ball to her guests. "Everyone is dancing and having a wonderful time. I do so enjoy these occasions."

Mrs Addleton smiled, used to Mrs Everington's unusual ways. "Yes, it is, indeed, a lovely evening."

"Mrs Addleton, I would like to make you known to a very dear acquaintance of mine. Mr Jonathon Westercott."

Millicent's head snapped up at the mention of that name, drawing her attention away from the dancers.

"It is a pleasure to meet you, Mrs Addleton," he greeted.

"Pleased to meet you, also, Mr Westercott," she replied, quite clearly impressed by the young man standing before them. She glanced at her daughter and noticed her sudden pallor. "Millicent, my dear, are you alright?"

"Yes, of course, mother." Just because her heart was flipping around in her chest and her breath didn't seem to be able to decide if it was coming or going didn't mean there was anything wrong.

"Mrs Addleton, as your daughter and I are already acquainted, I had hoped to be granted permission to ask her to dance."

Mrs Addleton beamed. "I am sure she would be delighted."

Millicent accepted the hand held out to her, having little choice but to be led onto the dance floor. Inside, however, she was seething. He had not even bothered to ask her if she wanted to dance. No. Instead he had asked her mother, of all people. Did she not have a say in what she wished to do and who she wished to do it with?

"People will think you are angry with me if you continue to look like thunder," he murmured quietly.

"Then they would be correct in their assumptions because I am angry with you."

"Why would that be?" he asked, a little surprised.

She looked at him in amazement. "You truly do not know?" When he shook his head, she pressed her lips together, afraid of saying something completely ill mannered.

They took their places and the dance began. Each time they passed each other, he would whisper her name. She pretended not to hear and ignored him.

"Miss Addleton, it is not polite to ignore me when I speak to you."

"And it was not polite to ignore me and ask my mother if I wished to dance," she hissed as she passed him.

"I see," he murmured and couldn't help the smile that tugged at his mouth.

He took her hand as they turned in the circle and she could not escape looking at him. When he had asked her mother if she would dance, her strongest feeling was to say no. And not having a choice had made that urge even stronger. But now, standing as they were, his face only inches from hers, she wasn't so sure it was such a bad thing after all. Their eyes held and Millicent felt a strange tingle run through her body.

The dance steps parted them and minutes later she was curtseying as it came to an end. He stood before her and raised her hand to his lips.

"Thank you for a most enjoyable dance, Miss Addleton," he murmured softly.

"Thank you, Mr Westercott," she replied automatically. Removing her hand from his, she turned and walked away. She continued past her mother, past Sara who was signalling for her to join her, out of the ballroom into the hallway, and then closed herself in the ladies room down the hall. She sat down on the padded bench set against the wall and leaned her head back.

What on earth was the matter with her? She had spent months avoiding the interest of gentlemen, avoiding her mother's matchmaking plans, determined to remain alone and focus her attentions on astronomy. Now this man had come into her life and was doing his best to turn it upside down. And she couldn't let him. She would not give up her astronomy for anyone. Not even Jonathon Westercott!

Amanda burst into the room, her face flushed and her eyes glowing. "Oh Millicent, I thought I saw you come in here. Hasn't it been the most wonderful evening?"

"You have obviously enjoyed yourself," Millicent observed.

"Yes, I have. Mr Jenson has asked if he might call on me tomorrow. I don't think Gerald is too happy about that but Richard had a quick talk to him and he seems to have accepted it. I never thought anyone would ever wish to call on me, Millicent. Isn't it just wonderful?"

Millicent tried to push aside her own worries and smiled brightly. She stood and hugged her friend. "I am very happy for you, Amanda. He seems very nice."

"He is. And so polite, and thoughtful. I am so glad I decided to attend this ball."

She continued to gush about the ball and Mr Jenson for several minutes and all the while Millicent stood there with a smile pasted on her face wishing she could go home. She knew she would never feel the way Amanda was feeling, had been determined not to feel that way ever, but that thought now made her envious and just a little sad.

"Millicent, who was that gentleman I saw you dancing with before you came in here?"

Millicent had only been half listening to Amanda and it took her a moment to realise the subject had been changed. "He is merely an acquaintance of Mrs Everington's. He asked me to dance and so I did," she added absently.

"He seemed most taken with you."

"What made you think that?"

"The way he looked at you, the way he watched you all the way until you left the ballroom."

"He watched me?" At Amanda's nod Millicent felt a little thrill. She quickly clamped it down. She could not allow herself to feel an attachment to any man. "Well, it makes no difference to me. I did not particularly like him and do not wish to see him again," she announced firmly. "Let's return to the ballroom, shall we?"

Amanda gave her friend a thoughtful look as they left the

room but was too caught up in her own joy of the evening to dwell on her friend's emotions for too long. She wandered over to her brother and Mr Jenson and Millicent made her way through the crowd towards her mother.

"There you are, Miss Addleton. I have been searching for you." Tristan Farley stood in front of her, barring her way. He was the last person Millicent wanted to deal with at this moment.

"Mr Farley, if you will excuse me, I am returning to my mother as we are about to leave for the evening."

"I was just speaking with your mother and gained the impression she was not returning home for some time. I was encouraged to think we might have another dance and that walk in the garden."

"As much as I would enjoy that, Mr Farley, I fear I have a headache and will be requesting my parents to return home as soon as possible."

"I am sorry to hear you are unwell," he said, much concerned. "Allow me to lend my arm for your support."

"Thank you but I do not need support. Please excuse me," she repeated and moved past him.

Her mother greeted the request to return home with anything but excitement. She was so enjoying the ball and had been hoping to stay long into the night. However, they were in attendance for Millicent and if their daughter was unwell then they would leave.

It took some time for her father to be located and convinced to leave the card game he was playing but Millicent was soon putting on her coat ready to step outside.

"You are leaving so soon, Miss Addleton?"

Millicent spun around to find herself facing Jonathon Westercott. If there was one thing to make the night the worst she had ever attended, this was it. She could hardly stop thinking about him if he continued to crop up in front of her.

"Yes, unfortunately I have a headache so my parents have agreed to take me home."

"I am sorry to hear you are unwell. My sisters had hoped to meet with you again before the evening was over."

"Please tell your sisters I am very sorry. Perhaps we will meet again at the next assembly."

"I am certain they would like that and I will pass on the message. I hope you feel better very soon. Good night, Miss Addleton." He stood for a moment as though he were about to say more but then, with a brief nod, he returned to the ballroom.

Millicent closed her eyes. He was the one person she hoped never to see again.

Chapter 6

"Thank you, Pemble," Mrs Addleton uttered excitedly as the butler left the room. She turned towards her daughters. "Millicent, quickly, come here and let me tidy your hair. You have a caller!"

All the girls turned to their sister, their excitement almost as overwhelming as their mother's. Millicent, however, sat very still, almost dreading further information.

Mrs Addleton motioned her over impatiently and Millicent all but dragged her feet to her mother's side. "A gentleman, Millicent. How exciting. Mind, I could tell he was quite taken with you and had hoped he would come calling but a mother hardly dares to rely on such things."

Millicent winced as her mother tugged a curl into place. "Who is it, mother?" She held her breath for the reply. Either possibility that she could think of were each as unpleasant as the other.

"It is Mr Jenson! I believe he is quite a wealthy man, a great compliment that he has singled you out so, Millicent."

Mr Jenson? She had barely exchanged two words with him and could not understand why he would be calling on her. She was soon being shuffled out of the room to join her morning caller in the drawing room.

Richard Jenson turned from the window as she entered. He held his hat in his hands and looked like he was enjoying himself immensely.

"Good morning, Mr Jenson."

"Good morning, Miss Addleton. How lovely you look this morning," he greeted.

Millicent was surprised by the unexpected compliment. "Thank you. Won't you sit down?" she invited and moved to the settee. He sat in the chair opposite and looked at her for a long moment. "It was very kind of you to visit," she said into the silence, hoping for some illumination from him.

He smiled suddenly and sat back in the chair. "Of course, you would be wondering what brings me to your home. We had barely an introduction at the ball so my visit must seem rather unusual."

Millicent nodded. "Yes, especially so given your connection with Amanda."

He looked at her approvingly. "Ah, Miss Bladestoke did say you were a very clever young woman. Most observant, too, it seems."

Millicent couldn't help smiling at him. He was unusual in his manner but she quite liked him already. "Might I assume you have visited Amanda today?"

"You might, indeed. In fact, I have come directly from her home with an important message."

"Why didn't she bring the message herself?"

He chuckled softly. "I think, Miss Addleton, I need not tell you of the quirky wit of your dear friend. It would appear that she wished me to call on you for your mother's sake."

Millicent's eyes widened. "My mother? What could she possibly mean by ...?" As realisation dawned, Mr Jenson's smile grew and Millicent could not help joining in the joke. "Well, her plan has worked as my mother almost fainted when your card was brought in. However, this will cause me some problems when you cease to call on me in the future."

"Oh, but that won't happen. You see, Miss Addleton, if your mother believes you are being courted by me then she will not push you to meet other gentlemen. I would only need to take you driving occasionally and Miss Bladestoke, as your dearest friend, would also come along as a chaperone."

Millicent's head was spinning. She rose from the settee and stood by the window to contemplate what he had said. Amanda was always coming up with crazy schemes and this one would have to be amongst the craziest. It appeared Mr Jenson was a good match to her with his own sense of the ridiculous for even considering the plan. But consider it he obviously had and had decided to put it into practice. She turned to him.

"Do you know, I believe this plan may work. My mother is already in raptures at the fact you have called on me and she would not push me towards anyone else if she thought you were interested. Amanda is very correct in her assumption there. But when you stop courting me and it is known you have an attachment to Amanda, that will cause me some problems, as you know."

"It has all been considered," he told her, waving her concerns away. "You will be the one to end the connection and, in my despair, I will turn to Miss Bladestoke for comfort. As the dear companion of her friend during my courting, she has come to know me quite well and we have determined we will suit. That shall be our story."

Millicent rolled her eyes and groaned to herself. Amanda was ever the actress and it was times like these that Millicent could understand her friend's passion for wishing to pursue the stage.

"I believe, Mr Jenson, that you are almost as bad as Amanda," she told him with a smile.

He laughed heartily and was in full agreement. "It is why we suit so perfectly. Now, I must take my leave of you but I will return in a few days to take you driving. Oh, I almost forgot," he added, handing a bunch of flowers towards her. "These are for you."

Millicent loved flowers and breathed in their scent as she cradled them in her arms. "Mr Jenson, these are beautiful." She then looked at him with a twinkle in her eye. "I do believe I will enjoy being courted by you."

His laughter echoed through the hall as he took his leave and when Millicent stepped back into the small drawing room her family were ready to pounce.

"Oh, Millicent, what beautiful flowers," Susan cried. "Did Mr Jenson give them to you?"

"As nobody else has called this morning, yes they are certainly from him."

Susan gave her a look and then bent her head over the bouquet. "I swear I like him already," she murmured with her nose in the blooms.

"Millicent, come and sit down, dear," urged Mrs Addleton, making room on the settee. "I want to hear everything he said to you."

Millicent handed her flowers to the maid who had entered the room. "Could you put these in a vase in my bedroom."

"Yes, miss." The maid took the flowers and left the room.

Millicent joined her anxious mother.

"Now, dear, every word, mind. So much can be determined by the simplest tone and structure of a sentence."

Never one for acting, Millicent was hesitant to say too much incase her clumsiness spoilt the plan.

"Mr Jenson said that he had been pleased to meet me at the ball and asked if he could return in a few days to take me driving in his curricle."

Mrs Addleton almost swooned off the chair. "We must visit Madame Le Cruz and ensure you have the most perfect dresses to wear for each occasion he calls."

"Mother, I have more than enough dresses."

"Millicent, dear, you just do not understand the honour that has been bestowed upon you. You simply cannot drive around with someone of Mr Jenson's standing in your old faded dresses."

"Mother," Millicent began but Mrs Addleton would have

none of it.

"Not another word, dear. Trust that your mother knows what is best. Tomorrow we will visit the modiste and have you fitted for several dresses."

Millicent's heart sank at the prospect. She would ring a favour from Mr Jenson for subjecting her to this.

*

Millicent visited Amanda later that day. Her friend was expecting her and they hurried up the stairs to Amanda's room without uttering a word. Once safely in the privacy of the room, she turned to Millicent. "Has he called on you?"

"You know very well that is the reason I have come to see you," Millicent told her.

Amanda shrugged. "You might be calling just because I am your dearest friend and you wished to find out how I enjoyed the ball."

Millicent laughed and Amanda joined in.

"So, he has told you our plan?" she asked eagerly.

"I hardly think Mr Jenson would have thought up this plan."

"Alright, he has told you of *my* plan?" she amended impatiently.

"Yes, he has. I must say, Amanda, I think he is as crazy as you are!"

"Yes, I know. Isn't it just wonderful?" she breathed.

Millicent rolled her eyes and shook her head. "Back to your plan. As crazy as it seems, I do think it will work and stop my mother from continuing to push me into the notice of every eligible man in the county."

"My thoughts exactly," Amanda agreed. "You are so insistent on remaining unattached and I struck upon this wonderful idea while visiting with Mr Jenson earlier today. He has a wonderful imagination and, just for fun at first, we worked out this plan. Then, afterwards, I realised how helpful that would be to you and he was very eager to join in the fun," Amanda finished, her eyes glowing and cheeks flushed.

"Amanda, I do believe you would be a huge success on the stage," she was told dryly.

"I must write to Mr Jenson right away and let him know it is time to set our plan in full motion."

"No need," Millicent stopped her. "He has arranged to call for me in a few days to take me driving. Information that sent my mother into a swoon, I might add. And, as my dearest friend, you will accompany me to ensure my virtue remains intact."

"Perhaps I had better sit between the two of you to ensure nothing remiss occurs. If that means I must sit quite closely to Mr Jenson, then I will just have to endure it as best as I can," she said on a sigh.

Millicent flung the pillow at her friend before they both fell on the bed in a fit of laughter.

*

Over dinner that evening, talk around the table centred on Millicent and her conquest at the ball.

"I'm pleased to find you had a successful evening, Millicent," Mr Addleton said.

"Thank you," Millicent responded, hoping guilt at her falsehood didn't show on her face.

"Yes, most successful," Mrs Addleton agreed. "Such great prospects if he were to make our Millicent an offer of marriage."

"Do you think it a possibility?" Mr Addleton asked.

"A great one. He has singled our Millicent out in a very particular way. Once he takes her driving in the park everyone will know of his intention."

"It's just a drive, mother," Millicent interrupted, alarmed at the progression of her mother's thoughts. "Besides, we have only just met and I may find I do not care much for him at all."

"Not care for him? Millicent, dear, do stop with your silly ideas. No young woman of sense could possibly resist a proposal from a man of such character as Mr Jenson. We must hold a ball!"

"A ball?" Millicent exclaimed. Things were moving much too quickly.

"My dear Mrs Addleton, please do not let your head run away with you and invite the whole town," Mr Addleton warned her. "I am not about to have my home invaded by riff raff, toadies, and silly school girls."

"Mr Addleton, as if there would be schoolgirls at a ball. Really! And I would only invite the best of people, as you very well know, sir. You may depend upon it that our ball will be one that will be talked about for seasons to come."

Mr Addleton grunted, expecting to be inundated with annoying questions and errand runners for days leading up to the occasion.

Susan's eyes had lit up at the mention of their own ball. "Mama, if we held a ball here, might I attend?"

"Definitely not, Susan. You are not yet out so how would that appear?"

"Yes, but with so many people I would not be noticed if I stayed to the side and out of everyone's way. But to be stuck in my room while the dancing goes on below would be too much to bear."

"Then you will just have to be strong, child, because you will not be attending."

Susan's face fell but she managed to control her tears before they escaped. She would find a way to sneak into the ball if she had to. Besides, Mr Farley would surely be in attendance and she simply had to dance with him. Her cheeks felt warm at the thought and she bent her head over her dinner so nobody would notice the change in her expression.

Chapter 7

Millicent sat alone in the drawing room trying to focus on her embroidery.

Pemble's entrance thankfully diverted her. "A young gentleman has called, Miss," he said, handing her a card.

Millicent stifled a groan.

"Shall I say you are not at home, Miss?"

"No, Pemble. You may show him in."

"Yes, Miss."

"But, Pemble," she called him back. "If he still remains here in ten minutes could you please think of a way to end the visit?"

Pemble hid his smile. "Certainly, miss."

Moments later, Tristan Farley entered the room.

"Good day, Mr Farley."

"My dear Miss Addleton," he greeted, coming towards her. "Please accept my apologies for not calling on you sooner. I had business that kept me occupied for the better part of yesterday but I have come at the first opportunity to see how you fared."

Millicent slid her hand out of his and invited him to sit down. "There is nothing to forgive, Mr Farley. As you can see, I am perfectly well."

"That news pleases me. It was a sad occasion when you left the ball unwell."

Her lips stretched in a tight smile but she found she had nothing to say to him. His manner annoyed her and made her suspicious of him. Searching for a topic, she asked, "How is your sister?"

"She is very well, thank you. She wished to come with me to visit you but I advised her it would not be a good idea if you were still unwell. However, perhaps she can visit another day."

"That would be nice."

"As you are feeling quite well, may I invite you to take a drive with me?" he asked.

"That is very kind of you, Mr Farley, but I have already made plans for today and am not available to go driving." Millicent's mind sought quickly for an errand that would keep her occupied for the day.

"That is disappointing. Errands can be so tedious. I would gladly lend my assistance if you wish it," he offered graciously.

"Thank you for the offer but my plans do not involve errands so I need no assistance."

"Then perhaps I could drive you to where you need to go?"

Millicent was wishing strongly that he would take the hint and leave, when Pemble entered. "Sorry to disturb you, Miss Addleton, but you have a caller. I have told him you are occupied but he was most insistent and happy to wait. He is in the library."

Millicent stood and took the card handed to her. Today was just not her lucky day. However, it did provide her with an excuse to be rid of Mr Farley.

"Oh. Oh, yes!" she exclaimed in what she hoped was believable surprise. "I have been awaiting this call. A very important matter, you see," she explained to Mr Farley. "I do hope you will forgive me but I must attend to this matter right away. Thank you so much for your visit and concerns."

Finding himself dismissed, Mr Farley bid her farewell. "I will return soon to take you for the promised drive."

Once he was out the door, Millicent turned towards the library. She hesitated for a moment, considering having Pemble tell her visitor that she had been called away. Before she could act on this thought, the door opened and Mr Westercott stood looking at her.

"Miss Addleton, I am pleased to see you looking so well," he greeted.

As Millicent had felt the colour drain from her face, she did not take his words as much of a compliment. "Good afternoon, Mr Westercott."

"Please forgive my intrusion. My visit has two purposes," he began.

Millicent joined him in the library and invited him to sit down.

"My first purpose," he continued, "was to make sure you were quite well after the ball. You left early, if you remember."

"Yes, I remember," she told him. "I am quite recovered, thank you."

"Excellent," he told her, a smile spreading across his face. He continued on while Millicent fought to return her breathing to normal. "My second purpose was to bring to you an invitation from my sisters. They were sorry to have missed you at the ball and Juliette would especially like it if you would attend a small tea party she is holding tomorrow afternoon."

He handed her a message as he finished speaking and Millicent took it, hoping her hands didn't shake as much as she thought they would.

Breaking the seal, she opened the note and read the neatly handwritten invitation. Juliette had seemed like a nice person, from the brief acquaintance they had, but Millicent wasn't sure if she wanted to become involved with anyone from this man's family.

As if reading her thoughts, he said, "I will not be at home tomorrow but I am certain my sisters will make you very welcome."

That helped her make her decision. "Please would you wait while I pen a reply?"

"Of course."

Millicent sat at the desk, pulled out pen and paper and quickly wrote a note to Juliette. She handed him the message. His fingers very slightly brushed hers as he took it from her and she quickly pulled away. Glancing up at him, it didn't appear as though he had noticed her abrupt action.

"Please tell your sisters I look forward to seeing them tomorrow."

He nodded. "Goodbye, Miss Addleton."

After he left, Millicent returned to the drawing room. She sat down on the large chair next to the fire, contemplating the day ahead with his sisters.

The embroidery still lay untouched in her lap when Millicent heard her mother and sisters returning from their shopping expedition. They entered the drawing room full of chatter about their outing. Millicent had thankfully been allowed to remain home after her gruelling morning with the modiste. On the one hand she was grateful but, on the other, if she had been out shopping she would not have had to endure her two visitors. To make matters worse, she had planned to spend the afternoon reading her borrowed book but as it reminded her of Mr Westercott every time she looked at it, she could not make herself pick it up. It would have to be returned to the library unread, she thought disconsolately.

"Is something the matter, Milly?" asked Catherine. "You look troubled."

Millicent forced herself to smile. "I am perfectly happy, just daydreaming."

They accepted her excuse and, as they were still so full of their outing, quite easily moved on to fill her in on everything they had done and seen.

Mrs Addleton handed her parcels to the maid, accepted a note from the butler and followed the girls into the room.

"Millicent!" she gasped.

"What is it, mother?"

"Two gentlemen!" She slid into the nearby chair and fanned herself.

"What are you talking about, mama?" asked Susan curiously.

"While we were out, your sister has been called upon by two more gentlemen! Mr Farley and Mr Westercott. Mr Westercott," she repeated thoughtfully. "Isn't he the friend of Mrs Everington's whom we met at the ball?"

"Yes, mother," Millicent replied quietly.

"My goodness. They are both very eligible gentlemen, too. And here you are already receiving the attentions of Mr Jenson. No matter, I am sure you can accommodate all three gentlemen until you become better acquainted and then you can have your pick."

"Mother! I do not want my *pick*. I do not wish to be courted by any of them."

"Millicent," uttered her mother aghast. "Well, I hope you have your best manners with you when you meet with these gentlemen because I can tell you right now that I expect a marriage proposal to be the outcome and a wedding to take place before the year is out."

Millicent hurried from the room. When she reached her bedroom, she closed the door firmly and slumped on her bed. This was worse than it was before the ball. Now that her mother had proof of three very eligible men showing an interest, she would have to attend every single assembly to ensure she remained in their view as much as possible. So much for Amanda's plan of preventing this very thing!

She looked to her bedside table where the library book sat waiting for her to read it. Determinedly, she picked it up and opened the cover. She really needed to bury her mind in astronomy and try to forget this day had ever happened.

Scant minutes later, she snapped the cover shut and threw the book on the bed. She could not read one page without Mr Westercott's face swimming before her smiling in such a friendly way as he had handed her the book. Blast that man!

With a huge sigh, she fell back against her pillows and stared at the ceiling. Her life was becoming complicated and she didn't like it one bit. All she had been aiming for was peace and quiet to read her books and concentrate on the heavens above. Now, she had three gentlemen callers and her mother planning a wedding in the not too distant future. How had things taken such a turn in so short a time?

Millicent opened her eyes as her door inched open.

"Milly?" Jemima popped her head in and looked around for her sister. "Oh, there you are," she continued as she spotted her spread out on the bed. "Why are you in bed so early?" she asked curiously.

"I am not in bed, merely resting," Millicent informed her, rising to a sitting position. "And please will you stop calling me Milly!"

Jemima looked at her with as much indignation as a ten year old could gather. "Well!"

Millicent looked at her ruefully, rolled her eyes, and swung off the bed. There had been no reason to bite off Jemima's head, even if she did continue to call her that odious name. "I am sorry, Jemima. Please forgive me, I am just a little tired, I think."

Jemima hesitated, deciding whether or not to accept her sister's apology, but the next minute was standing beside Millicent prying her with questions as to why she was feeling more than usually tired. Millicent groaned inwardly at her mistake. Jemima was always trying to mother someone and the slightest hint to her that you were feeling unwell had the girl cooing and soothing and, quite frankly, driving the person slowly insane.

"Shall I get you a shawl to put across your shoulders,

Millicent? I do think you may be coming down with a chill," the young girl stated, trying to feel her older sister's forehead.

"I am perfectly fine, thank you," Millicent tried to assure her, smiling to herself at Jemima's obvious use of her full given name. "We were out late at the Everington ball and I have been quite busy since. A good night's sleep is all that is lacking."

Jemima didn't look convinced and continued to fuss about. Millicent finally managed to get her sister out of the room by promising to call for her the moment she felt any worse. Left alone in her room, Millicent sat on the window seat gazing out across the scenery below. Jemima was a strange little girl and would not be completely happy until she had a small brood of children of her own to mother.

A knock sounded on the door and Millicent turned just as her mother entered. "Millicent, are you feeling quite well?"

"Yes, mother."

"Very good. I passed Jemima and she expressed concern at your state of health. I can assume she was trying to play at mother again?" she asked with amusement.

"Yes, unfortunately. I do hope she marries young and has many children to keep her occupied."

"As do we all, my dear. Which brings us to the reason for my visit."

Millicent looked at her mother warily. Something told her she wasn't going to like what was coming.

"Your father and I have spoken of a ball to be held here, as you know. Each of your new beaux will be invited and encouraged to dance and converse with you as much as possible. At the end of the ball, you will decide whom you wish to marry."

Millicent jumped up. "Mother! No!"

"Hush. The ball will be held in three weeks. During that time, I can assume the gentlemen will be calling on you so you will have ample opportunity to decide which suits you best. The ball will be a wonderful opportunity for them to profess their affection for you and, if we are very lucky, you will receive a proposal. But, proposal or not, you will make your decision and then encourage that chosen gentleman to offer for you."

Millicent sat heavily on the window seat as her mother talked on. She could not believe what she was hearing. She had known her mother and, indeed, her father, wished her to be married soon after this season but had been able to convince herself that she could do as she wished. Had planned to immerse herself in her study of astronomy and come out of the season none the worse for wear. All these plans were going up in smoke and she leaned her forehead against the cool glass as she gazed helplessly out of the window.

"Millicent! Millicent, did you hear me?"

"Yes, mother," she murmured, not looking around.

Mrs Addleton watched her daughter for a moment and softened. "Millicent, my dear, I know you are not as interested in receiving offers like the other young ladies of your acquaintance. However, you know that getting married is what you are required to do and you will enjoy the married state." She laid a hand on Millicent's shoulder. "Dear, you do at least have a choice," she continued gently. "Three very eligible gentlemen are calling on you which is more than many young ladies have. You can choose whichever of those men you prefer."

Millicent brushed a stray tear from her cheek and nodded her head. "Yes, mother."

Mrs Addleton watched her for another minute and then quietly left the room to begin instructions on the upcoming ball.

Chapter 8

The Westercott home was moderate in size, set beside a large pond on the outskirts of town. The sun glinted off the windows as Millicent alighted from the carriage and her eyes were drawn to the ducks paddling amongst the reeds near the water's edge. At the top of the steps, Millicent stopped and turned to look at the view. Across the pond were green hills, tall trees, and the sounds of birds enjoying the afternoon sunshine. Millicent had never felt more at home.

Reluctantly, she turned from the view to enter the house. She was shown into the large drawing room and Juliette was greeting her moments later.

"Miss Addleton, I am so pleased you could come."

"Good afternoon, Miss Westercott. Thank you very much for inviting me to your tea party."

Juliette smiled and led her further into the room. "I would be very pleased if you would call me Juliette," she said warmly. "I have heard so much about you I feel I know you already."

Millicent was not sure she liked the idea of who had been speaking of her but she felt drawn to Juliette. She found her arm tucked into her new friend's elbow as she was led through large doors leading out to a garden terrace.

"It is such a beautiful day, I thought it would be pleasant to take tea out of doors."

This part of the garden was just as beautiful as the front of the house and Millicent did not mind at all that they were to sit outside. "Miss Westercott, you have a lovely home."

"Juliette," she was reminded with a warm smile.

Millicent couldn't help smiling back at her. "Juliette, you have a lovely home," she amended. "And please call me Millicent."

"Thank you. It is actually the home of my brother but mother and my sisters and I have been living here for some time now. Ever since our dear papa passed away."

"I am so sorry for your loss," Millicent was quick to say.

"Thank you, Millicent. It was a difficult time, especially for mother, but Jonathon has been so wonderful and helped us all so much, the feeling of loss has been eased considerably."

Millicent didn't know what to say to this. She did not wish to speak about Jonathon Westercott and especially did not wish to hear what a wonderful person he was. She would much rather think of him as an annoying man that she never wished to see again.

Several young women sat at the tables placed on the terrace and Juliette introduced her sisters, whom Millicent had met briefly at the tea shop, and turned towards three other young women.

"Miss Addleton, let me introduce to you Miss Wilson, Miss Heathering, and Miss Tilden." The young women greeted each other and Millicent soon found herself seated next to Juliette just as the tea and refreshments arrived. There was a large assortment of cakes and pastries to choose from and conversation was mumbled as they sampled the fine food.

"Miss Addleton, I believe we may have met recently at the Everington ball," said Hanna Heathering.

Millicent looked at Miss Heathering and tried to remember her. She had not paid very much attention at the ball and, even with her flaming red hair, Miss Heathering did not stand out as a face she recognised.

"You were standing with Mr Westercott and Mrs Everington when we were introduced. I believe it is difficult for women to focus on anything else when Mr Westercott is standing beside them," she added with a titter of false laughter.

Millicent remembered her now. While Mrs Everington had introduced Mr Westercott to Mrs Addleton, a young woman had stood to the side, sending looks that were obviously meant for Mr Westercott. Looks that he was ignoring, much to her annoyance. She had sauntered up to their small group and Mrs Everington had no choice but to introduce her. Millicent didn't remember much else because it was at that point that Mr Westercott had led her away to dance.

"I must be very unlike most women, in that case, as I do not find myself attracted to Mr Westercott in any way," Millicent stated clearly.

"You do not?" asked Juliette.

"Forgive me, Juliette, for saying such things of your brother but he is not the type of gentleman I find myself attracted to."

"What type of gentleman would that be?" asked Lettie Wilson, pushing her spectacles further onto her tiny nose.

Millicent hesitated. She could hardly say what she thought of Mr Westercott in front of his sisters. All eyes were on her expectantly.

Young Miss Lilian Westercott came to her rescue. "I expect we are all attracted to a different type of gentleman and if Miss Addleton does not find our brother to her liking then there is nothing wrong with that."

Millicent smiled at her gratefully.

Miss Heathering's eyes took on a gleam as she murmured, "I am sure Miss Addleton is much more interested in gentlemen such as Mr Farley."

"What makes you think so?" Millicent asked, surprised.

Hanna Heathering shrugged her dainty shoulders. "I saw the way you looked at each other at the Everington ball. It was quite obvious you were enamoured of one another."

Millicent hid a shudder. "You are quite mistaken."

Hanna shrugged again and her manner was clearly disbelieving.

"Well I think Mr Westercott is a truly handsome gentleman," whispered Jane Tilden.

"You would think any man who looked your way was handsome," muttered Hanna in a manner that made Juliette frown at her. Shy Jane looked down at her lap and took a small bite of a biscuit.

"As Jane is one of the prettiest young ladies I know, I am sure there are many gentlemen wishing they could spend time in her company," announced Juliette. "Now, who would like some more tea?" she asked, putting an end to the subject.

Millicent remembered how much she had disliked Hanna Heathering at first sight at the ball. Her comments today showed that she could be mean and Millicent wondered why someone who seemed as nice as Juliette Westercott would have invited someone like Hanna Heathering to a tea party.

Millicent took a sip of her tea and nearly choked on it when Jonathon Westercott stepped onto the terrace.

"Good afternoon, ladies," he greeted. The women greeted him in return, the visitors eyeing him as though he were some grand prize.

Millicent pulled a face in disgust. Her cheeks turned pink as she realised Jonathon was watching her. She also wondered how long he had been standing in the garden and how much he had overheard.

"Mr Westercott," cooed the dreaded Hanna. "We did not expect to see you today. How fortunate for us that you are home."

Jonathon smiled politely but kept his eyes on Millicent. This did not sit well with Hanna Heathering at all and she glared at Millicent. Juliette stepped into the awkward silence and asked her brother the question that was burning on Millicent's lips.

"What are you doing here, Jonathon? Did your business finish early?" Her eyes twinkled at him.

"Yes, dear sister, it did."

"How fortunate," she murmured.

Jonathon narrowed his eyes at her, leaned very close and said something that only she could hear then bid the ladies farewell.

"You will not join us, Mr Westercott?" asked Hanna sweetly.

Millicent swallowed. Please, no. Please, no.

He hesitated the barest second before replying, "I do believe tea parties are a ladies-only past time so I will take my leave. Enjoy your afternoon, ladies," he said and walked into the house.

The three visitors watched him go as if mesmerised. Millicent watched the young women, disbelief clearly showing on her face. Their reaction to Mr Westercott was disgusting. If they really knew him the way she did they would know that he was a very annoying man. She turned to the Westercott sisters who were watching the reactions with amusement. Then, quite surprisingly, Juliette winked at her before turning away to pour more tea.

The rest of the afternoon passed uneventfully and, apart from a few comments made by Hanna Heathering, everyone seemed to enjoy the afternoon. When it was time to leave, Juliette laid a hand on Millicent's arm when the other ladies were escorted to the door.

"Please stay a moment, Millicent. There is something I need to ask you."

Millicent was curious and sat back down on her chair. "What is it?"

"Forgive me if I am being too forward and it is perhaps not my business but I have been wanting to ask you …"

"Yes?"

"Why do you not like my brother?"

Millicent almost choked. "I beg your pardon?"

"You said that Jonathon was not the type of man that you were attracted to and I wondered if he had perhaps done something to upset you. I would be truly surprised if he had, he is such a kind-hearted man, but if he has I will most certainly speak to him."

Completely surprised by this speech, Millicent could only stare. After several minutes, she said, "I don't recall him doing anything untoward."

"I am very pleased to hear that. Then what is it about him that repulses you?"

"I didn't say he repulsed me," Millicent told her. "I am simply not attracted to him. I must say, this is a very unusual conversation to be having with a man's sister."

"Yes, I do have a habit of being very direct, I am afraid. Are you offended?"

"No, just surprised."

"I am so glad. I do want us to be friends and was worried for a moment that my frankness had made you regret visiting today."

Millicent had regretted her visit the moment she set eyes on Jonathon Westercott but to Juliette she merely said, "Not at all. I don't mind frank speaking and, to be frank in response, there is no particular reason I do not find your brother attractive. I think it is just that I do not wish to be attracted to any man."

"Not at all?"

Millicent shook her head.

"Why ever not?"

"I don't like the thought of being told what to do and not being permitted to follow things that I am interested in," she blurted in a sudden bout of confidence.

"What are you interested in?" Juliette asked softly, leaning in close.

"You will find it shocking." She felt she could confide

anything in her new friend but was hesitant.

"No, I swear I will not. You don't need to tell me if you would rather not."

Juliette looked so sincere and a moment later Millicent found the words spilling from her lips.

"For quite some time now, I have had a passion for astronomy. I watched a balloon ascension in the park and heard the men speak of what it was like to be so high in the sky, and close to the stars and they spoke of planets and things I didn't quite understand. I was so overwhelmed with the need to know more. Ever since, I have borrowed books on the subject and tried to learn as much as I could. There is nothing more exciting than sitting beneath a night sky and watching a whole new world waken above me." She felt heat warm her cheeks as the realised she was rambling and exposing herself to Juliette's ridicule. But to her surprise, there was no hint of ridicule.

Juliette's eyes twinkled and she smiled. "How wonderful to feel such interest in something. But what does that have to do with marrying?"

"A husband would stop me from reading my books and dreaming on the stars. I cannot let that happen. Therefore, I am determined to remain unmarried and avoid all gentlemen where possible."

Juliette laugh. "How, pray tell, do manage to avoid them? I am always being surrounded by men at assemblies. I swear it can be a trial at times. I think you have the best idea I have ever heard. Perhaps you and I can provide company for one another and we could both avoid the mass of gentlemen at these events."

Millicent laughed. "Juliette, I think you would not be happy sitting on the outer circle while others had fun dancing the night away."

"I do believe you may be right," she admitted with a smile. "Jonathon!"

Millicent's head snapped up and her mood slipped as she

watched him walk towards them. His eyes gleamed with amusement and another emotion Millicent couldn't quite determine. She began to wonder how much of their conversation he had overheard.

"Excuse my intrusion, Juliette. I thought all of your guests had departed."

"Most have left but I asked Millicent to remain for a little longer," Juliette explained.

Jonathon sat on a nearby chair. "Did you enjoy your afternoon, Miss Addleton?"

"Very much. Juliette is a wonderful hostess."

He smiled. "I hope you don't mind me joining you ladies but I had an urge to enjoy the warm sun here on the terrace."

Millicent glanced at Juliette who was giving her brother a speaking look. "We were actually in the middle of an important conversation."

"Don't let me stop you," he said airily and leaned back in the chair, closing his eyes to the sun.

"It is getting late, Juliette, so perhaps I should begin my journey home," Millicent said, rising from her chair.

"I do wish you could stay longer," Juliette said wistfully, but she knew the moment for confidences was gone. "My sisters and I are going to the library tomorrow. Would you care to join us?" she asked hopefully.

Millicent glanced at Jonathon, remembering her last visit to the library. His eyes were still closed but she could swear his lips twitched. "Thank you for the invitation but I am already occupied tomorrow." At Juliette's obvious disappointment, she added, "But I would enjoy going with you another time."

"Then I will hold you to that. I do so enjoy a good story, don't you?" she asked, although there was no need for Millicent to reply as Juliette stood up and led her towards the house.

They had only taken a few steps when Jonathon appeared

beside them. "Please allow me to escort you home, Miss Addleton," he offered.

"Thank you but there is no need. My driver is waiting for me."

"I wish you a safe journey home, in that case. It was a pleasure to see you again." He held out his hand and Millicent had no choice but to place hers in his. His fingers closed gently around hers as he raised her hand to his lips. "Until next time," he murmured.

Millicent could barely breathe and felt the heat returning to her cheeks. She quickly slid her hand from his and turned away before he could see her reaction. Juliette walked with her to the front door and waited while the carriage was brought to the steps.

"I so enjoyed your visit, Millicent."

Finding her voice, Millicent replied, "As did I, Juliette." Everything except Jonathon Westercott's presence, that was.

Impulsively, Juliette gave Millicent a hug and, once her friend was settled in the carriage, waved until she was out of sight. She then returned to the garden terrace where Jonathon was waiting for her.

"Well, sister?"

"Why did you come out to the terrace?"

He shrugged. "I wanted to enjoy the sunshine."

"Millicent is a wonderful friend. It is only because I like her so much and felt you would both suit very well that I agreed to find out if she felt any attraction to you."

"And I do appreciate your help. From what she said earlier, it seemed pointless to pursue her if she truly did dislike me."

Juliette felt sorry for him. "I don't think any woman could truly dislike you, Jonathon, but I also know you are very particular about the women you spend time with."

He raised his brows. "And just what would you know about

that?"

"Enough to know that my brother is a respectable man. I know how much you care for Millicent but I don't know how good your chances are at winning her," she told him gently.

"I merely find her interesting and thought spending time with her might be enjoyable. Don't read more into this than there really is, Juliette."

"Whatever you say, Jonathon. Then if your interest is merely passing, it will not upset you to know that she is not attracted to you or any gentleman of her acquaintance."

Jonathon gazed across the garden, deep in thought. Millicent's reaction to any close contact with him was not usual of someone who felt nothing. He would continue to see her, at least until he determined if there was any hope of securing her affections. If not, he would leave town as he was meant to do some time ago.

"Thank you, Juliette. I do appreciate you asking Miss Addleton about her feelings."

"I did it for the both of you, Jonathon. I would not falsely be anyone's friend, not even for you," she told him firmly.

"I know you would not."

Edith and Lilian joined them on the terrace and both girls were looking expectantly at their older siblings.

"Well?" began Edith. "What was all that whispering at the tea party about? Are you both planning something?"

"And is it to do with Millicent Addleton?" added Lilian.

"I have no idea what you are talking about," Jonathon told them. "I think you read too many novels." With that, he threw a smile at them and walked away.

"Well!" they both huffed in unison.

"Juliette, please tell us what is going on," Edith begged.

"Nothing is going on. Jonathon merely wanted to know how Millicent was faring after her headache at the ball."

Both young ladies looked at their sister in disbelief.

"You cannot leave us out of this!" exclaimed Lilian. "It is too unfair."

"There is nothing to tell." At their pleading looks she relented. "Alright, but you must keep this strictly secret. If Jonathon knows I have told you he will be very angry. Jonathon is interested in Millicent."

"We know that," Edith told her impatiently.

"He was interested to know how she felt about him and asked me to find out during the visit today."

"But we know that she likes him, regardless of what she says. It is clear in her manner," put in Lilian.

"We assumed that she did but during the tea party you know how adamant she was that she did not find Jonathon attractive in the least. I suspected she was covering but one can never tell. Jonathon overheard her!"

"No," the sisters breathed.

"Yes! And so he joined the party briefly and asked me to find out for certain which is why I asked Millicent to stay behind so I could do some sleuthing."

"What did you find out?"

"Well, I cannot tell you all that she said in confidence but I do believe she likes him but is determined not to."

Edith and Lilian looked at each other and smiled. Edith turned to Juliette. "So, when will Millicent join us on an outing so we can arrange for Jonathon to come across us?"

"We are not arranging anything. At least, not just at the moment. I did ask her to join us at the library tomorrow but she is unavailable."

"Were we going to the library?" asked Lilian. "I don't remember planning this?"

"No, we weren't but Millicent needn't know that. I was not going to tell her that Jonathon would be escorting us."

"Oh," they breathed excitedly.

"However, she cannot go so that plan is scratched. I was thinking we could wait a few days and then invite her to take a walk in the park with us. It is a very public place and it would not be unusual for us to meet Jonathon during our walk."

"It is perfect!" exclaimed Edith.

Lilian nodded her agreement and so the plan was set.

*

Millicent stepped inside her home, relieved the tea party was at an end. Her nerves felt on edge after her encounter with Jonathon.

"Did you have a nice afternoon, dear?" asked Mrs Addleton when Millicent joined them.

"Yes, it was very nice, mother. Juliette Westercott is a lovely person."

"Who else attended? Anyone that we know?"

"The three Westercott sisters, of course, and Hanna Heathering, Jane Tilden and Lettie Wilson. I am not acquainted with any of them, although we were introduced to Miss Heathering during the ball. I had forgotten until she reminded me."

"Heathering," her mother said thoughtfully. "Flaming hair, dainty figure?" Millicent nodded and Mrs Addleton pulled a face. "Yes, I know the young lady you refer to. Although, I am not sure I would call her a lady."

"Mama!" Susan gasped.

"Excuse my frankness, girls, but throwing oneself at any eligible gentleman and making simpering conversation while ogling him is not my idea of a lady!"

Susan and Catherine giggled, until their mother gave them a

sharp look.

"Was she pleasant at the tea party, Millicent?" Susan asked.

"I found her to be rather mean and when Mr Westercott arrived she looked him over in a most disgusting manner."

"Mr Westercott was there? Millicent, why didn't you mention him the instant you came home!" exclaimed Mrs Addleton. "He is one of your admirers, after all. Has called on you in this very house!"

"I barely exchanged two words with him, mother. He was merely passing by so stopped to greet everyone."

"What did he say to you? Did he single you out in any way?"

Millicent briefly thought of her encounter with the gentleman. "No, mother, he did not."

"Well, that is most unusual after having called on you only yesterday."

"Mother, he only called on me to pass on his sister's invitation. He is not interested in me himself."

"Nonsense! A gentleman does not call on a young lady unless he is interested in her. His sister's invitation was merely an excuse."

Millicent did not believe this to be so but did not contradict her mother. It would have been useless to convince her otherwise, in any case.

Catherine was watching her sister curiously. "Are you meeting with the Westercott's again, Millicent?"

"Juliette did invite me to go to the library with them tomorrow but I declined."

"Why?"

"I have made other arrangements for tomorrow."

"What other arrangements?"

Millicent looked at her sister. "Just arrangements. I did not realise I needed to keep you informed of my every action."

"There is no need to get upset, Millicent. I was only curious."

Millicent curbed her annoyance. She was confused at her own reaction to the invitation. She enjoyed the library, it was one of her favourite places, but her last visit held only memories of her encounter with Jonathon Westercott and his expression as he handed her the astronomy book. He hadn't looked upon her as strange and that confused her the most. She was trying to avoid entering the library again, at least for a while.

With a small sigh, she told her sister, "Juliette Westercott has invited me to join her for an outing and will send a message when it is arranged. So, yes, I will be meeting with them again."

Mrs Addleton's eyes lit up. "Perhaps Mr Westercott will join you all as an escort. That would be wonderful but we mustn't hold our hopes too high, Millicent. Although, it would be the very thing."

As Millicent held no such hopes and, in fact, prayed strongly that he wouldn't join them, she made no comment.

"What are the other sisters like?" asked Susan. "Perhaps we could all go on an outing together. A picnic near the lake. I am sure there is a lake nearby."

The large pond at the Westercott home swam into view and Millicent dampened it immediately. She would not share the image with her sisters or they would surely have a picnic on the grounds arranged before anyone knew what was happening.

"All the Westercott ladies are very pleasant," she told Susan. "Edith, I think, is seventeen and Lilian is possibly your age Catherine."

"I do so enjoy meeting new friends," piped up Catherine. "I wonder that we have not met them before. Are they new to the area?"

"They have lived in the Westercott home for the past two years but I do believe they have not ventured into society much until recently."

"How odd," murmured Mrs Addleton. "One would have thought that with three young girls Mrs Westercott would have found the first opportunity to mingle with society. Millicent, we must invite them all to your ball." With that, Mrs Addleton left the room to make amendments to her arrangements for the ball.

"So, that would mean Mr Westercott would also be attending," said Catherine, with a sidelong look at her sister.

This thought had already run through Millicent's mind and she nodded. "He may, if he is not otherwise engaged."

Catherine and Susan shared a glance and bent their heads over the embroidery they had discarded on Millicent's entrance.

Millicent walked to the window and watched the sun sink lower in the sky. Would Mr Westercott come to the ball? And did she want him to be there?

Chapter 9

The next morning, the Addleton ladies were gathered in the hall about to spend several hours shopping for their upcoming ball. Pemble opened the front door in answer to a knock and the girls turned to see who their morning caller was. All eyes turned to Millicent when they saw it was Mr Jenson standing on the front step.

Ushered into the house, he walked towards them. "Miss Addleton, good day to you. I have called with the hope of taking you for a drive in the park but see you are about to set foot out of the house."

"Good morning, Mr Jenson. Yes, I am afraid we do have plans this morning."

Mrs Addleton stepped forward. "We can surely manage on our own, Millicent. It wouldn't be polite to keep Mr Jenson waiting."

Millicent opened her mouth to protest but found herself being ushered out of the house along with Mr Jenson.

She turned to the gentleman beside her. "I apologise for such unusual behaviour, Mr Jenson."

"There is no need, Miss Addleton. Although, I do see what Miss Bladestoke means by your mother's eagerness to see you attached," he said with a gleam of amusement in his eyes.

She smiled ruefully, acknowledging the fact, and allowed him to help her into the curricle. "Speaking of Miss Bladestoke, are we to collect her now?"

"Of course. We could not possibly continue without the company of your most treasured friend," he said smoothly.

Millicent tried not to laugh, did not succeed, and enjoyed the short trip to her friend's home. Mr Jenson stayed with the curricle while she entered the house to collect Amanda.

She stood in her friend's bedroom waiting impatiently while Amanda put the finishing touches to her toilette.

"Amanda, we are only driving in the park. Please, would you hurry up."

She turned from the mirror. "Do you think I look alright? I want to look my best for Mr Jenson."

"Amanda, you look beautiful," Millicent assured her. "Now, please, we must go. Mr Jenson is waiting."

When the two young ladies emerged from the house, Mr Jenson could only stare as Amanda approached. He leapt from the curricle and held out his hand to assist her. "Miss Bladestoke, might I say how lovely you look today."

Amanda blushed and settled herself onto the seat, Millicent joining her shortly after. Mr Jenson swung himself into the seat next to them and nudged the horses towards the park. They all sat quite close on the seat of the curricle but, as Amanda had been placed in the middle, she didn't seem to mind in the least.

The park was busy and the ladies acknowledged many acquaintances as they drove along. They chattered on about general nothings and enjoyed the warm sunshine and the freshness of the air. Millicent glanced at Amanda, who was trying very hard not to stare at Mr Jenson sitting beside her. Her cheeks had remained pink and Millicent knew it would not be long before an announcement was made. Which would make things just a little awkward for her if she were still thought to be enjoying the attentions of Mr Jenson.

"Perhaps we should walk for a while," she suggested.

Mr Jenson was happy to oblige and drew the horses to a stop. They alighted and he kept hold of the reins as they walked along.

"I am not sure this plan will work," Millicent blurted.

"Of course it will work," Amanda told her.

"Not if you two keep eyeing each other as you do," she replied bluntly.

Amanda blushed further and Mr Jenson had the sense to look away.

"The thought is appreciated," she continued, "but I don't wish to play gooseberry. Besides, the plan has not worked because I have since received other callers and now my mother believes me to be inundated with admirers and is pushing me even harder to make a choice!"

"Oh no!" cried Amanda. "But how can she wish you to continue looking when Richard is so eligible?"

"She believes my other callers to be just as eligible and it has quite gone to her head. You know how she is."

"Now that Richard has taken you driving she may stop pestering you. We will see how things go from here on."

"Rightly so," he agreed.

Millicent didn't agree at all but was willing to wait for a few more days before ending the farce. She looked up as she heard her name called and saw Juliette Westercott walking towards her. She was joined by her sister, Edith, and they greeted her with obvious pleasure.

"Millicent, what an unexpected pleasure," Juliette greeted.

"Good morning, Juliette. It is such a lovely day to be walking. Please allow me to introduce two great friends of mine. Mr Jenson and Miss Bladestoke. And this is Miss Westercott."

"It is a pleasure to make your acquaintance, Miss Westercott," greeted Mr Jenson. "I have heard my dear Millicent speak of you."

Juliette looked surprised at the endearment and glanced between him and Millicent. "Pleased to meet you, also, Mr Jenson."

"Are you headed in a particular direction?" asked Millicent.

"We are on our way to the library," Juliette told her. "It is a shame you could not join us."

"I would certainly like to join you for an outing another day," Millicent said.

"I look forward to it. We must be off. It was nice to meet you Miss Bladestoke, Mr Jenson. I will send a message to you soon, Millicent," she added and she and Edith continued on their way.

Juliette was thoughtful for the rest of the way to the library. She hadn't really intended to visit the building today but, after suggesting it to Millicent the previous afternoon, realised she wouldn't mind going after all. She was surprised to run into Millicent and equally surprised, if not more, to see her on the arm of a gentleman. She had said she didn't like Jonathon because she didn't want to be attracted to any man. Yet, if that were the case, why was she out walking with one in the park? Juliette did not like to think that her brother would find himself pushed aside but she felt he should know that Millicent already had an admirer. And a very handsome one, at that.

"What has you so glum?"

Juliette looked up to find her brother waiting for them near the library. "Not a thing. I didn't expect to find you here."

"I was nearby and thought it a good idea to escort my sisters home."

"We have not even been inside," Edith reminded him.

"I am happy to wait," he told her, his eyes scanning the park behind them.

"You will not see her," Juliette whispered as they walked past him and into the library.

Jonathon ignored her and continued to watch the visitors to the park. He could feel she was near. He had sat at home fighting the urge to find her but in the end it had become too strong. The library was right near the park and what better excuse than to escort his sisters home? He crossed the street and stood on the edge of the grass where he had a better view. His eyes were drawn to a curricle standing empty near a large garden bed. Two women were bent over some blooms and as they stood and turned towards him, he smiled to himself as he recognised Millicent Addleton. Her love of flowers, being such a feminine trait, seemed at variance with her love of the universe and it intrigued him further. He watched as a young man walked towards the women, picked a flower from the bed, and handed it to Millicent bending close to speak to her. Jonathon's stomach tighten at such familiarity. He watched as Millicent smiled up at the man, clearly happy to be in his presence. With a muttered curse, Jonathon turned away and strode along the street, away from the library and away from the park.

"Mr Jenson, the flower is truly lovely," Millicent told him as she bent her head to smell it.

"Flowers suit you, my dear. Besides, how must it look if your admirer does not give you as much as a flower during a walk in the park?"

Millicent smiled mischievously. "Ah yes, I do remember now that enjoying your company will bring forth beautiful flowers. Perhaps we will continue this play, after all."

He laughed and handed her back into the curricle. He then turned to Amanda, discreetly produced a flower for her and spoke quietly in her ear. Amanda blushed and allowed him to hold her hand longer than was expected as he helped her into the seat beside Millicent.

"Richard, I do believe it would be best to drop me off first before taking Amanda home. My home is closer and I assume you would wish to visit her brother," Millicent suggested.

"Do you know, Millicent, I believe you may have an excellent idea. And I do believe I will enjoy keeping company with you, especially with such a lovely friend to assist you."

"Yes, the dearest friend. How could I even consider joining you without my trusted friend by my side?"

"She is truly a joy."

"Please stop teasing me," Amanda said, trying hard not to laugh. "You are both worse than I when it comes to play acting."

They pulled to a halt outside Millicent's home and Richard accompanied her to the door.

"Thank you for a lovely day, Miss Addleton."

"Thank you, Mr Jenson."

"I will call again soon, if that is acceptable?"

"I look forward to it." With a smile and a wave at Amanda, Millicent entered her home.

Richard joined Amanda and was soon pulling up again, this time in front of her house.

"Do you wish to come inside and see Gerald?"

"I do wish to come inside but not to visit your brother," he said quietly.

He helped her down and she led him inside the house and to the small drawing room. "Would you like some tea?" she asked.

"No, thank you."

"I think our show went well today. Many people saw us in the park and would have been blind not to notice your attentions to Millicent."

"We must hope her mother learns of the outing and stops pushing other gentlemen into her view."

"I hope it won't be too long."

"Long enough to make it impossible for Millicent to attract attention after she and I have ended our friendship."

"Oh yes, because if you end it too soon Mrs Addleton will have Millicent at every ball and assembly in the county!"

He pulled a face of distaste. "Not something I would wish on anyone."

"Exactly. Therefore, we need to continue this for some time to come and then she will be free to do as she chooses. At least until next season."

"And when the time comes, I hope her dear friend will help console my broken heart," he murmured as he took her hands in his.

"Most definitely," she said softly, looking up into his eyes.

He raised her hands to his lips and let them linger on her skin for several long minutes. Amanda couldn't help the sigh that escaped her and before she could think, she found herself wrapped in his arms.

Richard slowly released her as footsteps sounded in the hall.

"I look forward to the day when I can hold you as truly mine." He pressed his lips to her cheek and left the house.

Amanda sat on the sofa, holding her hand to her cheek. She wondered how long she could continue this playacting with Millicent because all she really wanted to do was make it publicly known that she and Richard Jenson were in love.

"Did I see Richard here?" asked Gerald, entering the room.

Amanda sat up and hoped her cheeks were not as pink as they felt. "Yes, he had taken Millicent and I driving and brought me home. He was unable to stay and asked me to pass on his apologies."

"Hmmpphh. Strange," he muttered and just as quickly left the room.

Chapter 10

Millicent came upon Harry as he was about to leave the house.

"Harry, you are going out?" asked Millicent.

"I am off to the races today, Mill. No, don't even think of asking for my assistance," he added raising his hand. "Farley and I have had this planned for a week and I won't let you drag me off on one of your schemes to prevent me going."

"I never drag you off, as you put it," she protested. "Although, to be honest, I am surprised that you are spending the day with Mr Farley."

He narrowed his eyes at her. "And what is that supposed to mean?"

"Oh, nothing," she said airily. "It is just that he is not very well-mannered, don't you think?"

"Millicent Addleton, what are you up to?"

"Why must you always assume I have an alternative plan?"

He gave her a knowing look as he pulled on his driving gloves. "Mr Farley is every bit a gentleman and just because you do not like him, Mill, does not mean there is anything amiss with him."

Her face showed him she did not agree but her opinion held no weight with him when it came to his friends. "You can tell mother that I should be home by dinner," he threw over his shoulder as he left the house.

Millicent was not happy about this new friendship of Harry's. It would mean that Mr Farley would become a frequent visitor to their home and that she did not look forward to.

She went in search of Pemble who would need to arrange for

some strong lads to help move boxes of glasses and kitchen supplies from the basement in readiness for the ball. She had hoped to convince Harry to stay and help and so deter him from spending the day with Mr Farley but it was clear that was not going to happen.

Her errand complete, she returned to the drawing room where Susan and Catherine were busy poring over the latest women's magazine.

"I declare, these new fashions from Paris are not at all flattering," stated Susan to the room in general.

Catherine nodded her agreement as they continued to flip through the pages.

Millicent spared them a glance and sat by the window. She had arranged to meet with Juliette later in the morning for a walk in the park. While she enjoyed her new friend's company very much, she was anxious that her brother might join them. She hadn't seen him for several days and that suited her perfectly. His absence had not gone unnoticed by her mother, though, and Millicent felt it was almost time for his name to be removed from her mother's list of eligible gentlemen. That would leave only two and Millicent felt certain she could have Mr Farley dismissed just as easily.

"Millicent, when are you getting married?" asked Jemima as she skipped into the room.

"I am not getting married."

"But mama said you are," she retorted. "Will I be your flower girl? I am so looking forward to throwing petals on the ground for you to walk on."

"Jemima, hush!" remonstrated Mrs Addleton. "You prattle on far too much for a young girl who should be upstairs."

Not to be dampened, she replied, "Miss Crane said I might have a break from my lessons as we are to go outside and do some drawing shortly. I thought I could draw a picture of my dress for the wedding so wanted to ask Milly what it will look like." She turned to her sister expectantly.

"Jemima, one day, if I must, I will be married but it won't be for a while yet." Millicent didn't dare look at her mother whose face she knew would be creased with annoyance. "However, you can be sure when that day comes you will know of it."

"Then what shall I draw?"

"Whatever you wish to draw, I imagine, unless Miss Crane has something special in mind."

"Perhaps I will draw a picture of the wedding all the same," she announced and skipped out of the room.

Millicent watched her go with mixed emotions. Obviously, she had overhead more talk of a wedding and Millicent heartily wished her mother would speak just a little less vocally on the subject.

"It looks like we have a visitor," announced Susan, peering out of the window. "For you," she added to Millicent with amusement.

Millicent turned to the window in time to see Jonathon Westercott pass by on his way to the front door. She couldn't hold back the groan that escaped her and wished she had left earlier for her meeting with Juliette. Now there was no avoiding him.

Mrs Addleton frowned at the groan but fussed about making sure the room and her daughters were presentable.

"Mr Westercott, ma'am," Pemble announced, showing the gentleman into the room.

The ladies stood and curtseyed in greeting.

Susan and Catherine looked at him openly, waiting to hear what he would say to their sister.

Millicent tried hard not to look at him.

Mrs Addleton went towards him and welcomed him to their home.

"This is a pleasure, Mr Westercott."

"Mrs Addleton, I have come to collect Miss Addleton. She is meeting with my sister today and, as Juliette has been detained, she asked me to do her the greatest favour by escorting Miss Addleton to our home." He turned to Millicent. "I trust this meets with your approval, Miss Addleton."

What could she say with her mother looking on except that it, of course, met with her approval?

Mrs Addleton was all smiles. "Millicent, don't keep Mr Westercott waiting."

"Please excuse me while I get my wrap," she said and hurried up to her room.

A short time later she returned and was soon being led to the waiting carriage by Mr Westercott. She could feel her mother's excitement following her and suppressed the groan of annoyance and frustration fighting to escape.

Assisting her into the chaise, they were soon on their way. The journey would be short, only fifteen minutes, but Millicent did not look forward to that amount of time seated opposite Mr Westercott. She turned her face to the window and prepared to ignore him for the rest of the journey.

"Juliette asked me to express her sincerest apologies for this change of plans," he said.

"It is no matter," she replied politely.

"Although, it has provided an opportunity for us to become better acquainted with one another."

Millicent closed her eyes for a moment and looked more intently outside.

"Have you lived here long?" he asked.

"Yes, most of my life."

"It is a wonder I have not seen you before now."

"Yes."

Jonathon sat back and watched her. It was clear she did not want to converse with him but he was determined to gain her interest. With a small smile, he continued, "Did you enjoy the library book?"

Millicent swung her eyes to his and quickly looked away again. "I have not had the opportunity to read it."

"That is unfortunate, especially as I know how eager you were to borrow it."

"I would not say I was eager."

"You did look at it rather longingly."

"I most certainly did not!" she protested indignantly, turning to him.

"Well, there was only myself and the book before you at the time and I doubt it was me you looked at in that way."

Millicent felt her face grow warm with embarrassment and annoyance. "You can be completely certain of that!" she snapped.

Instead of giving him the greatest set down, she was surprised when he smiled at her. That put an end to their conversation as she found it very difficult to breathe for the rest of their journey. Much to her annoyance, he was still smiling when he helped her down from the carriage and led her inside the Westercott home.

When Millicent entered the small parlour, Juliette hurried over to her and took her hands. "Please forgive me for not meeting you as planned, dear Millicent. Mother required my help at the last minute and so I asked Jonathon to escort you so that our outing would not be too delayed."

At her sincere speech, Millicent could not continue to be annoyed.

"It was no trouble," Millicent assured her.

"Thank you, Millicent. You are such a kind friend. I thought we would have some tea before we go."

"Tea sounds lovely," Millicent said, trying to relax as she sat on the settee. It did not help that Jonathon was still in the room and she could feel his eyes on her.

"Jonathon, don't you have somewhere to be?" asked Juliette abruptly. She could feel the tension between the two of them and did not plan to be caught in the midst of her brother's dramas.

"I thought, dear sister, that you wished for my escort."

Millicent stiffened. The day was just getting worse by the minute. She relaxed a little at Juliette's words.

"I had thought we might need your escort but I am perfectly confident that Millicent and I shall enjoy our walk in the park alone."

Jonathon looked at her and he wasn't completely happy. They had planned the outing and it included him being present for the entire time, getting to know Millicent Addleton and allowing her to feel comfortable in his presence.

"I would feel happier knowing you were both safe by having my presence."

"Jonathon, we are grown women. Thank you for your gentlemanly offer but please don't let us keep you from your own errands," she said pointedly.

Knowing he was thoroughly dismissed, he took his leave and left the room. His sister, however, had not heard the end of this.

"I am so glad he has gone," Juliette said. "Now, tell me what happened to put you all out of temper."

Millicent was startled. "I don't know what you mean."

"You walked into the room with your face flushed and your eyes sparkling, and Jonathon followed with a smile that I know all too well. Did he offend you?" she asked concerned.

"No," Millicent said, although Juliette did not miss the hesitation in her voice.

"I do not want to pry but you know you can tell me anything in confidence."

Millicent gave her a small smile. "Yes, I know that. You are the greatest friend." She let out a sigh. "Your brother did not offend me but he is aware of my special interest in astronomy and teased me on our journey over here.”

“How did he find out about it?”

“He saw me reading a book in the park and then at the library, that day we first met, he found me in the science section. It was difficult to deny my interest under the circumstances,” she added ruefully.

“I see. Yes, I understand it would be and I also understand how you must feel. But Jonathon wouldn’t think any less of you because of your scientific interests. In fact – ”

“Oh, I know, and he has not once looked at me as though I were some freak,” Millicent put in. “I would just rather he didn’t know and, now that he does, it makes me somewhat vulnerable which I do not like.”

“I will speak to him and make sure he never brings up the subject in front of you again.”

“No, I don’t want you to make a fuss. I will deal with this and plan to ignore him from now on, even though he is your brother.”

Juliette poured the tea and was thoughtful as they sipped the warm beverage. She would have words with Jonathon later but, for now, she changed the subject and the two ladies were soon in higher spirits and left the house chuckling over some secret joke.

The day was cooler than usual and they wrapped their shawls tightly around their shoulders as they walked along. They nodded to several acquaintances who were also braving the cool weather in the park and Millicent found her mood had completely lifted and she was enjoying their walk immensely. Juliette whispered a comment and Millicent looked ahead to see Hanna Heathering walking their way.

“Good day, ladies,” she said sweetly.

“Hello Hanna,” Juliette replied.

“Is the weather not ghastly today?” she said with a little shudder.

"I am surprised you are out walking if you feel it so terribly," put in Juliette.

Hanna let out a small laugh. "One can be seen more easily if there are fewer people walking in the park. Which is why you are both out, I would think?"

"You would think wrongly," Millicent told her bluntly.

Hanna gave her a shocked look that was as false as her presumed good manners. "Of course, you have no need to be strolling in the open with such noted bachelors vying for your hand," she said, her jealousy peeking through.

"Enjoy your walk," Juliette said abruptly and hooked her arm through Millicent's as they walked away. "She is not a very nice person."

"I would agree. To be honest, I was surprised you invited her to the tea party."

"I didn't. Edith did. She is not acquainted with her fully enough to know what that woman is really like. She knows never to invite her again." After only a few paces, she continued. "I am curious about something, though, Millicent. You don't need to tell me if you prefer not to."

"Of course I will tell you. What is it?"

"Hanna mentioned your admirers and, I should tell you, I was surprised to meet you in the park several days ago with Mr Jenson. I was surprised because you had told me that you did not wish to become attached to any gentleman. Has he managed to change your mind?"

"Mr Jenson is a friend of mine."

"Yes, I could see that he was."

Millicent looked at her, clearly seeing the unspoken questions in her face. "Mr Jenson takes me driving but that doesn't change my mind about becoming attached."

"So, you find driving agreeable providing it is just with friends or acquaintances?"

"Yes." Millicent looked at her warily, feeling certain there was more to this query.

"Do you drive out with many gentlemen? Hanna mentioned several bachelors."

"Juliette, just because some gentlemen are expressing an interest in me does not change the way I feel." She sighed. "To be completely honest with you, my mother is driving me to distraction about it. She is excited about three particular callers I have received and is planning a wedding soon after the season ends!"

"You are not serious?"

"Unfortunately, I am. I don't know what I am going to do," she confided. "After the ball that is being held at our home, my mother wants me to decide which of the gentlemen I will accept an offer from. She is hoping I will receive a proposal on the night but I can tell you quite candidly that I will be doing my best not to be in such a position! I have yet to figure out a way to stop this whole fiasco but there you have it."

Juliette remained silent as they walked along. She could not imagine being forced into a corner the way her friend was. Her parents had always made it perfectly clear that all their daughters would choose their husbands, even if that meant they never married. To be forced to make a choice in a matter of weeks would be worse than she could imagine.

"Who are these gentlemen? Do I know them?" Juliette asked.

"One is Mr Jenson, the gentleman you saw me with at the park. One is Mr Farley, whom I dislike very much."

"Who is the third?"

"Third?"

"Yes, you said your mother was excited about your three callers."

"She was mistaken in the third man's intentions but I cannot convince her that he was not calling due to an interest in myself."

"Why did he call?"

"He was passing on a message. My mother does not believe it and so has added him to the list of eligible gentlemen for me to choose from."

"What is his name, do I know him?"

Millicent really did not want to admit to Juliette who he was. But Juliette was waiting expectantly and was not about to let her get away with silence.

In a rush, she blurted, "It is your brother." At Juliette's startled look, she added, "Yes, I know, it is truly ridiculous. He only called on me to pass on your invitation to the tea party but mother will not have it. When he called to escort me to your house this morning, she could not stop smiling in a most embarrassing way." She looked at Juliette and was surprised by the twitch of amusement around her mouth. "Why are you looking that way?"

"What way do you mean?" she asked innocently.

"Juliette, you don't seem very upset about this news."

"Oh, I am. To be forced to choose a husband as you are being forced to do is a terrible thing. I was just thinking how my brother would feel knowing he is looked upon as a man vying for your hand."

"Please do not tell him," begged Millicent. "It would be too embarrassing."

"You know," Juliette began thoughtfully. "He might not be upset by the fact."

"What can you mean?" Millicent suddenly felt a little breathless.

"I don't really know," she admitted, seeing the alarm in Millicent's eyes. "It was nothing."

She pulled Millicent forward and changed the subject, prattling on about books she had recently read and the upcoming assemblies they would both be attending.

Millicent walked along automatically contributing to the conversation but her mind could not stop thinking about Juliette's words and the thought that Jonathon Westercott might actually be interested in her.

Chapter 11

Dinner that evening was not a pleasant affair for Millicent. Harry had done the unthinkable and invited Mr Farley to dine. Seated around the table, she was conscious of Mr Farley's eyes on her several times. Harry kept up jovial conversation with his guest and papa about their luck at the races, although this conversation did not last long after their mother expressed her wish to keep any talk of gambling away from the meal table.

Susan was very happy to have Mr Farley dine with them and was not very good at keeping her emotions secret. Millicent had twice now given her a nudge to curb her staring and was thankful for her sister's sake that Mr Farley appeared to be unaware of it all.

"Mr Farley, how is your sister?" Catherine asked him. "Do you think she will visit us again soon?"

"Petunia is very well and was only yesterday expressing a wish to see you all again. I believe our mother is planning an outing nearby later this week."

"How wonderful. Would it be possible for you to take a message to her when you leave?"

"It would be my pleasure."

Catherine beamed at him and began composing the letter in her head while she ate.

Not to be outdone, Susan drew him into conversation about the upcoming ball at their home. "Will you be attending, Mr Farley?"

With a quick glance at Millicent, he replied, "My mother plans to attend and I will be escorting her." Any hoped for expression of pleasure at this news from Millicent went begging as she kept her head down. "I hope to have the pleasure of a dance or two with Miss Addleton during the ball," he added.

Susan was about to protest that, alas, she would not be attending when she saw he was looking directly at Millicent and the comment was meant for her. Her lips pressed together as jealousy flared in her chest. With false brightness, she told him, "I am sure every woman will be looking forward to dancing with you, Mr Farley. If I were to be attending, I am sure I would save many dances for you." She looked at him through her lashes in what she knew to be an attractive and flattering move and was rewarded with a spark of interest in his eyes.

"What a shame we will not have that opportunity," he told her in a manner aimed to bring a blush to her cheeks.

Susan gave a small laugh, turned her eyes away coyly and continued eating her meal.

Millicent could not believe her eyes at such a wanton show of flirtation and would speak to her mother at the first opportunity and request her to have a word with Susan on propriety. She looked across the table to find Mr Farley watching her with amusement. Anger flared inside when she realised he had been playing with Susan and, it would appear, with the sole purpose of trying to make Millicent jealous. He had been mistaken in his actions because rather than jealousy he had only stirred up a further dislike of the man.

Dinner thankfully came to an end and the men withdrew to have their cigars and port while the women had tea in the drawing room.

"Isn't Mr Farley the most charming gentleman?" Susan breathed.

"It's not a word I would use to describe him," murmured Millicent.

"He is very polite and well mannered," agreed Mrs Addleton. "I hope you dance several times with him at the ball, Millicent."

Millicent did not comment but was planning to do the exact

opposite. It wasn't very long until the ball and she had to move quickly to make her mother believe she was about to become attached to Mr Jenson. It was the only way her mother would stop pushing her towards Mr Farley or, for that matter, Mr Westercott. Several weeks after the ball, at a time when all gentlemen had stopped looking to her for marriage and her mother had stopped also, she would end her relationship with Mr Jenson. And that would be the end of that, she would be free to do as she pleased so late in the season.

*

The following evening, they attended a dance at the Assembly Rooms. Millicent wore one of her favourite peach gowns. Soon after entering, she spied Amanda and made her way towards her.

"Is your Mr Jenson here?"

"He is not my Mr Jenson," Amanda reminded her. "At least, not to everyone here. They all believe he is your Mr Jenson."

"That is true and I believe I will have to make strong use of him over the coming weeks if this plan is to work," Millicent told her quietly.

Amanda's eyes widened with excitement. "I should begin working on my role of soothing companion for when you throw over the poor man."

Millicent laughed. "I am sure it will be your greatest work."

"Here he comes," she whispered and they looked across the room to see Richard making his way towards them.

"Good evening, ladies," he greeted.

"Good evening, sir."

"Richard," Millicent began in hushed tones. "If you wish the patrons to believe you are interested in me, you will have to stop staring at Amanda in my presence."

He tore his eyes away from Amanda and looked apologetic.

"I am finding it harder, you may have noticed."

"Well, I will not let you out of this agreement now because I have finally decided how to use it in our favour." She told him of her plan and he agreed it would work. "I know it will mean several weeks before you and Amanda can show your affections openly but you know that I do appreciate your help."

"Don't worry about that, Millicent," Amanda told her. "This role will be the excitement of the season and I wouldn't miss it for the world."

"You will have your hands full with this one, Richard," Millicent warned him.

"I believe you may be right and I cannot wait for the day." Seeing several people looking their way, he turned to Millicent. "May I have the pleasure of this dance, Miss Addleton?"

"Most certainly, Mr Jenson," she replied and he led her onto the dance floor.

Amanda watched them go wistfully but, determined to play her best role, she schooled her features to one of pleasure for her friend and strolled around the room to speak to friends and acquaintances.

Richard claimed Millicent for several dances and it was enough to set people talking and whispering about an upcoming announcement. She was seated against the wall watching him dancing a set with Amanda when her view was blocked by Mr Farley.

"It has been difficult to find you alone, Miss Addleton. Might I say how lovely you look tonight?"

Millicent smiled her thank you and looked towards the dance floor.

Following her glance, he held out his hand to her. "Shall we dance, Miss Addleton?"

It was the last thing she wanted but she could not show such rudeness and accepted. He continued to watch her throughout the dance in a manner that made her uncomfortable and she was glad when it finished. About to walk away, he held her arm until the music began again and she had no choice but to remain for the next set. As soon as the music ended this time, she thanked him and turned away before he could take hold of her arm again.

She found Amanda standing by the refreshment stand. "Please save me from that man!"

Amanda looked at her with amusement. "You should not encourage him by dancing with him so much."

"I had no choice! He had the audacity to hold my arm until the music began again and I had no choice but to stay. I will not dance with him again, I swear to you."

"Then you had better move quickly for he is headed this way." Amanda almost laughed out loud at the stricken look on her friend's face. They were saved by the appearance of Richard who claimed Millicent for the dance before Mr Farley reached them.

"I could just hug you!" Millicent whispered.

"Now that would really cause tongues to wag," he laughed.

"It would at least stop Mr Farley from pursuing me."

"You do not like his attentions?"

"Most definitely not. I dislike him intensely."

"Then allow me to give him the hint to leave you alone." With that, he stopped mid dance, raising her hand to let his lips linger on her skin for a long minute. Nobody watching could mistake his meaning.

Millicent's cheeks turned pink at the looks she received but her eyes were brimming with amusement. "I am saved."

He grinned broadly and Millicent continued the dance with great pleasure.

The rest of the evening passed pleasantly. Mr Farley did not ask her to dance and she mingled with several friends and enjoyed the company of Richard and Amanda. She had even managed to escape the assembly room with them to a small garden terrace and found a secluded spot where her two friends could have a few private moments. Judging from Amanda's glowing face, it more than made up for having to watch the man she loved dancing the night away with her friend.

The evening came to an end and Richard helped them both with their cloaks. His hands lingered on Millicent's shoulders for the benefit of onlookers and then, making it known that he had been entrusted to see Miss Bladestoke safely home, he escorted Amanda from the room.

Millicent smiled to herself as she joined her parents in their waiting carriage. It had been a very pleasant evening and Richard's great acting skills had set the scene for their attachment. Freedom would soon be hers. Mrs Addleton set the tone for this success by her obvious approval of the evening's events.

"He could not have made his intentions clearer than if he had made an announcement this very night. I have to admit that I was concerned about your prospects, Millicent, especially with your unusual height because, while you are very beautiful, not many men see tall women in the same light. But to secure the affections of someone like Mr Jenson is more than we could ever have hoped for. I believe he will make an offer at our ball, dear. Mark my words."

Millicent sat in silence as her mother gushed on about her success. She was looking forward to the end of the play when she could take her books to the park and sit in peace, staring at the sky without the hint of any gentleman vying for her attention.

As the carriage pulled to a stop outside her front door, she let herself wonder for the briefest moment why Mr Westercott was absent from the dance.

*

"Were you able to give Millicent my apologies for not attending the assembly?" Juliette asked when Jonathon entered the breakfast room the next morning.

"No."

"Why not?"

"Because she was busy."

His sullen manner annoyed her and she stamped her tiny foot. "Jonathon Westercott, why can you not give me a straight answer?"

He turned to her. "I did not give your message to Miss Addleton last night because she was too busy flirting with her gentleman friend and making it obvious to everyone present that an announcement was imminent."

"You must have been mistaken!"

"I can assure you I was not. It seems your friend was not completely honest with you, Juliette."

Juliette shook her head. "No, you are wrong. She would not lie to me."

He gave her a sympathetic look and left the room. He was severely disappointed and realised too late just how much he cared for Millicent Addleton. It was time he left town.

Juliette made quick work of her breakfast and was determined to pay a visit to Millicent as soon as possible. Something didn't sit right and she would find out what it was. The pain in Jonathon's face was just too much to bear, not to mention the pain in her chest at the thought that her friend may have deceived her.

"Miss Westercott to see you, Miss," Pemble told Millicent, entering the drawing room.

"Oh, please show her in," Millicent told him. She was concerned about Juliette because she hadn't been at the assembly even though she had assured Millicent she was going to attend.

As soon as she entered, Millicent took her hand and looked at her closely. "Juliette, are you well? I was very concerned when you didn't arrive last night."

Juliette was heartened by the warmth and sincerity in Millicent's eyes and assured her she was well. "I had asked for a message to be given to you but, unfortunately, it did not happen. I thought I would visit you this morning and hear all about the ball and explain my absence."

"I am so pleased you came. It's so lovely outside, would you care to go for a walk?" Millicent didn't want anyone overhearing what she had to say to Juliette and hoped her friend felt the same.

"I think that would be perfect," she agreed. Donning their bonnets, they set out in the general direction of the park.

"So, tell me, Juliette, what kept you away from the assembly rooms last night?" Millicent asked, still concerned.

"Mother was unwell and, even though Jonathon could have escorted me, I didn't want to leave her alone. Sometimes it is better for family to look after you when you are sick instead of servants."

Millicent nodded her agreement, glad to hear her friend wasn't the one who had been ill.

"Now, tell me all about last night. Did you have an enjoyable time?" Juliette asked her.

"Yes, very much so. The one unpleasant moment was when Mr Farley claimed me for a dance and then would not let go of my arm and so I was obliged to stand up with him for the following set as well!"

"How shocking! I can imagine you were not at all pleased."

"No, indeed. You know how much I dislike the man. I think by the end of the evening he realised he had no chance of winning me, however," Millicent said with a triumphant smile.

"Oh?" Juliette held her breath, waiting for the truth of her brother's words.

"You remember my friend, Mr Jenson?" At Juliette's nod, she continued. "He stood up with me for several dances and behaved in a way that made Mr Farley realise I was not in the least interested in him."

"How did he do that?"

"I am afraid you will be shocked. I allowed him quite too much familiarity," she admitted. Now that the time had come to tell Juliette about the evening, she was feeling self-conscious about her role.

"You don't have to tell me if you don't wish to, Millicent, but know that I won't judge you."

"I am glad you came to visit today. If you had not, I would have visited you, instead. People will begin to talk, you see, and I wanted you to hear it from me."

"Go on," Juliette urged.

"You know that my mother is wanting me to commit to a marriage and that Mr Farley is one of the men on her list. However, as you also know, I dislike him intensely. His manner at the ball was disgraceful and I had to find a way to ensure he would not approach me in the future. Mr Jenson helped me to do that."

"What did he do, Millicent?"

"In the middle of the dance, he stopped, took my hand, raised it to his lips and kissed it for a very long minute. Right in front of everyone. And I let him." She didn't dare look at Juliette. What must she be thinking of such wanton behaviour?

"Are you ... Does this mean you are engaged to Mr Jenson?"

"No! Although, I fear the gossip will be that we have an understanding. I will understand if you no longer wish to spend time with me," she added softly.

Juliette stopped walking and waited until Millicent turned to face her. "Why would you think I wanted to end our friendship?"

"My behaviour was wrong, Juliette, so wrong. And then there is the matter of your brother and what I told you about my intentions of not marrying. I wouldn't blame you if you were angry and upset with me."

"So you are not engaged to Mr Jenson?"

"No, most definitely not."

"Everything you told me about wanting to remain unwed and your parents' plan to make you marry was true?"

"Yes, of course, Juliette. I would never lie to you." Millicent's eyes pleaded for her understanding.

Surprisingly, Juliette began to smile and she hooked her arm through Millicent's and gave it a squeeze. "I agree it was not the best move to make but I understand why you allowed it to happen. The question is, does Mr Jenson know that his actions do not mean that you and he have an understanding?"

"Oh yes, you can have no concern about that. He only did so to stop Mr Farley from bothering me."

"People will talk."

Millicent sighed. "I know. On the one hand, my mother will believe the talk and stop pushing me towards other men and I will not have to make that choice at the ball. She will think there is no longer any need. On the other hand, I fear I will hurt some people, especially when it is known that Mr Jenson and I are nothing more than friends."

"I thought he was hoping for more. He takes you driving and is seen in your company quite a bit."

"No, just a ruse," Millicent said without thinking.

Juliette gasped. "A ruse? Millicent Addleton, is there something you are not telling me?"

"Oh, please forget I said anything! Please. Just know that I will not be marrying Mr Jenson but, at the moment, it would not hurt if my mother suspected it to be so. Oh, Juliette, what a mess this is becoming."

"I am sure it will all work out in the end, Millicent," her friend soothed. Juliette was pleased to know the truth and now she could tell Jonathon that there was still hope for him.

Millicent, though, was beginning to wish this whole play acting was over.

Chapter 12

There was an air of excitement in the Addleton household. The Farleys were visiting town and were to join the Addleton women on an outing. Everyone was looking forward to it, except for Millicent. She knew Mr Farley would be present and did not wish to see him. It irked her that Susan was walking around with dreamy eyes at the prospect of seeing the man.

Young Reggie was squirming as his mother pulled on his jacket. "Why do I have to go? I want to go see the horses with Harry," he complained.

"You will not be attending the races with your brother, Reginald, so please do not even consider this option. You are far too young, as you well know. You will enjoy the boat ride and playing in the park. You know you will," she said encouragingly.

Reggie didn't look convinced and walked around glumly, waiting for the time to leave.

"Well, I know why Susan wishes to come today," piped up Jemima. "She is in love with Mr Farley."

"Jemima! I am not," Susan denied strongly, giving her sister the stare of death.

"You are so. I heard you tell Adelaide when she came here two days ago."

"You heard incorrectly, Jemima, and I will thank you to stop spreading such rumours." Susan's cheeks had grown pink but whether it was from anger or embarrassment at her true feelings being revealed, no-one was quite sure.

"In any case, Mr Farley will not be present," announced Mrs Addleton.

Her words had an interesting effect on the young ladies. Susan's face fell comically and Millicent's brightened considerably.

Soon they were bundled into the carriage and on their way to meet their friends. The sky was clear and blue and the sun was warm. The perfect day for an outing, Millicent thought as they rolled along. They were to meet the Farleys at the river where they would take a gentle boat ride up the river to a park that was said to be beautiful with its flowers and meandering pathways.

Mrs Farley waved as the Addleton's stepped down from their carriage. "June, so good to see you again," she greeted.

"And you, dear Mary. I have been so looking forward to this day."

Behind them, Catherine and Petunia greeted each other warmly and they all made their way towards the river. A stout man helped them all aboard and, finding a seat placed firmly on deck, they settled down for the relaxing ride.

Young Reginald caused his mother some alarm when he felt the only way to get a proper look at how the boat moved through the water was to hang over the side rail. Millicent pulled him safely back on to the deck but he made it clear he was not happy about this change of position. Sitting on the deck, he found he could hang his legs over the side beneath the railings. As these railings kept him from falling overboard, his mother was quite happy for him to remain seated there for the duration of the trip. Although, an eye was kept on him because you could never tell what these young boys would get up to the moment you looked away.

The girls sat in a group and chatted most of the way. Partway through the journey, Reggie found himself joined by his youngest sister who sat down huffily saying how horrid her sisters were for treating her like a little school girl. Reggie made no comment as he really was not interested in silly girl's talk.

Susan was the only one of the older girls who didn't appear

to be enjoying the day. Millicent could easily guess at the reason and was, again, glad that Mr Farley had chosen not to join them. She gave her sister a little nudge and smiled at her, indicating she should pick up her spirits. Susan gave a half hearted smile, which was better than nothing. For the rest of the trip, she gave at least a pretence of enjoying herself and by the time they arrived at the gardens, everyone seemed in good spirits.

There were an abundance of flowers and the scent that floated in the air was heavenly.

Catherine began to laugh. At the curious looks from her sisters, she explained, "We are going in search of petunias." She and her friend, Petunia, walked ahead still giggling.

A picnic hamper had been supplied and the mothers spread the blanket and gathered the children for refreshments. Amidst the colourful blooms and green grassland, contentment reigned as they enjoyed an assortment of cakes.

"Did you know, dear Mary, that our Millicent is soon to be engaged?"

Millicent almost choked on her food as her mother uttered these words.

Mrs Farley looked startled and, Millicent thought, uncomfortable but expressed her delight. "Might I ask who the young gentleman would be?"

"Nothing is certain," Millicent told her quickly.

"Of course it is," put in Mrs Addleton. "Or near enough that everyone, simply *everyone*, is expecting it. His name is Mr Richard Jenson," she said proudly.

"Well, you have done very well for yourself, Millicent. I expect my dear Tristan will be heartbroken," she added with a poor attempt at a smile.

"My dear, dear friend. Nothing would have pleased me more than to have your dear son engaged to my daughter. However, Mr Jenson has been so persistent I fear there will be a few broken hearts for those left lagging behind.”

“Well, things are as they are and no point worrying over those that have not gone as expected,” stated Mrs Farley. “Millicent, you must be very happy with your success.”

“Yes.” What more could she say? That she was excited at the prospect of being a free woman very soon with no man to bother her? She doubted that piece of news would be taken very well by either of the mothers.

“Oh, look, Millicent,” cried Susan. “Isn’t that your friend?”

Millicent looked around to see Juliette and her sisters walking along the path nearby. Juliette saw them and with a smile she changed direction. Millicent met her halfway and they hugged in greeting.

“What a lovely surprise. We did not expect to see you here today,” Juliette told her.

“Nor I. How wonderful that we both chose this location for an outing on the same day. Come, let me introduce you to my mother and sisters.”

Reaching the small group, Millicent introduced Juliette to her mother first.

“It is a great pleasure to meet you, Mrs Addleton,” Juliette said politely.

“And these are her sisters, mother. Edith and Lilian Westercott.”

“I have heard so much about you,” Mrs Addleton told them. “Juliette, it was very kind of you to invite Millicent to your tea party.”

Juliette smiled and Millicent turned to introduce them to the rest of the party. Susan and Edith were chatting away almost instantly and Lilian was welcomed warmly by Catherine. Millicent smiled at Juliette. “It seems we are one happy little party.”

Juliette laughed and agreed. They walked a short way from

the group to talk more privately, arms linked and heads close together.

"So, tell me, has your Mr Jenson committed anymore romantic gestures on your behalf?" asked Juliette.

Millicent chuckled. "No, of course not. However, mother is certain he is about to make me an offer and has stopped talking of other gentlemen. Oh, by the way, Mrs Farley whom you just met is the mother of the dreaded Mr Farley."

"No!" Juliette glanced back at the woman. "She seems a very nice lady and so does her daughter."

"Oh yes, they are wonderful. It is only the son that I dislike. I think Mrs Farley had hoped he and I would become engaged."

"I think Mr Farley hoped for the same thing."

"I believe you are right. My body shudders at the mere thought."

"Would that be a shudder of delight or a shudder of distaste, I wonder?" murmured a voice nearby.

"Jonathon, that is a very inappropriate thing to say!" Juliette remonstrated.

Millicent stood very still. She had not seen Jonathon Westercott for more than a week. He looked at her and bowed in greeting.

"Please forgive my forthright words. I was merely teasing to get a rise out of Juliette."

"It was in poor taste," his sister told him in no uncertain terms.

"It won't happen again," he said. "Miss Addleton, I am surprised to find you here. Is Mr Jenson with you?"

Millicent frowned. "No, of course not. Why should he be?"

"As a man almost betrothed to you, I would think he would want to spend every moment in your company."

So, he had heard the rumours. "He was otherwise engaged."

"A pity for him. Not so for us," he murmured.

Millicent felt her cheeks grow warm and wasn't sure why. Which annoyed her. "Juliette didn't tell me you were escorting them on their outing." Something she was also annoyed about although it wasn't Juliette's fault. She didn't know of Millicent's confused feelings when it came to her brother but, even so, it would have been nice to be forewarned.

"I am sorry, Millicent, it completely slipped my mind at the pleasure of finding you here unexpectedly," Juliette said apologetically.

Millicent squeezed her hand. "It is alright, Juliette. There was no reason, after all, for you to mention it."

"Were you looking for us?" Juliette asked her brother.

"Yes, mother is eager to return home."

"I will go and gather Edith and Lilian. Wait for me, Millicent, I will be only a few minutes."

She hurried away, leaving Millicent alone with Jonathon. She wanted to follow her friend but couldn't seem to make herself leave while Jonathon Westercott stood nearby.

"So, Miss Addleton. When can we expect to hear an announcement?" His voice was hard and cool.

Millicent looked at him and found his eyes matched his voice. The contrast to his usual behaviour towards her was startling.

"I don't quite know," she said quietly.

His eyes scanned the path ahead, impatiently waiting for his sisters to return. His eyes swung back to her when she next spoke.

"Mr Westercott, have I done something to offend you?"

"What on earth could you possibly have done, Miss Addleton?"

His sarcasm did not escape her and she was even more confused. "I can't imagine but it must have been something for you to be speaking to me so rudely," she told him frankly.

A reluctant smile tugged at the corners of his mouth but he pressed his lips together. "You wish me to be honest?"

"Of course."

"I do not appreciate my sister being used and lied to, Miss Addleton. She may have forgiven you but I have yet to be convinced that your friendship is anything more than on the surface."

Millicent's chest rose with indignation. "How dare you! I will have you know, Mr Westercott, that Juliette and I are the best of friends and I have never lied to her and have done nothing to harm her. Nor would I ever do anything so cruel. Your accusations are unfounded and mean and I demand an apology this instant!"

Jonathon watched the sparks flying from her eyes and for a brief moment wondered if he had misjudged her. "You led my sister to believe you were quite happy to remain in the single state and yet here you are, flirting with any man who will pay you a compliment and accepting the first offer sent your way."

Tears stung the back of her eyes. Without thought, she swung her hand hard and left a growing welt on Jonathon Westercott's cheek. Turning on her heel, she stormed away from him. Dimly she heard Juliette call her name but she didn't stop. She kept walking and walking until she was the only person amidst the flowers and finally allowed the tears to fall.

"What did you say to her?" demanded Juliette.

"Nothing that wasn't the truth," Jonathon replied.

"Whatever you said was hurtful. Before you deny it, I can tell by the handprint showing clearly on your cheek! Millicent is a good friend of mine and I will not have you or anyone else hurt her!"

"She lied to you, Juliette. What kind of friend is that?"

"You have no idea what you are talking about, Jonathon, but know this. Millicent Addleton is one of the kindest, most loyal friends I know and you will never again hurt her. Do you hear me?"

Her low voice and furious eyes let him know to keep his thoughts to himself and so he turned around and walked back to where his mother waited for them.

Juliette remained silent for most of the journey home while Edith and Lilian excitedly told their mother of their chance meeting with Millicent and her delightful sisters.

"They seemed very nice, mother, and we all got along famously," Edith said. "I do hope we have the chance to meet again."

"You must invite them around for tea," Mrs Westercott said.

"That is a wonderful idea."

"How exciting," Lilian agreed.

Not everyone in the carriage shared their excitement.

Jonathon kept his gaze fixed on the scenery as they travelled along, his hand moving unconsciously to trace the mark of Millicent's hand on his cheek.

Chapter 13

The morning sunshine filtered through the windows and a soft breeze lifted the curtains. It was another beautiful day yet Millicent felt decidedly glum. She entered the morning room to find Susan and Catherine poring over a magazine. She had hoped to have the room to herself but resigned herself to the fact that such a situation was hardly likely in this household. Gathering up her embroidery, she sat on a chair near the window and picked up the needle.

Her sisters' chatter faded into the distance and the needle dropped into her lap as Millicent gazed out of the window. Memories of their outing in the gardens floated back to her. It had been several days since the event but she could not get Jonathon Westercott's accusing eyes out of her mind. Try as she might, she could not understand what had made him turn so cold towards her. He had never shown more than a passing interest in her and she had never encouraged him in any way. So his reaction to her upcoming engagement and to herself, in general, was completely confusing. And it hurt. His cold words hurt her deeply. She put aside her embroidery and left the room.

Upstairs, she quickly changed into her walking dress and was soon leaving the house. Perhaps the fresh air would clear her head.

She had been walking for some time without knowing where her feet were taking her and was surprised to find herself in front of the library. She stood for a moment looking at the doors. To enter, or not to enter? Maybe the planets above held answers for her. Entering the building, she went straight to the scientific section. She was surprised and gladdened to find new books had been added to the shelves. Choosing one that contained coloured drawings, which was an exciting addition, she borrowed it and left the library.

She hesitated at the edge of the park. On such a nice day, it would be pleasant to sit in the park and read the book, however, she didn't want to run the risk of bumping into Mr Westercott. Her need for peace outweighed her concern and she headed for her private little spot away from the crowds and settled beneath the shade of the large tree. Taking a moment, she breathed in the peace around her and felt her body begin to relax. It had been a strange few weeks, a difficult past few days, and today's peaceful interlude was just what she needed.

The coloured pictures in the book took her breath away. She had no idea the planets contained such colours as these. She ran her fingers over the pages, enjoying this book more than she had enjoyed any others. Leaning back against the tree trunk she raised her face to the sky. Closing her eyes, she imagined the planets hiding so far above them but this time was able to do so with colours. She smiled to herself and sighed. She would find a way to purchase this book so she could always see the planets as they truly were.

A noise had her eyes flying open. Jonathon Westercott stood nearby watching her. Placing the book carefully on the grass, she rose to her feet. She had not forgiven him for his actions at the garden and was not particularly pleased to see him. Although, the strange breathlessness was coming over her again and she forced herself to breathe evenly and deeply.

"Good morning, Miss Addleton," he greeted softly.

"Mr Westercott," she replied stiffly.

"I was hoping I might find you here. I remembered it was one of your favourite places."

Millicent looked at him, surprised by his words.

"I realise you may not wish to speak to me and quite understand," he continued. "My behaviour at the gardens was unforgivable. My sister is quite upset with me," he added, smiling ruefully. Millicent made no answering smile or comment. He looked to the sky and said, "Each time I have come across you here, you have been looking at the sky. It is quite fascinating, don't you think?"

"Why are you here?" she asked bluntly. When he looked at her, she added. "You made it perfectly clear at the gardens what you think of me, Mr Westercott. I cannot even begin to fathom why you chose to seek me out. Do you wish to insult me further?"

"I see you are still angry with me."

"Oh, no, why should I be? I do so love to be insulted and called a liar. You surely misunderstand me." Her sarcasm struck home and he took a step towards her.

"Miss Addleton, I owe you a very large apology for my actions during our last meeting. I can offer no excuses but wish to make it up to you. Please accept this as a token of my apology." He held out a package wrapped in brown paper, with a roughly tied bow on top.

Millicent stared at it. Then she stared at him. None of this made any sense.

He took a few steps towards her until he was standing within arm's reach. Taking her hands, he placed the gift in them and stepped back. "I hope it makes up, even in a small way, for my hurtful words. I wish I could take them back. I am sorry, Millicent," he murmured softly. Then he turned away and disappeared out of sight.

Millicent watched him go and continued to watch even after he had disappeared from her view. This was very confusing. His words at the gardens had been so cruel and hurtful and now he had apologised with no excuse for his behaviour. She looked at the gift in her hands. Really, she could not accept anything from the man but was curious about what the box contained.

Sitting back down on the grass she turned the gift over. It wouldn't hurt to open it and take a look. Then she could return it with a message saying she could not accept it. That would work.

From the crudeness of the bow it seemed obvious that he had wrapped the gift himself. She undid it and removed the paper. She lifted the lid of the box and gasped. Her eyes had to be deceiving her.

With shaking hands, she reached inside and pulled out the most beautiful, elegant, delightful telescope she had ever seen in her life. Her hands stroked it lovingly as she held it to her chest. The one thing in the world she had been longing to own and it was Jonathon Westercott who had thought to give it to her. A lump formed in her throat and she covered her face with her hands as the tears fell.

*

"Jonathon, you promised to take us to the military display today!" Edith stood beside him, hands firmly on her hips. When he didn't respond, she stamped her little foot to grab his attention. "Jonathon? It was most upsetting. We sat and waited for you for such a long time," she informed him. Gaining no response, she left the room in a huff to complain to her mother about inconsiderate brothers who broke promises and then acted as though his sisters did not exist.

Jonathon leaned against the mantelpiece and gazed into the fire. His meeting with Millicent preyed on his mind, even now.

Juliette had informed him in no uncertain terms that he had been misguided in his thoughts about Millicent and her treatment of his sisters. He had not quite believed her but had spent time reflecting on all that he knew of Millicent Addleton. While it wasn't much, he had to admit that she appeared to be an honest, forthright young woman and if Juliette said she was a true and honest friend then he had no reason to doubt that. Juliette was a very good judge of character, after all.

It was her attachment to Mr Jenson that had really caused him to lash out. A reaction that he regretted almost instantly. He was usually such an even-tempered person, prided himself on his manners and ease with people, so his outburst had made him feel very uneasy. He recognised the jealousy burning within him and was surprised at the force of it. Juliette had tortured him with her remonstrations to the point where he had left town for a few days. He had decided it was time to move on, in any case, but the last thing he had needed at that point was his sister telling him how he should and should not go on.

The few days in the country had been of benefit and the one major result was his deep-felt remorse at his cruel words to Millicent. Whether she was engaged to another man or not, he had no right to react the way he had and a major apology was in order. He had debated how that apology should be and hit upon the one gift that he felt was sure to please her. And, at the same time, please him at the thought of the pleasure it would bring to her eyes.

On his return to town, he had begun his search. Finding the gift had been difficult, and keeping it secret from his sisters even harder.

That morning, as he was on his way to collect the gift from the shop, he had spied Millicent walking into the park. It seemed the perfect opportunity to offer her his apology. He purchased paper and ribbon and wrapped the gift as best as he could and hurried directly to the spot where he was sure to find her.

To say she was shocked by his gift would have been putting it mildly, he mused to himself as he stood back from the fireplace. But he hoped she liked it. Hoped it gave her some happiness to make up for his hurtful words.

"Jonathon, I do wish you would speak to Edith instead of ignoring her as you did. She is very upset about today's outing not taking place."

He turned towards Juliette as she entered the room. "When

did I ignore her?"

"Just these past few minutes. She came to ask you why you did not take them to the military display as planned."

Jonathon raised his eyebrows in surprise. "I do not recall her being in the room or speaking to me."

Juliette shook her head. "Where is your mind these days, Jonathon? You disappear for several days and upon your return you seem to be all at sea. Is there something wrong?"

He walked to the door and closed it firmly before turning to her. "I saw Millicent Addleton today."

"You did?"

He nodded and walked back to stand near the fireplace. It was not a cool afternoon but the warmth of the fire eased something within him. "She was not very pleased to see me."

"I can't say I am surprised."

"I went to apologise for my behaviour at the gardens." At Juliette's surprised murmur, he continued. "I am sorry I said those things to you about her and, even more so, to Millicent.

"Did she accept your apology?"

"I think so. I walked away before she could say much at all."

Juliette looked at him thoughtfully. "You are in love with her. Aren't you?"

His silence confirmed her thoughts and she smiled.

He caught her look and told her firmly, "I am not in love with Millicent Addleton and I would thank you to keep such rumours away from your sisters and mother."

"Of course." However, she continued to smile in a knowing way and sat down to write a letter the moment he left the room.

*

"A message for you, Miss Millicent."

Millicent took the letter from the maid and slit open the wafer seal. "Oh, it is from Juliette."

"What does she say? Is it an invitation? Are we to meet with her and her sisters again?"

"Shush, Catherine. Why would Juliette wish to meet with you again if you cannot stop gabbling?"

Catherine pressed her lips together but continued to wait expectantly. Susan entered the room and she gestured for her to join them on the settee. "It is a letter from Juliette Westercott," she told Susan in a hushed voice.

"And why is that cause for such excitement?" asked Susan.

"Perhaps it is an invitation to us all."

"I hardly expect Juliette Westercott would invite us to her house. She barely knows us. If it is an invitation, it will be for Millicent only."

Not to be deterred, Catherine continued to hope otherwise.

"Dear, dear friend," murmured Millicent. "She has invited me to visit with her tomorrow afternoon for tea. Her mother will be out, as will her sisters, and she would enjoy the pleasure of my company," she told them.

"Just you?"

"Yes, Catherine, just me." At her disappointed look, she said, "Perhaps we could invite them to join us on an outing?"

"That would be wonderful," Catherine agreed, smiling at the idea.

"Will Mr Westercott be present tomorrow?"

Millicent's face clouded briefly. "No, I am certain he will be away as Juliette mentions she will be alone."

"A pity," Susan muttered.

"Did you say something?" Millicent asked her. Susan shook her head and Millicent went back to reading the letter again. Juliette was a wonderful friend but the thought of seeing Mr

Westercott had her stomach tying up in knots. However, if Juliette said she would be alone that would mean no family would be present so she had to hold on to that thought.

She pictured her new telescope sitting safely on the shelf of her cupboard in her room upstairs. She hadn't dared take it out of its box since returning from the park. It would make it so much harder to return it if she took any enjoyment from it. But return it she must. She just had to find the right opportunity.

"Good afternoon, girls," greeted Mrs Addleton as she entered the room. "Millicent, I thought you were seeing that charming Mr Jenson today?"

"Yes, mother, he will be arriving very soon to collect me."

"Then you had better hurry upstairs and make yourself ready. He has not made you an offer yet and you cannot afford to be lax in any manner until he does."

"Mother, my dress is perfectly respectable for driving in the park," Millicent protested.

"Wear one of those new gowns Madame Le Cruz had delivered earlier in the week. I am sure there is something just right for this occasion."

"Mother, they are far too good for driving. I am sure Mr Jenson will not mind the dress I have on."

"Millicent, you must let me know what is best now hurry upstairs and change before he arrives."

With a frustrated sigh, she hurried from the room. She was only halfway up the stairs when a knock heralded the arrival of Mr Jenson. Glad that she would now not have time to change, she checked her hair in the mirror on the wall and descended the stairs to the foyer as he entered.

"Miss Addleton, how charming you look," he greeted.

"Mr Jenson, good afternoon."

"Dear Mr Jenson. I thought I heard your good voice." Mrs Addleton hurried towards him. "It is a lovely day for driving. I know Millicent has been looking forward to this afternoon's treat all day."

"As have I, Mrs Addleton," he told her with a smile and turned to Millicent. "If you are ready, Miss Addleton, might I suggest we be off?"

"Yes. Goodbye, mother." Millicent went outside to Mr Jenson's waiting curricle.

Giving her a helping hand, he then climbed up beside her and set the horses to. "I hope this outing is everything you have been looking forward to, Millicent."

Millicent rolled her eyes. "If it had been anyone but you, Richard, I swear I would have turned several shades of red."

He chuckled. "She is only trying to give you the best opportunity for an advantageous marriage."

"I know she means well but, really, sometimes it is too much."

"It won't be much longer and she will consider us engaged and will no longer bother you with such comments."

"Yes, this is true." She noticed they had passed Amanda's street. "Are we not collecting Amanda to drive with us?"

He shook his head. "She said that as it is so close to the announcement, she felt we needed to appear in public on our own. It gives a more obvious appearance of familiarity. Those were her words, by the way."

"It does not surprise me. It sounds like Amanda. We just need to hope there are many people in the park to witness such familiarity. Although, your actions at the assembly room have set so many tongues wagging I don't think we need to be concerned about any further shows of attachment."

"It did do the thing, didn't it," he said, very pleased with himself. "Perhaps I should join Amanda on the stage."

"Please do not encourage her, I beg of you."

He laughed as they entered the park and drew the horses to a slow walk.

"I will be seeing Amanda tomorrow morning. Is there any message you would like me to give to her?" Millicent asked.

His eyes twinkled. "It is the strangest thing but I do have a message in my pocket that I was hoping you would take to Amanda at your earliest convenience."

Millicent laughed. "Then I am happy to oblige."

"You are a true friend, Millicent. I know Amanda thinks very highly of you."

"As I do of her. And of you. There are not many gentlemen, if any at all, who would do something as crazy as you are doing for the friend of the woman they loved."

"Perhaps it is a measure of my love for her that I would go to such lengths to win her favour."

"No, not you. You are naturally a very generous man and I adore you for it." Millicent leaned forward and gave him a peck on the cheek. He smiled and squeezed her hand and anyone looking on would have been sure to believe they were deeply in love.

Which is just what Jonathon Westercott thought when he saw them rolling towards him. Once again, his stomach tightened painfully. Millicent was looking into Mr Jenson's eyes and openly leaned forward and kissed him. No matter what Juliette said or hinted at, it was clear that Millicent was lost to him and the sooner he accepted that fact, the better it would be.

Chapter 14

Preparations for the Addleton ball were in full swing and maids were busy making up the spare rooms for any guests that were staying overnight. A commotion broke out as two maids leaving adjoining rooms at the same time turned and collided with each other. Dirty linen flew everywhere and one found herself lying on the floor cradling her elbow in her hand. Pemble was sent for and came hurrying up the stairs. Orders were issued and the poor girl was taken to her room and the doctor sent for.

Poor Mrs Addleton was in a flap. With one maid down, it would slow the preparations and there was still so much left to do. She called Millicent to come at once to her sitting room.

"What is it, mother?" she asked the moment she entered.

"Millicent, the most bothersome thing has happened. Due to an injury, we are a maid short and I must ask you to go to the Registry to find us another to take her place until she can return to her chores. There is still far too much to do and Mrs Jones cannot manage short staffed at this moment. Now, I know Mrs Jones ordinarily arranges the employment of staff, even temporary ones, but I have many duties to pass on to her and she simply will not have the time. I want you to hurry over this morning and organise a young maid as soon as possible!"

Millicent's jaw dropped further with each sentence. "Mother, the ball is still some time away. Surely the maid will be well enough in a day or so to continue. Most of the work is done. There are just the rooms to prepare and the furniture to be moved, which can't be done until just before the ball."

"You just do not understand how much work is involved in preparing for a ball, Millicent. Now, I have asked you to do this one thing for me and I expect it to be done."

"Yes, mother." It dawned on Millicent that she would not find time to visit Amanda that morning as she had hoped and, depending on how her trip to the Registry went, she may not even be able to visit with Juliette either. She sighed as she left her mother's rooms. She was wondering if this ball would be worth all the fuss.

The day had grown cooler and Millicent hugged her cloak around her as the carriage rolled along towards the Registry office. The proprietress was rather severe in her appearance but very accommodating when Millicent told her of their need. The woman had several young girls who would suit and could arrange for them to attend an interview at the house that afternoon. Arrangements made, Millicent returned home. She would need to send a message to Juliette with her regrets as she would not be able to join her as planned. It was probably a good thing. She was beginning to wonder if visiting the Westercott home was something to be avoided from now on.

Going in search of her mother upon her return, she found her with Mrs Jones discussing the refreshments for the ball.

"Excuse me, mother. The Registry will be sending maids this afternoon for interviews. I will be happy to interview them if you wish me to. I know how busy you and Mrs Jones are at present."

"You are very kind, Miss Millicent, but if it is alright with you I would much prefer to interview the girls myself. Seeing as how I know what it is I need them to do," Mrs Jones told her.

"Mrs Jones, we have so much still to prepare. Do you feel you can fit in time to interview as well?" Mrs Addleton was not at all sure this was such a good idea.

"Ma'am, when I can no longer find the time to do all that my job requires then it will be time I should retire," she told her stoutly.

"Very well, then. Millicent, you will not be required to interview the maids. I will meet you upstairs for lunch momentarily."

"Yes, mother." Millicent left the housekeeper's rooms with mixed feelings. She was glad she would not have to take on interviewing duties but it also meant she would have to keep her date with Juliette. Nothing against Juliette, she was a wonderful friend, but she had just convinced herself that she should stay away from the Westercott home. With a deep sigh, she decided she should continue with her plans and remove any thoughts of certain members of that family from her head.

Everyone gathered for lunch and Mrs Addleton gave her husband a detailed account of the ball preparations to date. She listed the extra duties of the maids and their efficiency, the items needed to be brought out of storage, the refreshments she was planning … and the list went on.

Mr Addleton held up a hand. "Enough. My dear wife, I trust you have all arrangements under control for this ball. Please do not regale me with details as you know how heartily I detest such ramblings on. It has been bad enough I am overrun by errand boys and servants requiring details from me and goodness knows what else."

"Dear, you know very well you have not been bothered by any such people. All enquiries or problems are dealt with promptly by our very good staff. And what have you had to deal with at all but nothing. You spend most of your time at your club, as you very well know."

"I do so that I might not get in your way, as *you* very well know. Besides, all this fuss for a ball that is not required because, according to the gossip that is running rife in this town, Millicent is about to become engaged. Is that not so, Millicent," he said, looking at her over his spectacles.

"I am sure I don't know, papa." Millicent felt embarrassed by her father's kind and pleased acceptance of her supposed betrothal. She didn't like to deceive him but it was too late to change anything now. Not that she wanted to. She was just as determined not to become attached to any man and so this plan would continue to its fruition.

"Are you seeing your young man this afternoon, Millicent?" her father asked.

"No, sir. I am visiting my friend, Juliette Westercott."

"Westercott. I am sure I know that name. Isn't he the young man who took his whole family into his home when their father passed away? I am sure it is. A very decent young gentleman, not short of funds by any means, and very respectful of his sole remaining parent. You could not have done better than him if you had cared to throw your cap in his direction, my dear."

Beetroot didn't nearly describe the colour of her face, she was sure, if the heat rising from her skin was any indication. She could not find words to respond to such a comment. It was an effort to force any food past the huge lump that had formed in her throat at her father's words but, thankfully, he abandoned the subject to eat the remainder of his own lunch.

Susan watched her sister closely and did not miss her heightened colour.

"Millicent, why is your face red?" young Jemima asked.

"Are you feeling unwell, dear?" asked Mrs Addleton with concern.

"No, mother, I am quite well. It is just rather warm in here," she explained.

"Do you think so? I find it rather pleasant. Perhaps you should change your clothes to something lighter before you go visiting today. It would not do to arrive looking like a lobster."

Millicent nodded, glared at Jemima, who had no idea what she had said that was so wrong, and finished the rest of her lunch.

In her bedroom afterwards, Millicent opened her cupboard and pulled out the box containing the telescope. She didn't even open it, knowing that if she did she might lose the strength to return it. Wrapping it in plain paper with no adornments, she laid it on her bed. Visiting Juliette would provide the opportunity to return the gift to Mr Westercott without her having to see him personally to do so. It may be cowardly but it was for the best. The carriage waited below and, grabbing her warm cloak, Millicent picked up the box and left the house.

*

The sun broke through the clouds as the carriage pulled to a stop in front of the Westercott home. She was, again, struck by the beauty of the surroundings as she climbed the steps to the large front door. The butler let her in and led her to the drawing room to await Juliette.

"I was given this parcel to deliver to Mr Westercott. Could you please see that he gets it?" Millicent instructed the butler.

"May I say who it is from when Mr Westercott arrives, Miss?"

"I am afraid I do not know the gentleman's name. My father entrusted the parcel to my care when he heard I would be visiting."

"Certainly, miss. I will leave it for him to collect when he returns."

Millicent entered the drawing room, breathing a sigh of relief. Now the deed was done and she could forget all about the telescope.

"Millicent, I am so glad to see you." Juliette hurried towards her, giving her a warm hug.

Millicent had become used to Juliette's affectionate ways and returned her hug.

They sat down and Juliette wanted to know all about her Mr Jenson. "I heard you were seen driving in the park and behaving with great familiarity. Is it true?" she asked eagerly.

"We did drive in the park, yes."

"I think that even though you wish to remain unattached your heart might wish otherwise," Juliette told her with a knowing smile.

"What do you mean?"

"Millicent, with the way Mr Jenson is behaving towards you and the advances you allow him, it is clear you are in love with the man."

Laughter burst forth from Millicent before she could stop herself. "I can assure you I am not in love with him."

"Why is the thought so amusing?"

"I should not laugh but I can assure you that I still intend to remain unattached, no matter what anyone says."

Juliette wasn't so sure. She had hoped her brother might have a chance with Millicent but from the gossip floating around the town it seemed imminent that Millicent would soon be betrothed to Mr Jenson. While she was saddened for Jonathon's sake, she was glad for her friend that she had found happiness. It was just a little confusing as to why Millicent continued to deny it.

Changing the subject, she said, "I have begun to plant my own garden. Jonathon thought I might like to have my own little area to do with as I please and so I have been planting flowers. All by myself. Well, not completely. The gardener has helped me," she told Millicent excitedly.

"Juliette, that is wonderful. You are very lucky to have the land to work with as you do. Is it a large garden?"

"Not overly large but large enough that I might sit amongst my bushes and enjoy my own piece of solitude. Would you like to see it?"

"I most certainly would."

The two women left the drawing room and walked to the front door. "I'll just grab my shawl, Millicent. You can go on if you like and I will meet you below the steps in just a moment."

She ran up the stairs and Millicent stepped out onto the top step. Her eyes took in the sight that she never seemed to grow weary of. Not that she had had much opportunity to grow weary of it, this only being her third visit, but the view always gave her pleasure. She heard Juliette exit the house behind her and gathered her shawl about her shoulders, ready to descend the steps.

"Do you like the view?" a male voice asked her.

Millicent spun around at the sound of Jonathon Westercott's voice. "What are you – ?" Her eyes opened wide in alarm as she lost her footing on the step and began to topple backwards.

Jonathon's arm flew out and grabbed her about the waist, pulling her against him as he prevented her fall into certain disaster. She held on tightly, her heart pounding. She didn't dare think of what would have happened if he had not been quick enough to catch her. She raised her eyes to thank him and the words stuck in her throat. He was looking at her so intently and his breathing was not quite steady. His face inched closer to hers, she could barely breathe as she unthinkingly raised her face to his.

"Jonathon! What are you doing?" Millicent's eyes flew towards Juliette and at the same time his arm released its hold of her.

"Your friend almost fell down the steps. I was merely saving her from injury," he said evenly, taking a step back from Millicent. "Do not let your mind create situations that do not exist," he said softly to Juliette as he passed by her and entered into the house.

"Millicent, are you alright?" Her friend's colour was high and her breathing uneven. "You must be feeling shocked by what just happened."

Millicent looked at her. Did she know of the effect Jonathon had on her?

Juliette continued, "I have almost fallen down the steps myself and it gives one such a fright."

"Yes, it does," Millicent agreed, drawing on the excuse. "But I am recovered." Although, how she would ever recover from such an encounter she did not know.

"Are you sure? We can go to the garden another time."

"No, please, I would really love to see your garden." Millicent smiled at her and, looping her arm through Juliette's, they headed to the new garden. Millicent didn't risk a look back at the house. The last thing she needed was to find Jonathon watching them and him seeing her look for him. The longer they stayed away from the house the better it would be.

"Sir, a package arrived for you."

"Thank you." Jonathon took the box from the butler and walked into his study. His mind was filled with the thought of Millicent Addleton in his arms, how soft she felt, how perfect she felt. How close he had come to kissing her. Pushing his thoughts aside, he undid the parcel and opened the box. He stared at the contents for several minutes. He picked up the note inside and scanned the few words. Placing it back in the box, he replaced the lid and walked out of the study.

Minutes later, he was at the stable mounting his horse and galloping around the pond and across the fields beyond. He rode until the wind helped to clear the despair from his mind and the ache in his heart that he was trying very hard to deny.

"I wonder where Jonathon is riding to at such a pace?" queried Juliette as she watched him in the distance. "I was so surprised to see him. I did not expect him to return until tomorrow, which is why I thought I would be alone for today. Still, it is his house and he has every right to come and go as he pleases without explaining his movements to me. Although, I do pester him with questions to the point where I am sure he wishes I would marry and move to my own home," she added with a laugh.

Millicent laughed along with her but the day had been spoiled for her. She could not get the feel of Jonathon's arms from her mind. Her skin still tingled where he had held her.

"Have you chosen a gown for your ball, Millicent?"

She was glad of Juliette's change of subject. "Yes, although my mother kept insisting I wear something altogether unsuitable. I have managed to convince her, in some part at least, that as the ball is in my honour I should choose my own gown in preparation of becoming a married woman."

"My goodness, what did she say to that?"

"She almost swooned at the thought of me getting married and was so much beside herself she agreed that I should choose exactly what I felt best for a young lady about to become betrothed."

Juliette chuckled. "And is Mr Jenson's family attending the ball?"

Millicent felt surprise. "Do you know, I have no idea."

"Don't you think you should find out before the announcement?"

"Yes, of course. I shall speak to him the next time we meet."

There were many details Millicent had not thought of with regards to the ball. She had been so focused on having everyone believe she was in love with Richard Jenson that she had forgotten about the finer points. She would have to speak to him and Amanda tomorrow and develop their story. The last thing she needed was people asking awkward questions at the ball to find she had no answers.

They wandered through the small garden for a short while, it was not very big after all, before Juliette suggested they return in doors. The cooler weather made it unpleasant to remain outside for any length of time. When they returned to the drawing room, the maid brought in a welcome pot of hot tea. Millicent had no idea how long they had sat chatting and was surprised when she looked up to see the sky outside was beginning to darken.

"I had better be on my way, Juliette, or my poor mother will think I have been involved in an accident!"

Juliette turned her head to look out of the window and was also surprised by the passing of time. "It has been wonderful having you visit, Millicent. I hope we can do this again very soon. Perhaps you can even help me to plant some flowering bushes."

"I would like that," Millicent told her sincerely. She stood and picked up the shawl she had draped across the arm of the settee. Before she had taken more than a few steps towards the door, it opened.

"Juliette, we need to talk." Jonathon stopped suddenly when he realised she was not alone. "Miss Addleton," he murmured.

"Mr Westercott." Her slight curtsey was almost her undoing as her legs suddenly felt quite weak. "I was just leaving."

He nodded and moved away from them and stood looking out of the window. His actions spoke louder than if he had told her to her face that she was not welcome in his home. Ignoring the stabbing sensation inside, Millicent said farewell to Juliette.

"Don't worry about seeing me to the door," she said, glancing at Jonathon who was clearly impatient to speak to Juliette.

"Will you be attending the assembly rooms this week?" Juliette asked.

"Yes, I believe so."

"Then I shall look forward to seeing you there." She gave Millicent a hug, walked with her to the door despite her friend's protests, and waved her off.

Then she returned to her brother. "You were very rude to Millicent."

"Was I?"

"You know very well that you were. I know you must be disappointed at her upcoming betrothal but that is no reason to treat her so impolitely," she told him, part of her feeling sorry for him and part of her annoyed at his manners.

"I would appreciate it if you changed the subject."

"What had you bursting into the room, in any case?"

"I didn't realise your friend was still here."

"Yes, that was obvious by the look on your face. Now that she has gone, what was it you needed to talk to me about?"

"I don't want you to invite her here anymore," he said bluntly.

"I beg your pardon?" she asked, shocked by his words.

"There are some people I would rather not find myself running into in my own house."

Juliette took pity on him. "I know you love her, Jonathon."

"You are mistaken," he interrupted.

"Am I?" The look she gave him was full of sympathy.

He turned away from her. "I have no problem with you visiting Millicent or arranging outings with her but I would prefer she did not come here." He strode out of the room.

Chapter 15

The weather turned dull and wet and there was no opportunity to even go walking to relieve the boredom descending on the Addleton household. Reggie complained noisily about being cooped up and not able to run around outside and many thanks went out to Mr Drummond who suggested he take the boy to the stable where he could help with the horses. As Reggie loved horses, he fully agreed with the plan and everyone breathed a sigh of relief when he left the house and silence reigned.

The sisters were in the morning room. Susan and Catherine, as usual, had their heads in the women's periodical and were discussing the newest fashion ideas. Millicent sat beside them and peered at the article.

"I don't understand why fashions have to constantly change. If a style of dress is flattering or comfortable, why make any changes?"

Millicent's comments met with patronising stares from her younger sisters and she simply shrugged and continued reading her book. Not that the book was very exciting. It was nothing like the astronomy book hidden in her room upstairs. However, it passed the time and, as it looked like they would be stuck inside for many days, she had resigned herself to reading anything that was handy during the day knowing that her true reading enjoyment would come at night when she was alone in her room.

There had been a few clear nights when the stars shone brightly. She had felt a pang of regret at the telescope she had returned to Jonathon Westercott. What she would give to be able to accept such a gift and be watching the stars every night. She just had to hope that her parents would one day accept her need to see into the sky and purchase a telescope for her. She would not hold her breath for that day. Perhaps when she was married her husband would be forward thinking and would purchase one for her. She immediately dismissed that idea because she was never going to marry. So that put an end to that avenue of owning a telescope.

Jemima entered the room holding her doll in her arms. "Milly, my doll has torn her dress. Could you mend it for me?"

Millicent looked pointedly.

"Please," the young girl added.

"That is more polite but it was not what I meant," Millicent told her.

"Then what else was I to say?"

"You called me Milly."

"Oh, sorry, I always forget to call you Millicent."

"Don't look so worried, Jemima. After all these years I have come to realise that no matter what I say, there are some who will always call me Milly. Much as I detest the name."

"I will try to call you Millicent but I heard you say that you hated that name as well."

"That is true. Then I suppose it makes no difference what you call me as one is no better than the other."

Her other two sisters threw her a look that said clearly what they thought of her melancholy mood. Besides, they quite liked her name and it was much nicer than their own plain ones.

"If I call you Millicent will you fix my doll?" Jemima asked pleadingly.

"Of course I will fix it. Bring it here to me. What has happened to her?"

"She was playing too rough and now her dress is torn. I think her hair needs to be dressed also."

"Then we had best make her presentable. We cannot have her

wandering around with torn clothes and messed up hair.”

Millicent was glad of a project other than reading. Jemima sat beside her while she deftly mended the tear in the doll’s skirt and tidied the mop of wool that was the hair. Jemima was so pleased with the result, she gave her sister a huge hug before running back upstairs to continue her games.

Millicent looked at the rain swept streets outside and picked up her book with a sigh. Ordinarily, she managed to keep herself busy no matter what the weather but for some reason she felt very glum and quite bored. They were meant to go to the Veton ball that evening but she found it hard to get excited about the prospect. Juliette would most likely be there and she knew that Amanda would be in attendance because Richard had told her specifically that he would be there. Amanda could not spend time in his company if Millicent was not also present. It would create quite a stir.

“Millicent, come and look at this gown. I think it would be perfect for your ball.” Susan gestured for her to join them and Millicent half-heartedly did so. Peering over their shoulders, she looked at the flowing gown with a bejewelled bodice and pearls sewn around the wrist of the sleeves.

“Don’t you think it is a bit too much glitter?”

“How can you think so? It is the most beautiful gown I have ever seen,” said Susan in awe.

“Then you may wear it next year when you come out,” Millicent suggested.

“If it was painted with stars and planets she would wear it,” Susan muttered to Catherine.

Millicent pretended not to hear and soon left the room and went upstairs. In her own room she could relax and read the books she wanted to read and, if she was going to get herself out of the doldrums, then that was what she needed to do.

Pulling her book out from under her bed, she made herself comfortable on the window seat and flipped over the first page.

It was the book with coloured drawings that she had been reading in the park not so long ago. She had not been able to finish it on that day and looked forward to doing so now. At each drawing she looked to the sky and visualised the planet perched high in the heavens above them. Time disappeared and hours later she was still in her room re-reading this most fascinating book. She had decided to speak to the librarian and find out how she could go about purchasing such a book.

There was a knock on the door and she reluctantly slid off the seat to answer it. A maid gave her the message that Amanda had called and was waiting downstairs. Feeling her mood lighten, Millicent hurried down to greet her.

"This is a lovely surprise. I didn't think I would see you until this evening," Millicent greeted her.

Amanda took the hands held out to her and smiled. "I was bored to tears at home in this horrid weather and decided that if I was bored, so were you, and now here I am. If we must be bored, then we shall be bored together." Millicent laughed. "Besides," Amanda added as they climbed the stairs to Millicent's room, "Gerald is being painful and I could not stay in the house one minute longer."

"What has he done?" Millicent asked as they entered the room, closing the door.

"He is unhappy with me because of Richard. What is most annoying is that he was not happy in the beginning that Richard liked me and wished to spend time with me. But now that he is courting you, Gerald is asking me what I did to turn Richard away and how could I do such a thing to his friend who had obviously adored me. And so on and so on. It is very difficult to hold my tongue when he continues to rant."

"Amanda, I am sorry he is causing you so much trouble. This will all be over soon and then you can tell him the truth."

"Yes, I know. Don't you worry about me. I know how to handle my brother and having friends like you that I can visit when he becomes too difficult makes it all worthwhile," she smiled.

"I was meant to drive with Richard today but we had to cancel because of the weather."

"Yes, he mentioned it to me. I am glad he did not suggest you still go driving in a chaise with the windows pulled high."

"Why ever would he want to do that?"

Amanda shrugged. "It would be a more private drive and quite cosy in this weather."

"Amanda Bladestoke, are you inferring what I think you are inferring?" demanded Millicent.

"You do spend quite a deal of time together," she said uncertainly.

"I am upset that you would even think for one minute that I would do anything so terrible to hurt you or betray you. You should know me better than that."

Amanda turned to her. "I know, I know. Please forgive me for even suggesting it. It's just that …" She trailed off, not able to find the words to describe how she felt.

"Amanda, I know how much you love Richard and you know that he loves you as much, if not more. When we go driving or on any outing, all we do is talk of you. You know that. Almost every time he passes me a message to give to you. You cannot possibly think he would betray you, or that I would, for that matter."

"I know neither of you would. I am just being silly and feeling insecure. I am anxious for this to be over so that he and I can be together and a small part of me worries that it might never happen," she admitted.

Millicent threw her arm around her friend. "It will happen sooner than you think and you will wonder what bug got into your head to even make you think such silly thoughts."

"You are right. I am glad I came to visit."

"I am glad, also. Now that you have removed that weight from your shoulders, you can visit for real without any excuses."

This caused Amanda to laugh. Her friend knew her too well and she relaxed and settled in to enjoy a cosy visit during this otherwise wet and dreary day.

"So, now that you are out in the open with Richard, has your mother stopped pushing you towards other eligible gentlemen?"

"Thankfully, yes. I think she is expecting the announcement of our engagement at the ball."

"What will you do?"

"There will be no announcement, you can be sure of that," Millicent told her firmly. "I am hoping mother will be confident that an announcement will be made in the near future and, therefore, not require one at the ball. Mind you, she has hinted several times, but that is not the plan."

"I hope you can hold out against the pressure she will bring on you."

"My main goal is to remain single so there can be no pressure great enough to change that. Besides, it will be much easier to end my relationship with Richard if no official announcement is made."

"True enough. Oh, I saw your friend, Juliette, yesterday."

"You did?"

"Yes. She was with her brother purchasing some items for the ball."

Millicent had paled at the mention of Jonathon Westercott and turned away from Amanda so that she would not notice. "And how were they? Juliette, that is."

Amanda gave her friend a curious look. "Are you asking about Juliette or are you asking about her brother?"

"Juliette, of course. Why would I want to know anything about her brother?"

Amanda lifted her shoulders in a slight shrug. "I am not sure.

Why would you?"

Millicent turned to face her, although couldn't quite look her in the eye. "There is no reason whatsoever why I would want to know about Jonathon Westercott. In fact, I would be happiest knowing I would never have to set eyes on him again!" Amanda remained silent but her mind was ticking over. "How was Juliette?" Millicent repeated.

"She seemed very well. We spoke only a few words to each other. Mr Westercott was very polite and held the door of the shop open for me."

"I am not particularly interested in anything Mr Westercott did," Millicent murmured.

"Of course not," Amanda agreed, although a secret little smile tugged at her mouth. "Juliette will be at the Veton ball tonight so we will see her there."

"I don't know if I will be attending," Millicent said, beginning to feel a little down in the dumps. She didn't know what was the matter with her.

"But you must!" Amanda exclaimed. "Richard will be there."

"You can speak to him without my presence."

Amanda pulled a face. "Yes, I can say 'good evening' and 'how are you' but I cannot spend a lot of time in his company as I wish. I can only do so if you are there with us. Millicent, you must attend the ball."

Millicent sighed. Yes, she did have to attend. Amanda and Richard were doing so much to help her, it would be churlish not to do all she could to help them in return. But Jonathon Westercott would likely be there. She would just have to make sure she avoided him at every turn.

She gave Amanda a quick hug. "Never fear, my dearest friend, I will be there. I just wish the weather were a little warmer," she added, trying to lighten the mood.

"I am sure I will freeze in my gown but at least we know the ball will be quite a squeeze and that will keep us warm.”

They continued to discuss more details about the evening ahead and then Amanda realised it was time for her to leave. “I must prepare for tonight. I will see you there.”

Millicent accompanied her to the front door and then returned to her room. Amanda’s visit had been a pleasant diversion to this dull day but she still felt somewhat apprehensive about the evening ahead.

Chapter 16

Blankets kept them warm during the carriage ride to the Veton ball and Millicent was thankful for her warm cloak that would protect her from the cold during her move from the carriage to the Veton home. There was no dallying by any of the guests as they arrived at the large house, it was far too cold to remain outside any longer than necessary. It was a bit of a squeeze entering the front doors but, once inside, they found it warm enough to discard their cloaks and greet their hosts.

Leaving her mother talking to friends, Millicent went in search of Amanda. Richard would be arriving soon and she wanted to make sure she was standing with Amanda at that time. Her journey around the room was stopped several times as she met other friends along the way. Her gaze roamed the room and she gasped as her friend pointed out a new arrival to the ball. The orange gown was hideous and did not at all suit the young woman. It was clear, however, that she thought herself beautiful and she swayed into the room as if expecting all eyes to be on her.

"If I were Lydia Farnsworth, I would burn that gown this instant," whispered Lettie. "How can she believe she looks anything but a fright in it?"

"She believes orange makes her look young and fresh," replied her friend. It was not clear how Lydia had come to that conclusion but they were impressed by her calm confidence.

Millicent was a very confident young woman but she would not be seen dead in a gown as horrid as the one Lydia Farnsworth was wearing. Her older husband appeared beside her, was obviously pleased with her appearance if his look was any indication, and they both disappeared into the crowd. The young women chatted a bit more and Millicent moved on in search of Amanda.

Two pair of male eyes watched as she made her way around the room.

Jonathon had known the instant Millicent entered the room. He had felt it. He also knew the evening would be bittersweet for him. His eyes watched her as she moved about the room. Her laughter reached him as she spent time talking to some friends and he wished that laughter had been caused by a conversation in his company, instead. He knew that would never be, however. She moved gracefully through the crowd, her height making it easy for him to follow her. A stray dark curl had escaped from its pins and rested softly against her shoulder. For a brief moment he thought of going to her with the excuse of re-pinning the stray curl in place but, in the next moment, realised he would never again be spending time in such close proximity to her. He had accepted that she was not meant for him and it was time he moved on. Tonight he was sure to find someone else to pay his attentions to. He turned away and strolled towards his sister and the group of young ladies surrounding her.

Tristan had not been pleased about being passed over for Richard Jenson. He felt himself to be a much better prospect. His mother had urged him to try his hand at securing Millicent's affections once more. According to her, the young lady did not love Jenson and was merely spending time with him because no other suitable gentleman had tried to court her. This had given him some hope and tonight's ball would be the beginning of his plan to win Miss Millicent Addleton for his own. He smiled to himself and began weaving his way through the crowd towards her.

"Good evening, Miss Addleton," he greeted.

"Good evening," she replied politely. Her eyes flicked quickly over the nearby crowd in search of Richard.

"It has been some time since we last spoke. I trust you have been well?"

"Yes, very well, thank you."

"I hope to have the pleasure of dancing with you this evening, Miss Addleton." At that moment, the musicians began warming up. "If you have not been claimed for the next dance, shall we join the other dancers?" he asked, holding out his arm.

"Thank you, Mr Farley, but I am about to join a friend of mine. It would be impolite of me to desert her," she added quickly.

"I am sure she won't mind," he said smoothly and looped her hand through his arm. Unless she wanted to cause a scene, Millicent had no choice but to follow him.

As soon as the dance began, she wished it would come to an end. Mr Farley came far too close and looked at her far too intently. At each opportunity, she scanned the room for Richard. Finally, she saw him talking with Amanda. If he looked her way, he would no doubt see that she was not enjoying dancing with this particular gentleman and be there to lead her away the moment the music stopped. However, each time she turned and looked his way, he was looking away from the dancing.

The music came to an end and Millicent curtseyed. When she turned to walk away, Tristan gently but firmly took her arm.

"Another set, Miss Addleton? Or perhaps some refreshment would be more appealing. It does get quite warm during the dancing."

He smiled at her and she was surprised by his confidence that she would so easily wish to spend time in his company. She tried to find some excuse to escape him but nothing came to mind. They had only taken a few steps away from the dance floor when she was saved.

Richard stepped in front of them and greeted Tristan Farley. He then turned to Millicent. "My dear, how lovely it is to see you this evening." He raised her hand to his lips. "Thank you for looking after her, Farley, until I arrived." He turned to Millicent.

"Your friend is waiting for you, Millicent, and anxious to speak with you."

"Of course. Thank you for the dance, Mr Farley," she said and gladly walked away on Richard's arm.

He smiled down at her, aware of her feelings for Mr Farley, and patted her hand where it lay on his arm. To anyone looking on, they appeared to be a couple very much in love.

Tristan Farley watched them go with a frown. How dare Jenson be so familiar with Miss Addleton and call her by her given name. Jenson would find it did not do to trifle with the affections of young ladies. He would learn that Millicent Addleton did not care for him at all. Tristan looked forward to the day when he would be the one leading her away from Richard Jenson, triumphant in winning her for himself.

"I saw you dancing with Mr Farley," Amanda said softly as Millicent joined her. "Are you alright?"

"Yes. I am so thankful Richard arrived when he did. It seems Mr Farley believes he has a chance of gaining my affections, if his actions were anything to go by. I would have thought your actions last time would have been enough to convince him otherwise, Richard. But apparently not."

"His sort finds it difficult to believe any woman would not prefer to be in his company than any other man's. Perhaps he heard about our plan?" he suggested.

"I don't see how. I have not told anyone," replied Millicent.

"Perhaps he is merely trying his hand to see how much you react to him," he said thoughtfully, watching the man wander the room.

"Then he should know without a doubt that I am not in the least attracted to him," she said firmly.

"He would be blind not to. Still, we might need to keep a watch out for him and be careful how we go on in his presence."

Millicent glanced at Amanda. She didn't feel it would be right to show signs of affection in front of her.

Amanda caught her look and squeezed her hand. "You will do what you have to do to convince Mr Farley to stay away from you. And I will be your devoted friend who loves your man and will be standing by waiting to grab hold of him when you throw him over." They all laughed at this and Richard took both their hands in his.

For onlookers, it was a simple gesture for his lady and her friend. For him, it was the opportunity to hold Amanda's hand tightly in his own and discreetly bestow on her a look that brought colour to her cheeks. Millicent smiled at them. They were so lovesick she didn't know how much longer they could continue with this play. It wouldn't be much longer, though. The ball was to be held at the end of the week and soon after that she would end her relationship with Richard and that would be that. Her eyes became dreamy as she thought of all those days ahead, free to wander the library and the park and immerse herself in her passion. If one small part of her longed to be loved as Amanda was, she ignored it. That life was not for her.

"Richard, would you do me a great favour and dance with Amanda? I don't like to see her missing out on the fun," Millicent told him with a twinkle in her eye.

"It would be my pleasure," he replied, holding out his arm for Amanda.

"Just try not to gaze into each other's eyes, if you can," she suggested as they wandered off. She smiled and turned away to wander the room in search of her friends.

The room was quite crowded and rather warm. She managed to squeeze past a small group of people, only to find herself face to face with Mr Westercott. Their eyes locked for the briefest moment and then, with a nod of acknowledgement, he continued on his way. Without a word.

Millicent watched him go, a mixture of emotions running

through her. His eyes as he looked at her were clouded. She had always found them to be warm and welcoming, when he wasn't angry with her that is, but this evening they were empty. He looked at her as if she were a stranger and it cut deeply inside her. She only wished she knew the reason for his behaviour and then perhaps she could make it right. Why it meant so much to her for him to look at her as he used to, she didn't want to think about.

She spotted Sara waving to her and moved through the crowd to her side. Sara took hold of her hands. "What has you looking so glum?"

"Nothing of importance," Millicent told her. "How are you enjoying the ball?"

"There is a sad lack of eligible gentlemen but I am enjoying myself. I see your friend, Mr Farley, is present."

"You know very well he is not my friend and I give you leave to set your cap at him and drag him away from me."

Sara laughed. "Do you know, I might just do that. He is extremely handsome, and such a physique. I don't know why you don't care for him."

"I agree he is handsome but there is just something about him that repels rather than attracts me."

"Well, all the more for me," Sara declared airily.

Millicent left her soon after and went over to Juliette. She was standing with a group of friends and introduced Millicent to those she did not already know.

"Isn't this a lovely ball?" Juliette said. "I have been asked to dance twice by Lord Shelton!" she told her excitedly.

Lord Shelton was relatively new to town and said to be quite eligible, indeed. Both young ladies looked across to where he was standing and he nodded his head in salute to Juliette.

She smiled shyly back at him and then turned to her friends. "Isn't he wonderful?"

Millicent watched her friend closely. She had only known Juliette for a short time but had come to know her very well. There was always a group of men surrounding her at any event but this was the first time Millicent had seen her show any sign of attraction to one man in particular. She was pleased for her.

"He is coming this way," Juliette breathed.

Lord Shelton joined the group and was made known to Millicent. They discussed the ball and moments later Jonathon Westercott joined them with a young lady on his arm. The woman was beautiful, with golden hair and ivory skin. Her figure was elegant and she barely reached Mr Westercott's shoulder. Beside her, Millicent felt like an awkward giant. Mr Westercott leaned close and said something to his friend that made her giggle. His hand rested on hers where it sat on his arm. Millicent tore her eyes away and tried to focus on the conversation going on around her. She barely heard a word, her whirling emotions confusing her.

"Millicent?" She realised belatedly that Juliette had been talking to her. Thankfully, her friend continued before an excuse was needed. "Lord Shelton knows your Mr Jenson. Isn't that such a coincidence?"

"Yes, it most certainly is," she said, turning to Lord Shelton. "He is present this evening."

"Yes, I have already spoken with him. He was with a charming young lady. Miss Bladestoke, I believe."

"Yes, she is a very dear friend of mine."

"I understand you and he are soon to become more than mere friends."

Millicent hesitated. She could not very well lie to the Lord but she could not bring herself to confirm such a comment either. "Well …"

"Sir, it is being kept quiet just for the moment," Juliette told him softly.

"Oh, I see," he said knowingly. "My lips are sealed on the subject."

Millicent smiled but felt like hiding away. She was thankful to Juliette for stepping in so that she didn't have to give any explanation. And Jonathon held his lady friend close the whole time, his hand resting on hers the whole time, his lips close to her ear as he spoke to her the whole time.

"Miss Addleton, please excuse my interruption." Mr Farley stood beside her and she had never been more thankful to see anyone. "I believe this next dance is ours?" It was a lie, of course, but she gladly jumped at the excuse to leave the group.

"Yes, I believe you are correct. Please excuse me," she said to the others and left on Mr Farley's arm.

Tristan Farley didn't question Millicent's acceptance of his ruse. It was clear she felt affection for him and felt confident of claiming her. He led her to the dance floor and, before taking his place, raised her hand to his lips. She caught her breath in surprise and he smiled, misinterpreting her reaction. Too late, Millicent realised the consequences of her acceptance of the dance but could do nothing except continue the set with him.

The movements brought Juliette and her group into view just as Jonathon Westercott raised his lady's hand to his lips. Millicent's stomach twisted, her face drained of colour and her legs felt weak. The moment the dance ended, she excused herself and hurried away to the ladies room before Mr Farley had time to blink.

She sank down onto the seat and covered her face with her hands. She tried to keep the tears from falling but a few squeezed out and trickled down her cheek. What was she going to do? The worst possible thing had happened.

She had fallen in love with Jonathon Westercott!

Chapter 17

The next morning brought no further relief from her emotions. For so long, Millicent had fought any attraction to any man and now this had happened right under her nose, without her even realising what was happening. Now she had to fight harder than she had ever fought to remove these feelings. If she was going to remain single and keep her freedom to enjoy all things astronomy, she had to stop these feelings burning inside of her.

Richard arrived to take her on an outing. It had been arranged to travel to the outskirts of town for a picnic and Amanda and Lord Shelton would be joining them. Spending the day with her friends would hopefully help to clear her mind and Millicent was thankful to have something to do.

It was an enjoyable carriage ride and Lord Shelton proved to be an amusing companion. He and Richard had known each other for several years and they shared many interesting stories about each other. It also became clear that Lord Shelton had been taken into Richard's confidence, much to Millicent's surprise.

"Richard, if this gets out …" she began.

"You have no need to fear, Miss Addleton. I have no intention of passing on this information to anyone. Richard and I have shared confidences since we were lads and I have never yet betrayed anything he has asked me to keep secret," Lord Shelton informed her sincerely.

"I suppose you think we are all rather mad," she said.

"On the contrary, I think it is most amusing. Richard was always one for a joke and it's good to see he has found a young lady perfectly suited to him," he added, looking at Amanda. "I am assisting you at this moment, you see, by coming along as Miss Bladestoke's companion for the day. Now, if you and I, Miss Addleton, find ourselves wandering off leaving these two alone, well, it can't be helped."

They all joined in the fun and Millicent liked him instantly. She only hoped Juliette did not find out about this outing and be upset to think that Lord Shelton was courting Amanda.

The countryside was green and refreshing and Millicent sighed deeply as she walked along the hill. The fresh air was helping to clear her mind and relax her inner turmoil. Strolling along the open land, Millicent found herself partnered with Lord Shelton. Amanda and Richard had lagged quite a way behind and soon would disappear from view altogether, Millicent thought.

"Lord Shelton, I understand you have only recently moved to town," Millicent commented.

"Yes, I have found my business often brings me to London so thought it prudent to purchase a house here. I still have my estate in the country which I can travel to when the need arises."

"I have always enjoyed the country. My aunt and uncle have land near Somerset and we visit them each year."

"A lovely area. My estate is further west but you will have to come and visit and enjoy our country air and ride the horses," he invited.

"Thank you for the invitation."

"You are welcome. Perhaps you might like to bring your friends. I believe Miss Westercott enjoys the country, also."

Millicent smiled. "Perhaps you could invite her yourself," she suggested.

"Perhaps I could. Do you think she would accept?"

Millicent laughed. "Lord Shelton, I have no doubt that she would accept any invitation from you."

He smiled, pleased at her confidence. "She is a charming

young lady."

"Yes, she is. You could not find a kinder person or a more caring friend."

"Her home is not within the town, I believe."

"No, she lives with her brother on the outskirts of town, only a fifteen minute drive."

"As you have given me confidence regarding her interest, I will send a message this afternoon and request the pleasure of her company for tomorrow. Do you think that will please her?"

"Very much."

Millicent grew quiet. The reference to Jonathon had shaken her control loose but only for a moment. She soon pushed thoughts of him aside and she and Lord Shelton had a very enjoyable walk.

Far behind them, Amanda and Richard walked slowly, her hand hooked through his elbow, heads close together. "I feel as though there is nobody else in the world except you and I," Amanda told him.

"Thanks to Lord Shelton and Millicent," Richard agreed. "I wonder if he and Millicent might suit, after this is all over?"

"No, she doesn't wish to become attached to anyone, as you know. Although, I think her heart may already be taken by someone, despite her attempts to stay unaffected."

"Who has captured her affections?" Richard asked surprised.

"It is only a thought and one I can't speak about. But we will see. For now, let's not talk about Millicent or anyone else. We won't be alone for very long."

It was a starry-eyed couple who joined Millicent and Lord Shelton at the picnic blanket. Lord Shelton chuckled to himself and Millicent looked at them both as they sat down. She could not ask personal questions with the gentlemen present but she would certainly be taking Amanda aside after their lunch to find out what had happened during their walk.

After eating, the men took a stroll to enjoy a cigar and Millicent asked Amanda for an explanation of her obvious happiness.

"Oh, Millicent, it was so wonderful. Richard has asked me to marry him!"

Millicent was surprised. She knew they would marry, it was impossible not to see the love they shared, but that he would propose now was a surprise. "I can see that you accepted."

"Oh, yes," she breathed. "Of course, we will have to wait quite some time to make it known and he will have to ask my father for permission, but to know it is so makes me very happy."

Millicent hugged her. "Congratulations, Amanda. I am very happy for you both. It looks like there will be a wedding soon after the season, after all."

"Perhaps we could have a double wedding," she said, looking sideways at Millicent.

"Who else is getting married?" Millicent asked, puzzled.

"Maybe your plans might change."

Millicent paused for a moment but shook her head. "No, my plans still remain the same. I will not be getting married with you, my dear friend. Although, I think Juliette may be joining you at the church."

"Juliette?"

Millicent nodded. "She and Lord Shelton struck up quite a connection at the ball last night. She was quite taken with him and he with her. He is calling on her tomorrow and it wouldn't surprise me if he continued to call with the view to offering for her."

"My goodness, this is becoming quite an eventful season, after all." She looked at Millicent, noting the shadows lurking in her eyes. "Is there no-one who has caught your eye, Milly dearest?”

Millicent looked away. “No, I am completely fancy free.”

Amanda knew her suspicions had been correct, regardless of her friend’s words. She wanted Millicent to be just as happy as she was and would make sure that happened. For now, she pretended to believe her and they chatted on happily about the wedding and how soon the announcement could be made.

The men returned and Millicent congratulated Richard. It was wonderful to see two dear friends find happiness. The sooner her role with Richard came to an end the better it would be. A change of plans needed to be determined.

*

Upon her return home, Millicent was informed that Mr Farley had called on her. She was thankful she had not been home and realised she would need to, once again, convince him that she was not interested in his advances. Unfortunately, her friendly actions towards him at the ball had not helped the matter.

Susan was waiting for her when she entered her room. “Are you encouraging Mr Farley to court you?”

“Susan, what are you doing in my room?”

“Are you?” she pushed.

“I hardly think it is any of your concern who calls on me, Susan.”

“You know how I feel about him. Yet you encourage him and flirt with him so that he is interested in you!”

Millicent was startled by her attack. “Susan, you are not even out yet. How could you think Mr Farley would possibly court you? And, to answer your impertinence, I have not encouraged Mr Farley but the fact that he continues to call is something I cannot at this moment control. Now, please leave my room and never bring up this subject again!”

She was so annoyed but regretted her mean words to her sister. It was so unlike her but her reaction had nothing to do with Mr Farley or with Susan. It was the fact that she had wished so badly that it had been Mr Westercott that had called and she knew that would never happen. Not now that he had a lady friend. Not now that he, for some reason, did not wish to know her. She lay on the bed and hid her face in her arms. This was not how she had envisioned her season to be.

Chapter 18

"Mother, I believe you were right about Miss Addleton. Once I started paying more attention to her, she was putty in my hands," Tristan informed his mother triumphantly.

"That is wonderful, dear. I knew persistence would win out. You know I have only ever wanted you to be happy so if Millicent is the one for you then I will support you all the way."

"It was stupid of me to give up on her so quickly. It was more hurt pride than anything else but now it has all turned in my favour. The Addleton ball will be held soon and I will use that event to make her mine. Everyone will know of it by the end of the night."

"A wedding, how exciting. And I know Mrs Addleton will be pleased because she told me herself that a marriage between you and Millicent was what she dearly wished for."

"Then it is done. I will call on her tomorrow and begin courting her in earnest." Tristan went to his study, completely confident that Millicent Addleton would become his wife in a few short months. When he had first journeyed to town with his mother, the last thought on his mind was that he would soon be wed. However, from the moment he had set eyes on Millicent he knew she was the one that could change his mind. She would not be sorry she chose him.

"Is Tristan really going to marry Miss Addleton?" Petunia asked her mother.

"He most certainly is."

"But I thought it was Susan Addleton who wished to marry him."

Mary Farley laughed. "Susan is still a child. Why would

Tristan be interested in her?"

Petunia shrugged. "I know she likes him very well and she thought he liked her. It is just that I didn't think Millicent particularly liked Tristan at all. Besides, I thought she was almost engaged to Mr Jenson?"

"Then you thought wrong, didn't you? You are young, you do not know how it is. However, you can be sure that before long you will be calling Millicent Addleton your sister."

Petunia went to her room to begin a long letter to her friend. No doubt Catherine thought the relationship between their siblings was a secret to all but she would surprise her friend by telling her that she was also aware of the secret. A secret they could share until the announcement was made.

*

Harry happened to be standing in the foyer the next morning when Mr Farley came to call. He greeted his friend, expressing his surprise to see him.

"Did we have an arrangement to meet today? I don't recall but I'd be pleased for you to join me," Harry said.

"Thank you for the invitation but it is not you I have come to call on," Tristan said, gesturing to the flowers he held in his hand.

"You have come to call on Susan? I am surprised. She hasn't even been presented yet but if that's the way the wind blows."

Tristan frowned at his friend's words. "No, not Susan. I am calling on Millicent. Why you would think I have come to call on your younger sister I can't imagine."

"Sorry about that. It is just that I thought the two of you… Well, nevermind, sorry for the misunderstanding." He was curious about his friend calling on Millicent. As far as he knew, Millicent was not partial to the man at all. Maybe things had changed. "Well then, if it is not me you are here to see, I will bid you farewell. The races do call," he said cheerily and left the house.

Pemble showed Mr Farley into the small drawing room and went to present his card to Miss Addleton. She was, not surprisingly, not happy with the news of her guest.

"Perhaps you could tell him I am unwell and not home to visitors," she suggested.

"He will do no such thing!" exclaimed her mother, appalled at her daughter's lack of manners. "He has done you the courtesy of calling on you and you do not turn away eligible gentlemen who take the time to call."

Millicent pulled a rueful face and went to greet her guest. Pasting on a smile, she entered the room. "Good morning, Mr Farley."

"My dear Miss Addleton. You look charming as ever. Please accept this small token," he said, handing her the flowers.

"They are lovely. Thank you." Placing the flowers on the sidetable, she then invited him to sit down.

He took a seat next to her on the settee, which startled her. With the excuse of rearranging her skirts, Millicent managed to move a bit further away from him. He turned slightly and rested his arm along the back of the settee.

"I cannot tell you what a pleasure it was to dance with you at the ball," he told her.

"Thank you. It was an enjoyable evening," she replied politely.

"Yes, very much so. I must admit, I had thought you were not interested in building our friendship so it pleased me very much to find I was wrong."

"Oh. Well. Of course."

"Miss Addleton, it would give me the greatest pleasure to take you driving in the park this afternoon. Might I call upon you at, say, two o'clock?" He looked at her in such a way, Millicent was confused as to why he thought she would be eager to spend time with him.

"Mr Farley, I am flattered by your invitation, however – "

"You have no need to concern yourself regarding Mr Jenson," he interrupted. "He cannot be upset at your driving with a friend." He leaned in closer. "I am sure, in time, he will realise where things truly stand."

Millicent stood up. "Mr Farley, I fear there has been some misunderstanding. Mr Jenson and I have an understanding."

"Yes, I know of this, as does everyone else in society. However, I know the truth, my dear Miss Addleton, and you have no need to fear I will expose your true feelings on the subject. After the ball he will know that his false affections will not win you."

She frowned at him, confused by his words. "I can assure you, Mr Farley, that Richard and I are very dear to each other."

He was startled by her use of his given name. "It would be unusual for you not to become better acquainted when spending so much time in each other's company. But let's not talk about this any longer. I understand your position and will be very discreet. At least until it is our time to show the world how we feel." Before she could utter a sound, he stood. "Now, I must go but I shall return for you later today."

The next moment he was gone and Millicent felt completely dumbfounded. What on earth had just happened and what on earth was Mr Farley talking about? One thing she did know was that she would have to do whatever she could to prevent him from continuing his courtship of her.

*

"Did your visit go well with Miss Addleton?" Mrs Farley had

caught her son just as he had returned and followed him to his study.

"Yes, it went well. Her actions were confusing, though. She kept insisting that she and Mr Jenson had an understanding and her actions towards me were not quite what they had been at the ball."

"She was likely surprised to see you, and surprised by her own feelings towards you. To spend so much time in one man's company and then find the man you truly desire is taking an interest can confuse a young lady. She would wonder if she is perhaps in a dream. You can be certain she is open to your attentions."

It sounded plausible and Tristan chose to believe his mother's words. He was sure to find on the drive this afternoon that Millicent Addleton was more than happy to spend time in his company.

As it turned out, her reaction to him during the drive only further confused him. She had seemed less than eager to leave the house in his company and had barely spoken during the drive through the park.

"I am wondering at your change of heart, Miss Addleton. You are less friendly then you were at the ball."

Millicent felt guilty for her dull company but she could not let him think she wished to repeat the outing. "I am truly sorry if my enjoyment of that evening has given you a certain impression of my feelings, Mr Farley. I am bound to tell you that my feelings have not undergone any change and, while I know our mothers are good friends, it does not automatically transfer to their children. However, I do very much appreciate the honour you have paid me by escorting me out today," she added, trying to soften her words.

"If you would allow me, I would escort you every day, no

matter what the task."

"That is very kind and thoughtful of you, Mr Farley."

"Would you allow me to do so?" he asked, looking at her.

"I don't believe a daily escort is necessary. Indeed, I find an escort is something I can well do without most days of my life."

He watched her for a moment and then turned his attention to the path ahead. "As you have felt honoured to be taken driving, so shall I feel honoured by your allowance of my escort."

Millicent glanced at him. His words confused her but it seemed that he had not taken her words of rejection seriously. She should have been more determined in her efforts, used firmer words. But now it was too late. He smiled at her and looked very pleased with himself as they continued their drive through the park.

Her return home wasn't much better for the first person she encountered was Susan who looked at her so reproachfully for going out with Mr Farley. Millicent chose to ignore her and, removing her bonnet, went into the drawing room where her mother and other sisters sat mending or reading.

"Millicent, dear, did you have a nice drive with Mr Farley?" asked her mother.

"It was pleasant enough," she replied.

Mrs Addleton put down her mending. "You don't sound as though you enjoyed yourself. Did something go wrong?"

"No, mother, it is merely that I prefer the company of Mr Jenson. You know we have been spending much time together."

"Yes but it wouldn't hurt you to be open to all offers. Mr Farley is very eligible, you must know."

It appeared her mother had not stopped looking for gentlemen as Millicent had hoped but she was not going to be caught up in a discussion of which gentleman would be best. Millicent knew exactly which gentleman would be best and it definitely was not Mr Farley.

Chapter 19

A whole day spent with her dear friend, Amanda, was just what Millicent needed. They had ridden in the carriage to visit Amanda's aunty who lived an hour away from town. Far enough away so that Millicent didn't run the risk of seeing Mr Farley in one of his attempts to be her escort on errands.

Aunty Mabel lived in a quaint cottage with flowers surrounding the driveway. Millicent breathed in the glorious scent as she stepped down from the carriage. A round elderly lady wearing a white lace cap came out of the house, waving in greeting.

"Hello, my dears. What a lovely day to visit."

"Aunty Mabel!" Amanda rushed to give her a hug, then turned towards the carriage. "May I introduce you to my friend Miss Millicent Addleton."

"Oh tosh, we don't need to be so formal. Millicent, is it? A lovely name. You look charming, dear. Well, come on inside, girls. There is tea and cakes waiting."

Amanda exchanged a grin with Millicent as they followed Aunty Mabel inside.

Millicent's gaze roamed around the interior taking in the tapestries, comfortable looking furniture and an abundance of colourful cushions on all chairs.

"Sit down, my dears. Amanda, you may pour," Aunty Mabel instructed. "Then you can tell me all of your news."

Amanda poured tea for them all and selected a cake. "There is not much news, Aunty Mabel. We have been attending assemblies and balls and enjoying the season, mostly."

"Sounds boring. In my day, we held little gatherings, unplanned and open to all who wished to attend. Sometimes we went driving to the country. And many a time found a quiet, secluded bit of park to enjoy the company of a special person."

"Aunty Mabel!" Amanda's eyes widened with shock.

Aunty Mabel laughed. "My dear, it was most respectable, I assure you."

"If you say it is so then …"

"It has always been easy and most amusing to shock you, my dearest Amanda."

"Aunty Mabel, you are a tease," laughed Amanda.

"Millicent."

Millicent had been enjoying their teasing conversation and was startled to find herself address directly.

"Yes, Mrs … oh, I don't think I know your name," she said uncertainly.

"Aunty Mabel will do just fine. Now, tell me how many beaux you have dangling this season."

Millicent's cheeks grew warm. "None, in fact. I am happily fancy free."

"Hmppff, nobody is ever *happy* to be fancy free. They just tell themselves they are."

"Oh, but I assure you, Mrs … Aunty Mabel, it is so."

Aunty Mabel turned to Amanda. "Does she tell the truth?"

Amanda hesitated the barest second but it was enough for Aunty Mabel.

"Ha, so you do have danglers!"

Millicent's cheeks burned.

Amanda took pity on her. "Oh, Aunty Mabel, please stop teasing her. She will want to go home all too soon."

Aunty Mabel laughed loudly. "Young people do so give me much amusement."

"She likes to put people on the spot for amusement," Amanda explained to Millicent. "She has a wicked sense of humour, but we do love her."

"Oh, now it is my turn to blush," said Aunty Mabel.

Millicent joined in the laughter and felt herself relax. Aunty Mabel certainly had an interesting way about her but Millicent could spend hours enjoying her company.

Lunch out by the pond had been arranged. The grounds behind the house were more extensive with trees surrounding a small pond and further gardens leading a trail away from the house. Millicent and Amanda sat on a blanket spread over the grass and Amanda unloaded a hamper of food. Aunty Mabel seated herself on a chair beside them.

A nearby noise showed them Aunty Mabel's two spaniels had followed the smell of food and sat nearby in the hopes of a morsel.

Aunty Mabel laughed. "They are my two little terrors who follow me everywhere. Always into some form of mischief," she added tenderly.

Food was laid out and they enjoyed a tasty feast.

The dogs livened up the day by chasing birds into the water and coming out dripping wet with no birds to show for their efforts. They then proceeded to shake off the water from their coats, spraying all present and the remainder of the food with dirty pond water. Nobody cared, though, and a quick towel dry got rid of the water. As for the left over food, Aunty Mabel declared it was only fit for the dogs, who made very short work of it.

Over a cup of tea in the charming sitting room, Aunty Mabel asked Amanda about the gentleman in her life.

"What makes you think I have a young gentleman, Aunty

Mabel?”

“I can see it in your eyes, girl. They are alive, they sparkle. I know what I know. So, who is he? Is he rich? Can he look after you?”

Amanda gave a nervous laugh. “I don’t have a man in my life.”

“Of course you do. Maybe your friend will enlighten an old woman. Well, Millicent? Would I like her young man?”

Millicent looked to Amanda. She didn’t want to lie to this lovely woman but she couldn’t betray her friend, either.

“Ah, a secret!” Aunty Mabel was more observant than they thought. “Just what I need to liven up my day. You have a secret lover, perhaps?”

“Aunty Mabel, of course I do not!” exclaimed Amanda, shocked that she would even suggest such a thing.

Aunty Mabel sat back against the cushions of her large chair and looked at both young women sitting in front of her. “Two guiltier expressions I have never before seen. Perhaps I can help.”

“We don’t need help,” Amanda told her.

“So, there is something!”

Amanda looked to Millicent helplessly. Aunty Mabel was far too clever and she knew they would not leave without filling her in on everything.

Which is just what they did. They told her the whole story, from their agreement not to become attached and the reasons why, to the meeting with Richard Jenson and their crazy plan to help Millicent at the same time. Aunty Mabel listened without interruption as the girls poured forth their story.

“That is the secret, Aunty. You must promise not to tell a soul,” Amanda said.

“Child, just who would I tell? No, your secret will not pass my lips. I do, however, have a few words to say on the matter!

Firstly, I think you are a silly girl to allow your gentleman to court another young lady when he should be courting you. Secondly, Millicent Addleton, you are equally silly to allow such a plan to take place, especially when it hinders the marriage plans of your dearest friend."

Both girls looked effectively chastised.

"Now, on to how to proceed from here," continued Aunty Mabel. "Amanda, you say this Mr Jenson has made you an offer?"

"Yes," she smiled.

"Then at least his intentions are honourable even if he has gone about it in a very unconventional manner. Your parents would approve of him?"

"Yes, I am sure they would. At present, though, they believe him to be courting Millicent."

"Yes, yes," she waved that aside. "Millicent, when do you plan to end the relationship?"

"Well, we had thought to wait for several weeks after the ball, which is to be held on Saturday, but now that Amanda and Richard have become secretly engaged, I think we should end it much sooner."

"I have a question. Why on earth would you think your parents would stop pestering you to marry just because you ended an understanding with a gentleman? I would think they would want to fix you up quick smart to stop any gossip and get you married off!"

"No, they wouldn't." Millicent looked alarmed at the thought.

Aunty Mabel shrugged. "Perhaps not but it is what I would do if my daughter suddenly found herself unattached after the whole world believed her to be about to walk down the aisle. Stops the tongues wagging if the girl is suddenly attached to an even more eligible gentleman. They forgive anything when the woman becomes indecently wealthy."

Both girls looked at each other. It was a scenario neither had considered. And, knowing Mrs Addleton, neither of them would put it past her to carry out such a plan.

"Oh no," Millicent groaned, putting her head in her heads.

"Now, don't go all melodramatic on me. There is a solution."

Two hopeful faces looked at her.

"Millicent, you will end your understanding with Mr Jenson today."

"What? But I can't."

"You can and you will. At the ball, he will turn to your dear friend, Amanda, for consolation. This part of your plan will still work and, as he has been seen many times in her company, nobody will think it strange that he seeks her out. After a few weeks of courting, they can announce their engagement."

"But …" Millicent closed her mouth. She felt it was not right to complain about how this all affected her.

"You were right not to say anything, my dear," Aunty Mabel said kindly. "As for your situation, perhaps if you sit down and have a nice long chat with your mother, she may take a backward step and allow you a bit of space with regards to finding a gentleman to wed."

Millicent and Amanda looked at each other and laughed. "You do not know my mother."

"That is unfortunate. However, I do feel strongly this is for the best."

A thought struck Millicent. "Aunty Mabel, when I end my understanding with Richard, I have a feeling that another gentleman will think it is because of him. He can be very persistent and I am not sure how I should deal with his advances."

"Do you like this gentleman? Would it be so bad if he courted you instead of your Richard?"

"It would be very bad! I don't like him in the least but, the thing is you see, his mother is a dear friend of my mother and I don't want to offend either of them. However, I do not like being in his presence but find it hard to make him understand. As soon as I show the least bit of polite attention, he believes me to be under his spell. It is very frustrating and is becoming worrisome," she admitted.

"Millicent, you didn't tell me he has been bothering you," cried Amanda.

"It has only been recent and I didn't want to worry you, especially with everything else going on. I had thought I could deal with him myself but yesterday he showed that nothing I said would make him believe I did not wish to be courted by him."

"Is there another young man who you would feel happy to have court you?" Aunty Mabel asked. Millicent hesitated and she jumped in. "I see that there is."

"No, there is no-one. At least, no-one who would be interested to take Richard's place."

"I knew your heart had been touched," exclaimed Amanda triumphantly. "And I know by whom!"

"No, you do not, Amanda, you could only take a guess. Besides, it is irrelevant as he is already courting someone else. I will deal with Mr Farley myself and, if he becomes a problem, I will inform my father and he will take care of things."

"Are you sure he will?" Amanda asked, not so sure herself.

"Yes, he will. Or even Harry, if it comes to that. However, first things first. I will speak to Richard and end this play and as far as the rest of society are concerned, they will see us spending less and less time together and we will not even dance at the ball."

"I hope you are right about this, Aunty Mabel," Amanda said uneasily.

"Don't you worry your pretty little head, Amanda. I am rarely wrong. Come back to visit me in a month and tell me if I am."

She expressed such confidence in her plan that both young ladies felt more convinced by the time they left. It had been a very pleasant day, a very interesting and eventful day, and they both knew that tomorrow would be the beginning of a whole new life for them both.

*

When Millicent returned home, there was an air of excitement about the place. Susan was walking around with a smug smile on her face and Catherine gave Millicent a secret knowing look. She had no sooner sat down than both girls joined her, eager to pass on their news.

"Mr Farley called today," Susan said with suppressed excitement.

Millicent groaned inwardly but merely said. "What a pity I missed him."

"Yes, it was. However, I explained that you had gone visiting with a friend and would not return until the end of the day."

"I had already sent him a note explaining I would not be home," Millicent put in.

"Perhaps he did not receive it. However, it worked out quite well. As he had gone to all the trouble of calling, I had the maid bring refreshments for him and we spent a pleasant few hours together in the drawing room."

"You met with him alone?"

"Mother was busy and I am sure if she had been aware of his presence she would have come into the room but it all happened so quickly I simply forgot to send word to her," Susan said easily.

"Susan! You know it was wrong of you to visit with a gentleman on your own."

"Oh rubbish, Millicent. You do so there is no reason why I

cannot, also. I am only a year younger than you are, after all. Besides, nothing happened. We merely chatted. It was surprising how much we both have in common. In fact, I think it surprised him as well. He seemed to have a very enjoyable visit. He even commented how sad he would be not to see me at our ball."

Millicent saw the clear signs of infatuation in her sister's face. A young gentleman had paid her special attention and she now believed herself to be in love. Everyone knew it could not happen so quickly and she had best set Susan straight on how things were before she had her heart broken. Before she could say a word, Catherine piped up.

"Well, I had a letter from Petunia today. It appears that all of their family believe Mr Farley to be practically engaged to Millicent."

This bombshell had both sisters staring at her in amazement. Susan looked at Millicent, doubt beginning to cloud her excitement.

"I can promise you that I am most definitely not engaged to Mr Farley and have absolutely no intention of becoming engaged to him."

She sounded so sincere but Susan wasn't sure. And Catherine continued to sit there as though she knew better.

"Then why would they think so?" Susan asked.

"I haven't the slightest idea," she replied. "Mr Farley has taken me driving a few times but I have made it clear to him that, although our mothers are very close friends, it did not necessarily spread to their children and that I was not looking to him for any courtship of any kind."

"Maybe he didn't believe you," suggested Catherine.

"He is difficult to persuade, that is certain," Millicent told her. "Susan, as for your visit, I don't think it is a good idea to encourage him."

"So, you do want him for yourself," she accused.

Millicent let out a short laugh. "I most definitely do not. I barely like the man but can hardly be rude to the son of mother's friend, can I? I swear to you both, though, that their belief that he and I are about to become engaged is false."

Catherine frowned. "Then what should I tell Petunia?"

"You tell her nothing. Gossip will not help this situation, Catherine, and I am surprised you would believe something spread about us from outside of this family."

"If you do not like Mr Farley, then why is it not alright for me to set my cap at him?" Susan asked.

Millicent looked at her. She kept forgetting how much Susan had grown up. Many girls her age were already out and some had even married. Why could it not be the same for Susan? If it were anyone but Mr Farley perhaps she would feel more positive but she did not like to encourage her in that direction.

"Mama was very happy for me to have accepted a visit from him," Susan added. "She came into the hall when he was leaving and thanked him for taking the time to chat to me. She would be quite happy for me to become attached to Mr Farley, I daresay."

Millicent knew that nothing she could say would dissuade Susan from continuing her chase of Mr Farley. After all, if their own mother was happy with the situation, really Millicent could say or do nothing. She was not happy about it, but she could hardly fail to see how happy Susan was at the prospect of a union with the gentleman. Just because she did not wish to become attached did not mean her sisters did not, Millicent reminded herself. She would step back and allow whatever was meant to happen to happen. It would also keep Mr Farley away from herself if he were encouraged to seek out Susan.

Perhaps she should convince their mother to allow Susan to attend the ball!

Chapter 20

Richard Jenson was about to step out the door to go to his club when a message arrived for him. He took it from his butler and quickly broke the seal. It was from Millicent and he frowned as he read the few lines. She insisted on seeing him first thing the next morning to discuss some urgent changes to their plan. He couldn't think what it could be but was not overly concerned. Putting the letter in his desk he grabbed his cane and hat and left the house.

The club was noisier than usual tonight with several card games already under way. He moved through the rooms until he reached his friends.

"Jenson, we weren't sure if you would show tonight," greeted Tom.

"And why would I not?"

"Word is you are about to become a prisoner of marriage. Thought you might be spending your evening with the lovely lady."

"No need to concern yourself, my friend. You won't find me missing from the club for some time to come," Richard assured him, taking a seat at the table. He ordered a drink and looked around the room. "I am surprised at how busy it is here tonight. Is there something going on that I don't know about?"

"Nothing I have heard about. Maybe all the men are escaping their women tonight," laughed Tom.

They moved to a table where a card game was starting up. Richard found luck was in his favour and had a few winning hands. Not so lucky his friends but, as they were not short of funds by any means, their losses did not cause them much concern. New players took the seats of those who had cut their losses and removed themselves from the game. Greetings passed around the table and Richard found himself seated across from a man he did not particularly like. Tristan Farley. He was looking back at Richard with a triumphant gleam in his eye that was puzzling.

The cards were dealt and play continued. The first hand went well but then Richard suffered several losses to Tristan Farley.

"It seems my luck has changed," Farley told him. "In many things," he added cryptically.

"Well done to you, Farley," Richard said politely.

"How is your lady friend?" he asked.

Surprised and suspicious at the same time, Richard merely commented, "She is well."

"Yes, I found her to be so during our outing. She is a delightful companion. Most friendly."

Tom looked from one to the other. "I say, it's not right that you speak of Jenson's woman in such a familiar way."

"Oh, but she and I are great friends. Didn't you know? We spend a great deal of time together."

Richard wondered what Farley was up to. He knew Millicent's thoughts regarding the man. He also knew that he did not like Farley's inference regarding Millicent's affections one bit.

"Miss Addleton has spoken of your outings and one could not expect anything less of her when you consider the friendship between your two mothers. She is very mindful of duty and is very well mannered."

His friends nodded their agreement and looked at Farley, daring him to say anything that would give them a reason to knock him off his chair.

"Yes, very dutiful. I am honoured by her friendship and her wish to drive with me so often. She really is very charming."

Why Farley was insinuating that Millicent had grown fond of him Richard did not know but something was definitely amiss. He thought of the letter he had received from Millicent. Perhaps his visit with her in the morning would shed some light onto Farley's renewed confidence in her feelings towards him. For the time being, Richard remained polite and smiling which led others at the table to disregard most of what Farley was saying.

Richard stood up from the table. "I'll be calling it a night, gentlemen."

He gathered his winnings and moved away from the table, his friends following closely behind.

"Jenson, what was all that about?" Tom asked him.

"I have no idea," he replied, pulling on his gloves.

"Do you think your Miss Addleton is wandering?"

"With that fellow?" Richard let out a short laugh. "I can assure you she is not."

His confident denial convinced his friends but they remained curious about Tristan Farley and his strange words.

It was late when he arrived home but Richard instructed his servant to wake him early. The sooner he spoke to Millicent, the sooner he would find out what Farley had to do with their pretence.

*

Millicent had barely begun her day when Pemble announced the arrival of Mr Jenson. She entered the small drawing room where he waited for her.

"Good morning, Richard. I didn't expect to see you so early but am very glad you wasted no time in coming here. There is something important I need to discuss with you. Please, won't you sit down?"

Richard looked at her closely before greeting her and taking a seat. "Your message did say it was urgent."

"Yes, very true. Richard, certain things have changed and I believe we should end our pretence immediately."

"I beg your pardon?" he asked, completely surprised.

"I cannot keep you and Amanda apart any longer. It is most unfair and selfish of me. We had thought that ending our so-called understanding nearer to the end of the season would prevent my mother from bringing me to the notice of other gentlemen. It has recently been made clear to me that, even after our break up, she will push harder to secure a husband for me to stop any gossip that might come out of our broken relationship."

She looked up to find Richard watching her curiously. "Does this have anything to do with Mr Farley?"

She was startled by his question. "Mr Farley? How could this possibly involve him?"

"I met him last night at the club. He seemed to think that you and he had become quite close. I did not believe him, knowing your feelings towards him. But now I am wondering if I was wrong in my thinking."

"Richard! How could you possibly believe that I am attracted to that man! You know how much I dislike him. How could you even believe a word he says?"

"Millicent, I don't mean to upset you but this is very sudden and what else am I to think but that you have found someone with whom you wish to spend your time? Mr Farley was telling any who would listen of your growing friendship and your regular outings together."

Millicent stared at him. "And everyone believed him?"

"No, I managed to convince them it was not the case. However, on top of your announcement this morning, what else can one believe?"

"You can believe that you and Amanda are my dearest friends and I have decided to end our relationship so that the two of you can finally be together. You can believe me when I tell you of my dislike for certain gentlemen and you can believe that I would never deceive you or lie to you." Tears stung her eyes and stood abruptly, turning away from him.

"Millicent, please, I am sorry if I upset you." He went to her and put his hands on her shoulders. "Sit back down and tell me what has happened between you and Tristan Farley so that I might understand his thinking. If he is about to cause trouble, it would be best if we remained in our relationship for a little longer."

After a moment's hesitation, she returned to her seat and told him about her recent outings with Mr Farley and how he would not believe her lack of interest in him.

"I know when he hears the news he may think our break up is due to him but I can assure you it is not. I am a little worried about how to handle that situation but I am sure my father or even Harry will come to my aid, if needed."

Richard wasn't so sure. They were more likely to push her into a marriage with the man to save embarrassment. But he held his tongue. "When did you decide to end this play? And what caused you to make that decision?"

"Amanda and I visited her Aunty Mabel yesterday and she managed to drag out the secret from us. She convinced us that it would be best to end this pretence now and take the consequences." She looked at Richard. "It isn't right that I should be keeping my friends from being together. I appreciate your help more than you can imagine but I have to stop being selfish and stop being afraid. As from today, we will not see each other and then at the ball we will not even dance. But you will spend time with Amanda, she will be seen to be consoling you. It is only a matter of time before you can make your feelings for each other known." She looked down at her hands. "My mother will not be happy and will no doubt start putting me in the way of every eligible gentleman again but I must deal with that as best as I can. Aunty Mabel is certain this is the best way."

Richard reached out and held her hand. "For myself, I cannot deny it makes me happy knowing I can spend time with Amanda and let everyone know how much I love her. For you, however, I am worried about what this means."

"Don't worry about me, Richard. If it becomes too bad I will find shelter with my dearest friend or I could always escape to Aunty Mabel. She will protect me from the wolves, I am sure," she added with a smile.

Richard chuckled. "If everything I have heard about her is correct then you can be sure you will be safe with her." He took a deep breath. "Well, then. If we are truly to end our relationship, we should start now. But first." He pulled her to her feet and held her in a tight brotherly hug. "You are a dear friend, Millicent, and I thank you for everything."

"It is I who should be thanking you. You put your own happiness on hold for me."

"Let us just say we helped each other. You realise I will have to be very impolite to you from this day on if our plan is to work. Please forgive me in advance for anything I might say or do and know that I will not mean one single word or action."

"That goes both ways, Richard. Now go. I will be suitably upset for the remainder of the day and make it known that you and I are no longer seeing each other."

"And I will make it known that it was you who ended the relationship and ensure you are not ruined in any way through this."

She nodded and, with one last hug, he took a deep breath, gave her a wink, then stormed out of the house letting everyone know he was one very unhappy man.

Millicent bowed her head, hurried from the room and up the stairs. Her bedroom door closed firmly behind her and the household knew something was amiss with Miss Addleton and Mr Jenson.

Millicent sat at her small desk and penned a quick message to

Amanda. The deed was done. She could begin her role as consoling friend to both parties and gradually find herself drawn into the arms of one Mr Richard Jenson. Millicent smiled at the thought. At least for those two people everything would work out perfectly.

When lunch was laid out, Millicent went down to the dining room. Her mother looked at her with concern. She had not seen her daughter look so unhappy for a long time. She glanced at her husband but he was ignorant of any change in his daughter and bid them all to eat.

"I saw Mr Jenson this morning," Catherine said.

Millicent said nothing and kept her head bent over her food.

"Are you going driving with him today?" she continued. "It's such beautiful weather."

"No, I will not be driving with Mr Jenson," Millicent said quietly.

Nothing more was said but after the meal Mrs Addleton took her eldest daughter aside.

"Millicent, is something wrong? Did something happen during Mr Jenson's visit this morning?"

Now was the time for the best acting performance of her life and Millicent hoped that she could pull it off. "We… We had a disagreement," she said.

"These things happen to the best of couples. I am sure when you next see him you will find it is nothing," her mother soothed.

Millicent shook her head and looked away. "No, mother, it won't be better. I have told Mr Jenson I no longer wish to see him."

"You did what?" To say Mrs Addleton was upset would be an understatement. "Millicent, do you have any idea what you have done? You will write to Mr Jenson this instant and apologise for whatever it was you said or did and you will beg his forgiveness. You will be a very lucky girl if he takes you back but you will do all that is needed to make it happen.”

“No, mother, I cannot.” She stood tall and confident. “I have made my decision and Mr Jenson and I have discussed it. He will no longer be calling on me.”

Mrs Addleton’s face turned red then pale. She groped for a chair and sat down. “No, no, this cannot be happening.” She sat up straighter. “I will not allow you to throw your chance of a good marriage away. Your father shall hear of this and then you will find you have no choice but to set matters right.” She stood and rushed from the room, going in search of Mr Addleton.

“George, you must speak to Millicent this instant!”

He looked up from his newspaper as she exploded into the room. “What is wrong, my dear?”

“You will never believe what that daughter of ours has done. I am so vexed with her I can scarcely speak! She must be ill to be so completely mindless of what is her duty. To throw it all away for no good reason! It is unbearable to even think about. But you, dear husband, can make her change her mind and see to it that she takes him back. You must go to her at once. We cannot waste a minute if we are to set things right. Before anyone knows of it. Come on, George. We must hurry!” She stood beside him and grabbed his hand.

“June, what in the world are you talking about? Before I move one step from this room, you will please explain what is wrong with Millicent.”

“She has ended her relationship with Mr Jenson!”

“Is that all? I expect the girl knows her own mind and if he is not the man for her then I am sure she has a good reason for telling him so.”

Mrs Addleton stood open mouthed. “How can you condone her behaviour? Mr Addleton, she was almost engaged to a very wealthy gentleman and now she has thrown it away. How can you just stand there and do nothing?”

George Addleton carefully folded his paper and laid it on his desk. When his wife started referring to him as Mr Addleton he knew it was in everyone's best interest to do whatever it took to soothe her feelings. "Alright, my dear, I will speak to her."

He followed his wife to the drawing room where Millicent sat waiting for his arrival. It had not gone pleasantly with her mother but at least she had believed her. Papa might not be easily fooled and she was not looking forward to his interrogation.

"Millicent, your mother has told me some very distressing news. Is it true?"

"Yes it is, papa," Millicent told him nervously.

"Mr Jenson is a very eligible young man. You have been very fortunate to come under his attention. This far into the season, you may not find another man so eligible."

"I understand, papa. Mr Jenson has been very attentive but I find I can no longer spend time in his company."

"Did he hurt you, Millicent?" he wanted to know. If that were the case, he would deal with the man himself.

"No, papa, he would never do so. He is a good man." She could not have her parents thinking Richard was anything but the best of men.

"Then why have you thrown him over, girl?"

"I merely decided we would not suit."

"Would not suit? You are not making much sense, my dear. Mr Jenson is a good man and it appeared you got along quite well together. You need to rethink the matter and I am sure you will find he suits you very well, indeed."

Mrs Addleton slumped onto a chair. Her daughter was losing her mind.

"It's those books, that's what it is," she said. "All that time she spends reading those horrible books has warped her mind. Oh, what is to become of her," she moaned.

Millicent looked from one to the other. This was not going

easily at all. "Mother. Papa. I know you must be extremely disappointed but surely you do not want me to wed someone that does not suit me?" She looked at them pleadingly.

"I do not understand you, Millicent," her father told her. "This is very disappointing."

Mrs Addleton shook her head and straightened in the chair. "No, I won't have it. This *simply* will not do. If you truly have decided Mr Jenson will not suit you as a husband, Millicent, then you will make a choice from the two other gentlemen as originally planned," she said determinedly.

"Mother?"

"Mr Farley and Mr Westercott will both be present at the ball. You will choose one of them."

"Mother, no!" Millicent felt the colour drain from her face. This was an outcome she had, stupidly, not considered.

"I agree with your mother's plan, Millicent. You may not find Mr Jenson suitable but I am sure one of the other gentlemen will be. We will allow you to end this relationship but expect you to be betrothed to either Mr Farley or Mr Westercott before the month is out."

Millicent could only stare in utter dismay. Her parents left the room and she sat on the edge of the settee, completely stunned. Now what was she to do?

Chapter 21

Amanda arrived later that day. She joined Millicent and her sisters in the drawing room.

"I think you'll find Millicent isn't the best of company today," Susan told her.

"I expected it might be so. It's a terrible shame what has happened but I am here to lend my support to my dearest friend," Amanda said, sitting beside Millicent and placing a comforting hand on hers.

"Thank you, Amanda," Millicent said softly. "You are a true friend, indeed." She turned to her sisters. "Would you mind if Amanda and I spoke in private? I believe it may help to improve my spirits."

"Of course," Susan agreed, speaking for them both.

She and Catherine stood and walked to the door.

"I am sure Amanda will do a lot to help ease poor Millicent's heartache," Susan whispered to Catherine as they left the room.

As soon as the door closed behind them, Amanda's eyes filled with excitement. "I can hardly believe it is finally done. Mind you, you know I was more than happy for this little play to continue for some time to come but now that the time for Richard and I to be together is so close, I am filled with excitement. What did he say when you told him?"

Millicent smiled at her friend. Seeing the glow in her eyes, she knew she had done the right thing. "He was very surprised at first and thought the reason for my change of heart was that I had found someone else. I soon set him straight on that thinking."

Amanda laughed. "I can imagine his surprise. But you know, dear Millicent, this means you can now set your cap at the man you truly love."

"There is no such person. I intend to remain single as always," Millicent told her firmly.

Amanda clearly didn't believe her, especially after the visit with Aunty Mabel which had brought about much information on the subject. But she did not press the matter. Besides, she was too excited about her own future.

They stopped talking and put on serious expressions when the tea tray arrived. They waited impatiently for the maid to finish and leave the room but finally she was gone. Millicent poured the tea and offered Amanda a pastry.

"Have you told your parents?" Amanda asked.

Millicent pulled a face. "Yes."

"What did they say?"

"They were very disappointed and mother wanted me to write to Richard immediately and beg his forgiveness and ask him to take me back. But, of course, I did not," she added, seeing the doubt flicker across Amanda's face.

"They finally agreed, I am assuming?"

"In a manner of speaking, yes."

"What do you mean?"

"Once mother overcame her fainting spells, she and papa agreed that I should find another man to wed."

"We suspected she would not give up on her attempts to have you married," Amanda reminded her.

"That is true, although I had hoped she would leave me in peace for a little while."

Amanda could see that something was not quite right. "Have your parents already chosen a man for you?" she asked, her suspicions growing.

Millicent sighed heavily. "In a manner of speaking."

Amanda put down her cup and turned to her friend. "Tell me what they have done, Millicent. I can tell something is wrong so please don't pretend otherwise."

Millicent placed her cup carefully on the table and walked to the window. This room overlooked a small garden and the scene was very pleasant in the afternoon sun. She wished the sun would always shine for her but in a few days things would change forever. She slowly turned to face Amanda.

"Do you remember when my mother had three gentlemen lined up for me to choose from as a husband?"

Amanda nodded. "Yes, it was around the time Richard and I came up with our little plan. Not that it worked as completely as we had expected," she added, with a rueful twist to her mouth.

"No, it didn't work at all. You see, my parents have allowed me to end my relationship with Richard but, in his place, I must choose a husband from the two remaining gentlemen of their first choice."

"You cannot be serious!"

"Much as I loathe the idea, I am," Millicent told her unhappily. "My mother insists I choose either Mr Farley or Mr Westercott as a husband. She does not require me to announce that choice at the ball which is a small blessing, I suppose. Merely to make my decision at the ball and encourage the chosen gentleman so that he makes me an offer by the end of the month." She looked at Amanda, her helplessness clearly written across her face.

"Oh, Millicent." Amanda hurried to her side and hugged her tightly. "I never expected anything like this would happen. None of us did. But you cannot choose Mr Farley! You detest the man."

"Yes, I do. Unfortunately, he somehow has decided that my affections for him have grown and when he hears of Richard and I ending our relationship, you can be sure he will think it is because of him. I have no other man to make him think otherwise."

"You could choose Mr Westercott. He seems like a very nice man," Amanda suggested gently.

But Millicent was shaking her head before Amanda had finished speaking. "I can never choose Mr Westercott. He would not be interested. Besides, I believe he is already courting a very eligible young woman."

"Then we will have to find someone else. I fear that, like it or not Millicent, you are going to have to get married," she told her gently. "What we must do is make sure it is not to Mr Farley."

The truth of this had also struck Millicent and she slumped into the nearest chair, wondering how her plans had gone so wrong.

After Amanda left, Millicent didn't have to pretend to be down in the dumps. She truly was down in the dumps. Their conversation had only borne it home to her that she was to be married before the year was out.

It was growing late but Millicent grabbed her cloak and left the house. She needed to walk. She needed to think. There must be a way out of this situation.

She knew without a doubt that Mr Farley would be descending on her more and more and it would take all her strength to make him understand she was not interested in his courtship. But then what? She had to choose a husband and he was the only possible choice from the men her mother wished her to consider.

What of Mr Westercott? her mind pushed. Much as she wished it were otherwise, Millicent knew that Mr Westercott was lost to her. Perhaps at one time it might have been possible to encourage him to at least like her. He did seem to enjoy her company. But things had changed and often when she heard his name mentioned it was linked with his new lady friend.

She had purposely walked towards the park and entered, heading for her special place. She had no book to read and only her imagination to see the heavens beyond but it was the only place she would find some peace. She sat beneath her usual tree and stared off into the distance.

No answers came to her and with a sad sigh she rested her head against the trunk and closed her eyes. She was becoming more and more afraid that she would end up having to marry Mr Farley.

For a short while, she imagined what it would be like if Jonathon Westercott was the man wanting to court her. Even marry her. It was a wonderful dream, but an empty one. He would never want her.

The air was growing chill and with a resigned sigh she opened her eyes and rose to her feet. She found herself looking into the hazel eyes of Jonathon Westercott. For a moment she thought she was still daydreaming.

"Good afternoon, Miss Addleton."

"Mr Westercott." Her voice was barely a whisper.

They stood looking at each other for several moments.

He did not miss the sadness in her eyes and, having heard the rumours already spreading around town, could guess at the cause.

Millicent could not drag her eyes away. Her racing pulse confirmed that she still loved him and her heart ached knowing she could never have him.

Finally, she looked away. "I wonder, Mr Westercott, if you could take a message to Juliette for me?"

"Certainly." While not exactly warm, his voice at least was not as cold as the last few times they had met.

"Please could you ask her if she would be free to visit with me tomorrow? There is something I wish to speak to her about if she is available."

"I will pass on the message."

"Thank you. If you will excuse me, I must go."

"Good day, Miss Addleton."

"Good day, Mr Westercott." Then she was gone, feeling sadder than when she had set out.

Jonathon watched her go. He had convinced himself that he felt nothing for her anymore. Had taken other young ladies on outings to remove her from his thoughts. Yet, seeing her had proved just how naïve he had been to ever think he could stop caring.

Chapter 22

Millicent paced the morning room. She had hardly slept the night before. The announcement from her parents was, naturally, unsettling but her encounter with Jonathon Westercott had been even more so. She was finding it hard to come to terms with the fact that she could never be with him. During her pretended courtship with Richard, she had not thought too much about her future apart from the need to be free to study the stars. But now that the pretence was over and she had the prospect of marriage ahead of her, she finally realised what was important and had to accept that she couldn't have that. And the man she did not want was about to arrive on her doorstep any minute.

Today she had to make sure Mr Farley realised without a doubt that she was not attracted to him. If he took the step back then her mother could hardly force her to choose him. It would be most unseemly. Convincing him would be the hard part.

"Mr Farley, miss," announced Pemble.

He entered the room and bowed before her. "Miss Addleton, what a pleasure it is to see you today."

"Good morning, Mr Farley."

He moved towards her. "I must tell you, my dear, that I have been somewhat disappointed that you have not taken advantage of my offer to escort you. I don't make this type of offer lightly, you know."

"Forgive me, Mr Farley, but as I mentioned at the time, I really don't need an escort during my daily errands."

"Far be it for me to argue with a lady so I will take your word for it. Now, there is something in particular that I wish to discuss with you."

"Please, won't you have a seat," she invited and sat down on a comfortable chair. She was not about to risk the settee where he might sit right beside her.

He took a seat opposite. "I know you won't be surprised to learn that the news that you are no longer being escorted by Mr Jenson is already about town."

"I expect nothing stays secret for long."

"That is true but I am sorry that you have had to deal with the innuendo surrounding it."

"I have not heard of any innuendo. On the contrary, people have generally been kind and understanding."

"Naturally. As one would expect. However, it does not come as a surprise that some feel you threw him over for another." He smiled at her.

"Then they would be misinformed," she told him firmly.

"Come, Miss Addleton, you know you cannot hide your feelings forever. And why should you want to? I believe it won't be surprising if we show the world who you truly wish to be with." He knelt before her and took her hand in his. "We could take a drive and show our feelings in public," he suggested.

Millicent stood quickly and stepped away. "Mr Farley, I am afraid you mistake my feelings for you. My end with Mr Jenson was not due to anyone but myself. To think otherwise is … is foolish."

"Yet, I am no fool, Miss Addleton. I do not understand why you continue to deny it," he commented as he moved towards her. "Why, even my mother has noticed your continuing attraction to me and it was she who encouraged me to pursue you further."

Millicent frowned. "Your mother put you up to this?"

"I had begun to think you had no feelings for me and, I admit, did find it a blow to my ego and took a step back. But her confidence in your feelings enabled me to see more clearly and then when you ended your understanding with Mr Jenson, I knew it to be true." He reached for her hand but Millicent moved quickly away.

"Mr Farley, please believe me. And please listen to what I am about to tell you. Mr Jenson and I found we would not suit. There is no other man at this time who I feel would suit me in his place. I have no intention of becoming attached to anyone. Forgive me for being blunt, sir, but I do not find myself attracted to you."

"Surely you jest."

"Surely I do not."

He stood watching her, puzzlement clear on his face. "You have driven out with me several times. Allowed me to call on you several times."

"I was merely being polite, Mr Farley. Our mothers are very good friends, after all."

He seemed to take this in and took a turn about the room. "This is most unsettling. I do not offer my affections to just anyone, Miss Addleton. Even though you appeared unfriendly on our first acquaintance, I was certain your feelings had changed during our meetings. Do you mean to tell me that they have not?" he demanded.

"It is not that I dislike you, Mr Farley." She lifted her hands helplessly. "I don't mean to be rude but I need you to understand. I just do not feel we would suit at all."

"Hmmppff. This is most unusual," he muttered as he continued to pace the room. He stopped to look at her and then paced some more.

"I am sorry if I have hurt you," Millicent said, trying to be gentle.

"I find, Miss Addleton, that my pride is badly bruised. Perhaps I am a fool, after all. Might I ask, if you did not end your relationship because of me, who did you end it for?"

"As I explained, I did so because I felt he and I would not

suit."

"Miss Addleton, forgive me for saying so but I don't believe it. I have seen you both together and you appear to get along quite famously. However, I will not push you to reveal your true reasons. Instead, I must unravel this information you have given me and accept that it is not my suit that you are after."

Millicent felt relief that he had accepted her rejection, and surprise. Her experience of him to date had not led her to believe he would be so easily swayed, but so it was.

As he said his farewells and left the room, Susan entered the main hall. Millicent saw him pause to greet her. Susan's cheeks grew pink as he raised her hand to his lips. Millicent watched on with surprise and then the idea dawned that the reason he no longer seemed to be worried about pursuing her was because his fancy had been caught elsewhere.

It seemed Mr Farley would not become a problem after all. Except, perhaps, when mother found out that her younger daughter might receive an offer before she had even made her debut.

A short time later, Susan entered the morning room. Her cheeks were still pink and her eyes glowed. "I saw Mr Farley when he was leaving. Did he come to ask you driving?"

"Yes, but I told him I was unable to go," Millicent informed her, keeping a close eye on her sister's reactions.

"But why not? It is such a lovely day and he is such charming company."

"I don't think Mr Farley will be calling here anymore, unless it is to visit Harry, of course."

Susan's brow creased. "What do you mean?"

"I have finally managed to convince Mr Farley that I do not wish him to call on me." Susan's face was a mixture of surprise and hope. "Now, you must not tell mother. I don't want her to know until after the ball. You must promise me."

"Why is the ball so important?"

"It is too detailed to go into but mother must believe him to be eligible until after that night. Promise me."

"I don't understand but I promise." She looked uneasy and, surprisingly, shy. "Do you know if Mr Farley will be escorting another lady to the ball?"

Millicent hid her smile. "I don't believe so, although he did not take me into his confidence. Speaking of the ball, I have made up my mind to speak to mother about your attendance."

"You have?" Susan almost squeaked.

"Why should you not attend? Many girls your age are already out in society. Why, some have even obtained very suitable connections. I don't believe attending one ball in our own home would be looked upon in any way but acceptable."

"Oh, Millicent," breathed Susan. "Do you really think mama would agree?"

Millicent was less than confident but it would be the ideal solution with regards to Mr Farley. "I will speak to her directly."

"You wish your sister to what?" Mrs Addleton was so startled by the suggestion she had to sit down on the nearest chair.

"Only think, mother, how very suitable it would be. Susan is almost seventeen and has attended many dinner parties held in our own home and even small impromptu dances. I am not recommending she attend any event outside of our home but a ball under this very roof would do her no harm."

Mrs Addleton stared at her daughter as if her mind had gone begging. To bring her younger daughter into the notice of all those highly respected in society before she was even officially out was unthinkable.

"I do believe, Millicent, that your recent unfortunate falling out with Mr Jenson has sadly affected your thinking. You must know that it is just not done. Everyone, simply *everyone*, of worthy note will be in attendance. What must they think when they see a daughter of mine barely out of the schoolroom being introduced at such a grand occasion? It just won't do. It simply won't do!"

Millicent's hopes faded as she watched her distressed mother vigorously fanning herself, trying to prevent a fainting spell which she simply *knew* was about to overtake her.

She left her mother in the capable hands of her lady's maid and went to her room. She would have to tell Susan, of course, but that could wait until later. Her sister would be crushed at not being able to attend. Millicent realised too late that she would have been better to speak to her mother in the first instance before raising Susan's hopes.

She gathered her bonnet and gloves and left her room. It had been some time since she had visited the library. Today was the perfect day to fill her mind with anything astronomy. She slipped out of the house without anyone seeing her. It would take some time to walk there but today she needed that time to clear her head of all that was happening. Because nothing was going according to her plan that she had made several months ago.

There were very few people in the library and Millicent walked purposefully towards the scientific section. One or two women glanced at her, most likely wondering what she could possibly want from that section, but Millicent paid them no heed. She found a book that would suit, proceeded to the librarian to sign it out, and was walking towards her quiet corner of the park in record time.

It was a little cool today and she was thankful for the warm cloak she had pulled on at the last minute. It also served as a blanket as she sat down, its length reaching to her ankles.

Leaning against her favourite tree trunk, Millicent opened the book and was soon lost in its words and pictures. As always, she imagined what the planets looked like, their colour, their beauty surrounded by stars.

She opened her eyes and slowly looked around.

This time, there was no Mr Westercott looking down at her, or wanting to find out what she was reading.

This time, the park in front of her was empty.

She returned her attention to her book, trying to pretend that the emptiness was not mirrored inside her.

Chapter 23

Juliette arrived just in time for afternoon tea and was ushered into the small drawing room where Millicent waited for her. It only took one glance to see that her friend was not feeling at her best and, once the door was closed, Juliette went to her side.

"Millicent, my dearest friend, I heard the news." She hugged her and added, "You poor thing. Has it been very dreadful?"

It took Millicent a few seconds to realise Juliette was referring to Mr Jenson. "Well, yes it was not easy, however, it has not been as bad as one might expect."

"Jonathon said he had seen you in the park. He also said that you were sadder than he had ever seen you before."

"He did?" She swallowed the lump in her throat that appeared at the mention of his name. "I was not feeling very happy. I had a lot to think about."

"Do you feel up to telling me why you are no longer seeing Mr Jenson? I thought you both went along quite well together."

"Oh, yes, we did. He is a very nice man," Millicent told her. "Juliette, there is something I need to tell you. It will no doubt shock you and I hope you still consider me a friend once you know it all."

"Millicent, what could possibly be so bad?"

She took a deep breath. "I am afraid I have deceived you. Not because I wanted to," she added earnestly. "It was a secret and one I could not tell. Not even to you. But when you know all you may not like me very much," she admitted. The thought saddened her and she wouldn't blame Juliette if she never forgave her, but she could keep it from her no longer.

Juliette pressed Millicent's hand as they sat beside each other on the settee. "Tell me, Millicent."

Millicent told her about Amanda and her crazy plan to stop Millicent having to marry, and about the true relationship surrounding Mr Jenson. She explained how his show of strong affection towards her was merely to prevent other gentlemen from approaching her. Then she told her of the reason behind her decision to end the relationship with Mr Jenson, and her parents' reaction.

"When we first met, everything I confided to you was true. Things began to move a little out of control after that and I could not tell you the truth because it involved other people that could be hurt. I am truly sorry, Juliette. So very sorry for deceiving you. You have been such a dear friend to me but I will understand if you find you no longer wish to continue that friendship."

Juliette had sat through the whole story, more amazed as the tale went on. While Millicent had intimated that her relationship with Mr Jenson was not serious, their actions had led her to believe, like everyone else, that an announcement was merely a matter of time.

"Jonathon was right," she said quietly.

Millicent looked at her with surprise. "Jonathon?"

Juliette nodded. "Do you remember that day when he was so rude to you?"

Millicent nodded. She could hardly forget something so hurtful.

Juliette continued, "I was so angry with him for the way he treated you. But the reason he lashed out was because he thought you were deceiving me and he is so protective it angered him greatly."

"Oh." Millicent felt even worse. Apart from everything else, when Jonathon found out the truth he would surely despise her.

"Mind you, he thought your deceit was that you were telling me you did not wish to become attached to any gentleman when, in fact, you were already attached to Mr Jenson. He thought you were trying to gain my sympathies or some such thing. You explained your friendship with Mr Jenson and, as your friendship grew, I considered it only natural. I felt there was no deceit in that."

"That was kind of you," Millicent murmured. "And now?" She was apprehensive about the answer.

"I must be honest and say that I am a little hurt that you did not feel you could confide in me. However, I can see that if the truth became known it would cause much upset with your family, not to mention harm any chances Amanda and Mr Jenson might have to be together. Can you imagine the scandal?" She turned to Millicent. "I think it was all most exciting and you all carried out such an excellent performance. I don't think anybody suspected."

Juliette was smiling and Millicent studied her to try to gain her true feelings. "You are not angry?"

"Millicent, what kind of friend would I be if I pushed you away because of something that did not even concern me?"

"But I deceived you. I shamefully lied to you."

"Because your friends loved you enough to help you. You could not betray that trust after all they had done for you."

"I don't know quite what to say," Millicent murmured. "Thank you."

"Thank you for finally telling me," Juliette said. "So, now that you and Mr Jenson are no longer an item, and he will now pursue Amanda, what will you do? You said your parents were not at all happy. I expect they will continue to push you towards a connection of some kind?"

Millicent took a calming breath. "While the outcome is good for Amanda and Richard, and I am truly happy for them, my own situation has taken a terrible turn. You might remember that my mother had three gentlemen lined up for my choice. Now that Richard is no longer a possibility, my parents accepted my decision on the condition I choose one of the other gentlemen. I have to make my decision during the ball."

"You cannot be serious?" exclaimed Juliette.

"Unfortunately, yes. Mother feels that the only way to scotch any kind of scandal is to become betrothed as quickly as possible. In fact, I have only until the end of this month."

"But, Millicent, how could that possibly happen? You have told me yourself that you strongly dislike Mr Farley, for a start."

"Yes, although he will no longer be a problem. I spoke with him today and was able to convince him that we would not suit. After his strong attempts to secure my affections up until now, he accepted my rejection quite easily. In fact, I think he is interested in Susan! It would not surprise me if he begins to look to her from now on. To be honest, I don't think he truly cared for me. I think he was only interested because I was not. It hurt his pride more than anything."

"I suspect you are right. It would explain how he so easily shifted his attentions to your sister. At least you don't have to be worried by his unwanted advances."

"We just cannot let mother know of his change of heart until after the ball. If she believes there is still a possibility of securing his affections, and if I allow him to hold a conversation with me and stand up with him for several dances, she will expect an announcement from that quarter. Of course, that won't happen and by the time mother realises there will be no announcement he will have shown his interest in Susan. I think as long as one daughter is a success in that area, it will keep her happy for a little while. And by then the season will be all but over."

"But think, Millicent. If it appears you yourself have been thrown over, that will seriously affect your chances in the future. It could ruin you!"

"As I don't plan to ever marry, it hardly presents a problem."

"If you change your mind, it could very well be a problem."
She hesitated a moment. "The third gentleman was Jonathon."

"Yes, it was," Millicent agreed. "However, I believe he has
made it quite clear that he would not consider that possibility.
Not to mention the fact he is in the almost constant company of
his lady friend."

"Things are not always what they seem."

Millicent's heart did a little flip. "Has he told you as much?"

Juliette wished she could give another answer but could not
do so. "No, he has said nothing to me on that score."

"Well then. It remains for mother to believe in Mr Farley's
affections for me and then we can forget any of this has ever
happened." Millicent stood up and walked to the bell rope. "Our
tea has grown cold. I'll order a fresh pot."

"Please don't on my account," Juliette said. "Unfortunately,
I can only stay a few moments longer. Millicent, is there no-one
you wish to have call on you?" she asked curiously.

Millicent clasped her hands together as she returned to the
settee in an effort to stop the slight trembling that the thought of
Jonathan Westercott had caused. She shook her head even as his
face swam before her. "No, I do not find myself attracted to any
of the gentlemen I have met. Which is just as I had planned."

Juliette felt sadness for her friend at the thought of her
spending her years alone. She had hoped at one time that
Jonathon may have been the right man for her but it seemed it
had been false hope. "If you need my help for anything, I hope
you know you can call on me. I promise to keep your secret with
regards to Mr Farley."

Millicent gave her a hug. "Thank you for remaining my friend
after all I have told you, and thank you for your help. Perhaps
one day, when all this is over, I can find myself a telescope and
hide in a corner to watch the sky and be left in peace," she said
lightly.

"I wish you could find a man who had the same interest as you do. Then you could marry him and enjoy watching the stars together. It would be so romantic. And so perfect."

"In a perfect world it would be just the thing but a man who encourages his wife in studying the stars does not exist."

"One never knows what possibilities lay ahead," Juliette said encouragingly. "Now, though, I must take my leave but I have a suggestion, if it is suitable to you."

"What is it?"

"After the ball, why don't you come and stay with me for a few days? You can help me in my new garden and it will give you an opportunity to avoid any added persuasion your mother might put on you to encourage any of the gentlemen."

"That sounds lovely," she replied, but wasn't certain she should accept.

"It will only be mother and I. Jonathon will be leaving town the day after the ball. He has neglected some business affairs or some such thing. My sisters will be visiting friends. I would dearly love your company."

The absence of a certain member of the family helped to make up her mind. "I would love to come. I accept your invitation. Thank you, Juliette."

"I so look forward to it." She hugged Millicent goodbye. "I will see you again at your ball."

Chapter 24

Amanda looked crossly at the group of young women as she and Millicent approached them. At the centre was Hanna Heathering, mean words as usual spilling from her lips. By now word had spread about Millicent and Mr Jenson's falling out. He had been a man of his word and told others that it had been Millicent who put an end to his courtship. However, young persons like Hanna chose to spread their own lies and rumours and put doubt in the minds of those who would listen.

The whispering stopped as the two young ladies walked past but started up again before they were out of earshot.

"I heard that Mr Jenson threw her aside because, naturally, a man of his standing requires true beauty in a wife. One should not be surprised at the outcome," Hanna said loudly enough for them to hear.

Amanda frowned at the meanness of the words. She paused in her steps but Millicent urged her on. "Don't listen to her. Nobody with any sense will believe a word she says."

The group of young women giggled and then, much to Amanda's annoyance, fell in step behind them. Their conversation did not cease and they continued to speculate on the dead relationship, always insinuating that Millicent was the one pushed aside.

Amanda turned so suddenly the group of women bumped into each other as they came to a stop. "Hanna Heathering, I find your actions very ill-mannered and lacking in any sense. The situation between Millicent and Mr Jenson is none of your concern but anyone with a brain and the ability to listen would know that the decision was Millicent's. If any of you are unsure, please feel free to speak directly to Mr Jenson who is very happy to tell the truth to any who wish to hear it." She glared at the young women standing around, most of whom now looked very uncomfortable about their part in this little gathering.

"Hanna knows everything because Mr Jenson told her. He has been paying special attention to her!" announced a voice from within the group.

"I am truly surprised that you believe such a thing. Have you ever known Hanna to be completely honest about anything?" Amanda scoffed. She turned to Hanna. "If you have truly become on friendly terms with Mr Jenson, pray tell him to escort you to the Addleton ball on Saturday night. We would all be very interested to see you on his arm."

Hanna looked uneasy but quickly covered by putting a confident expression on her face. "I am not certain he means to attend or, if he does, may be arriving late," she told them, giving excuses ahead of time as to why she may not arrive with him. "However, you can be certain that once he arrives we shall be very much in each other's company for the evening." She lifted her chin, daring Amanda to contradict her.

Amanda merely gave her a superior smile and turned away.

"It is hoped that one day Miss Heathering will mature into a young lady," she told Millicent, with a sympathetic glance back at Hanna. "Perhaps then she will find a gentleman who will truly wish to court her."

Gasps were heard behind them but they paid no attention as they continued on their way. "Amanda, that wasn't a very nice thing to say," Millicent whispered. "But, I must say, she deserved every word. Her lies were outrageous. Nobody could possibly believe her."

"I hope you are right, Millicent. She makes me so cross. Wait until I tell Richard. He will make sure he avoids her during the ball and serve her right."

They crossed the street, walked along the path running beside the small patch of green grass on the corner, and crossed into Main Street where most of the shops could be found. A new pair of gloves was on Amanda's list of purchases and they went directly to Mrs Lind's premises for this purpose. While Millicent browsed the shop, Amanda went over to the gloves and found exactly what she needed. She made her purchase and joined Millicent who had stopped to look over a stand of delicate shawls.

"Why don't you purchase one for the ball?" suggested Amanda. "It would look lovely draped across your arms." It had silver thread running through it that would be sure to catch the candlelight and appear to sparkle. "It would look like you had the evening stars gathered around you," she added, in awe at the very thought.

Millicent hesitated but her friend's words did catch her imagination. She let the fabric slide through her fingers. It was quite expensive and she did have many shawls already. But not one that sparkled as this one would. It was her ball, she thought. Why should she not have something special? Before she could change her mind, she took it to Mrs Lind and made the purchase.

As they stepped out of the shop, they almost bumped into the Westercott sisters.

"I didn't expect to see you again until the ball," Juliette said. "Are you both making purchases for the special night?"

"Yes, we are. I have bought myself a new shawl," Millicent told her, still excited about the purchase.

"It is so beautiful, Juliette. The silver thread will sparkle in the candlelight," Amanda told her.

"I cannot wait to see it. We are shopping for gloves and linen items for our mother. The gloves are for me, though, not mother."

"Are you planning to be out shopping for very long?" Millicent asked her.

"Once we make our purchases here we are finished. We were

planning to stop at the new little shop around the corner where you can sit and have a pot of tea and scones at a very reasonable price."

"That sounds lovely."

"Why don't you and Amanda join us?"

"Yes, please do," piped up Lilian. "It will be so nice to have you both join us while we wait."

"Wait for what?"

"For our carriage to return," Juliette answered. "I sent our driver on an errand while we did the necessary shopping. He will not return for some thirty minutes yet."

Millicent looked to Amanda who was more than happy to accept the invitation. "We would love to join you. We can browse the shop while you make your purchases and then we can walk to the tea shop together."

And so all five women entered Mrs Lind's shop chatting about their purchases and the upcoming ball. Even though Lilian was not able to attend, she felt the excitement of the older girls and, as she said, it gave even her a good excuse to go shopping.

It didn't take long for the Westercott sisters to make their necessary purchases and a short time later they were all seated around a table drinking tea and nibbling on tasty scones with jam and cream.

"These are delicious," murmured Lilian as she bit into her second scone. "I must ask Cook to teach me how to make them."

Juliette smiled. "Lilian is fond of cooking, much to our mother's surprise, and often disappears into the kitchens to try to learn culinary skills. The housekeeper and the cook try to discourage her but they learned very early that she was too stubborn to do what they asked of her."

Lilian smiled around her scone and poured herself another cup of tea.

Edith motioned to Juliette that their carriage had arrived.

"Oh, so soon," Juliette said, disappointed. "I had thought he would take longer."

"Enough time to finish our tea, at least," Millicent added. "It was delicious. We should come here again."

"Most definitely."

They all took final sips of their tea and left the tearoom, stepping outside onto the footpath.

"I am so glad we ran into each other," Juliette said. "I am looking forward to the ball. It should be a very interesting night," she commented with a secret smile for her two friends.

"Why should it be interesting?" asked Edith.

"Because it is the first one ever held at my home," put in Millicent quickly. Edith appeared to accept this and she and Lilian stepped into the carriage behind them.

"I must go. I will see you both very soon," Juliette said and hurried over to the carriage.

A man stood beside it talking to the driver and Millicent froze.

Amanda followed her gaze and took her arm. "Perhaps we should go now," she suggested softly.

Millicent nodded and turned away.

Jonathon Westercott stood for a moment longer and watched Millicent walk down the street then climbed into the carriage and they were on their way.

"We had tea and scones with Millicent and Amanda," Edith told him. "Wasn't it great luck that we happened to bump into them today? I had been worried about Millicent, what with her situation with Mr Jenson, but she was in fine spirits. I think he will be at the Addleton ball. Is that what you meant when you said the ball should be interesting?" she asked Juliette, turning towards her.

"No, I meant no particular thing when I said that."

"Well, it would be interesting. Just think of it. They would pass each other during a dance or moving through the rooms. It would be most uncomfortable for Millicent. Perhaps she should uninvite him."

Juliette glanced at her brother who sat impassively while their sister rambled on. Jonathon had informed her that he would not be attending the ball but Juliette was not about to let him disappear on such a special evening. She would find a way to make him escort her. Besides, she could not possibly allow him to disappoint Mrs Addleton who had one eye on him as a possible future son-in-law!

It took Millicent several minutes before she felt calm enough to speak again. Even then she didn't quite know what to say. Beside her, Amanda squeezed her arm as they walked. She was certainly a dear friend and knew just when to be supportive while saying nothing. They took the long way home and walked across the green parkland that would eventually lead to the street where Millicent lived. The grass was soft beneath their feet and eventually Millicent's steps slowed to a more sedate walk. She took a deep breath and exhaled slowly, feeling the remnants of her unease melt away.

"Better?" Amanda asked.

Millicent nodded. "Yes. I am sorry for hurrying away as we did. It was unexpected, seeing him like that."

"I am surprised Juliette didn't mention that he would be there."

"I don't think Juliette knows the affect he has on me." Realising she had just confirmed Amanda's suspicions, she glanced at her friend and hoped it had gone unnoticed.

No such luck.

"He is the gentleman, isn't he Millicent?"

"Which gentleman?" she asked evasively.

"The gentleman that has touched your heart. The one you hinted at during our visit to Aunty Mabel. I know you too well, my dear friend. I suspected it may be the case. I have never seen you react in such a way to any gentleman of your acquaintance before. He certainly is handsome."

"None of it makes any difference. I have to remain unattached. I must," Millicent said with as much conviction as she could muster. Sadly, however, her conviction did not seem to be holding in the presence of Jonathon Westercott.

"Millicent, would it be so bad if you allowed yourself to admit you are in love with Mr Westercott? I believe he likes you. It is quite obvious by the way he looks at you."

Millicent shook her head. "No, you are wrong. He doesn't like me at all. Perhaps at one time he may have but not anymore. And when he finds out about my deceit towards Juliette he will loathe me, I am sure."

"Surely not."

"When he thought I had lied to her once before he became very angry. I daren't think of his reaction when he finds out all that has gone on."

"Do you really think Juliette will tell him?"

"I am not sure. She has no reason not to, but it makes no difference. No matter what my feelings are, I have to forget all about Jonathon Westercott."

Amanda squeezed her arm and they walked along in silence. Finally, her dearest friend had found a man who could take her mind away from the heavens and bring her back to earth. As her friend, Amanda was bound to do whatever she could to bring the two together.

There were many others taking a stroll through the parkland and neither Millicent nor Amanda were oblivious of the looks and whispers directed towards them. "Are those ladies invited to the ball?" Amanda asked.

"Most of them."

"Well, I don't believe any of them deserve to be in attendance after the way they are behaving but you can be sure that during the ball we will find a way to put a stop to all of these rumours. They will know, once and for all, that you and Richard are still on good terms and it was you who threw him over."

This caused Millicent to let out a soft laugh. "And just what do you expect Richard to do?"

Deflating just a little, Amanda admitted, "I have not the slightest idea. I will think of something, though."

Thankful to have such a caring and wonderful friend, Millicent hugged her and continued the rest of their walk in a much better frame of mind.

Chapter 25

The day of the Addleton ball finally arrived and the household was a hive of activity. Servants moved the last pieces of furniture from the ballroom and smaller rooms that would be used during the evening, and last minute preparations were under way in almost every part of the house.

Millicent tried to keep as far out of her mother's way as possible. She certainly did not want to be swept up in any preparations. Thankfully, she had managed to evade the duty of arranging the flowers, a task that found its way into Susan's hands. That young lady appeared happy to take part in whatever preparations mama wished her to do, which was very surprising considering her desolation at not being permitted to attend the ball.

In the afternoon, a large bathtub was brought into Millicent's room and filled with warm, scented water. She was looking forward to immersing herself in it and easing her anxiety about the evening. She was not the type who usually became anxious. Normally, she was quite confident and looked upon balls and assemblies as something she had to do but that would quickly pass, allowing her to return to her books. For this evening, though, she felt nothing but apprehension. Her parents' hopes that she would make a decision with regards to the man she would marry added pressure. They weren't to know that Mr Farley was no longer a possibility or that Mr Westercott was not the least bit interested and would most likely not even be in attendance. During the course of the evening, she was sure these things would become apparent to her mother and she was not looking forward to the lecture she was bound to receive the next morning.

Millicent stepped out of the tub and dried herself with a thick, warm towel. Standing near the fire, she let the warmth spread through her body, helping to ease some of the remaining tension. The evening would progress well, she told herself. She would have her two friends, Amanda and Juliette, to support her. As they both knew the truth about her parents' expectations, it would help having them close. It was natural that people would talk of her ended relationship with Richard and she knew there were rumours that she would need to quench but, with the help of her friends, she would easily manage the task. She would glide about the room showing confidence and happiness and by the end of the evening everyone will have had a wonderful time and go away with the knowledge that she and Richard were on friendly terms and he had graciously allowed her to call an end to their unofficial understanding. She would be praised for her strength of character and her success as the hostess of the ball. She smiled at herself in the mirror. She was now quite looking forward to the ball.

Her maid came in and dressed her hair, which was swept up into an elegant style. Silver and blue ribbons were threaded through her dark curls and small flowers were pinned into place.

Millicent stepped into her gown of deep blue and her maid fastened the small buttons at the back. She had taken some suggestions from a picture in her sister's magazine and had Madame Le Cruz sew tiny seed pearls around the edge of the puffed sleeves. The pearls also adorned her bodice and, with her silver thread shawl about her elbows, she was ready for her ball. A quick glance in the mirror lifted her spirits several levels. Never being much interested in fashion, this evening her gown of deep blue reminded her of the sky at a certain time of the evening and her shawl of the stars. She felt like she was a part of the heavens themselves.

"Millicent, you look so beautiful," Susan breathed, coming into her room.

"Thank you, Susan." She looked at her sympathetically. "I

am truly sorry mother did not approve of my suggestion to allow you to attend this evening."

"There is no need to be sorry, Milly. Things always have a habit of working out for the best." Millicent forgave her sister the use of that horrid abbreviation, she had been denied the opportunity to dance with Mr Farley after all, and was impressed by her mature attitude to the situation.

"Do you know, I am sure Mr Farley will be very pleased to wait until your season next year, at which time you can be sure he will be your most ardent caller."

Susan smiled and a dreamy expression crossed her face. "I believe he may well be."

Something about her words puzzled Millicent but she didn't pay much attention and was soon downstairs, ready for the ball to begin. If her apprehension had not completely left her, it had lessened considerably and she was determined to enjoy the evening.

Millicent was to greet the guests with her mother and stood at the door as the time approached.

Within one hour she had greeted dozens of people and felt quite overwhelmed. Mrs Addleton, on the other hand, was in her element and was already congratulating herself on the success of the ball. Everyone, simply *everyone*, would be talking about this evening for many days. At ten o'clock she chose to leave the door and mingle with the guests. She had released Millicent from her hostess duties earlier and saw she was already dancing with Mr Farley. Her eyes lit up. Perhaps she and her dear friend, Mrs Farley, would have good cause to celebrate after this evening.

"I am pleased you agreed to dance with me, Miss Addleton, after our last meeting," Tristan Farley told her.

"I believe we came to an understanding at that time, Mr Farley, and am sure we can meet each other as friends during these events."

"Of course."

Millicent smiled, determined to make sure her mother would believe the two of them to be quite taken with each other. When the dance came to an end, she allowed Mr Farley to lead her from the floor.

"I see your mother is talking to mine. Shall we join them?" she asked.

They made their way through the guests. Both parents greeted the couple warmly.

"Mr Farley, I could not help but notice you and Millicent dancing together. What a lovely couple you make," Mrs Addleton told him profusely. "We have not seen you at the house recently but I am so glad you were able to attend the ball and reunite with each other."

"I have been detained elsewhere, ma'am, but hope to call again very soon." If Mrs Addleton believed he was calling on Millicent and not, as was his plan, on her younger sister, he was not about to alter her thinking.

"What wonderful news. I know Millicent will be delighted to receive you. Is that not so, my dear?" she asked, turning to Millicent.

Millicent looked at Mr Farley and in that moment he knew that she was aware of his intentions. "I am sure we will all be pleased to see Mr Farley."

"If you ladies will excuse me, I see someone I must speak to," he murmured.

The two mothers watched him walk away with growing hopes gleaming in their eyes. A match to unite their families was something they had talked of for many years and now it seemed all of their plans would be about to come true.

"What are you smiling at?" Amanda asked as Millicent joined her.

"Mr Farley and I just had the most interesting encounter with our mothers. I believe he means to call at the house tomorrow and I was imagining mother's surprise when he requests to see Susan instead of me."

"Do you think she will permit it?"

Millicent laughed softly. "Oh, I believe mother would welcome a match with the son of her dearest friend and once she realises it is Susan he prefers, I am sure she will be happy to accommodate him. As for papa, I am sure he will be equally pleased."

"After the way he pursued you, who would have thought he would have preferred Susan in the end," Amanda commented.

"I know it is an outcome Susan has longed for since the first day she set eyes on him. She has been languishing after him ever since."

"Is that Lord Shelton with Juliette?" Amanda asked, nodding towards their friend.

"Yes. They met at the Veton ball and I believe he has been calling on her ever since. They seem quite taken with one another and I am very happy for her," Millicent said, smiling across at a radiant Juliette.

Her friend smiled back, obviously enjoying the evening immensely. They moved away to join the dancing and then Amanda caught Millicent's attention.

"Look! Richard has arrived."

Sure enough, he was making his way slowly through the guests being careful not to look in their direction. Millicent felt people watching her and hoped she could carry off the last act of this performance convincingly. She turned to Amanda and gave the appearance of one who was uneasy and, perhaps, embarrassed by his arrival.

"Millicent, you must look at this," Amanda told her in an urgent whisper.

Both ladies watched as Hanna Heathering made her way to Richard's side.

"Good evening, Miss Heathering," he greeted politely as he almost bumped into her.

"Good evening, Mr Jenson. If you don't mind my saying so, I am quite surprised, but of course delighted, to see you here this evening."

"Oh? And why would that be, Miss Heathering?"

"Everyone knows of your recent relationship with Miss Addleton," she told him softly. "I am not sure how she will feel having you arrive after dismissing her so," she added with pretended concern.

"And her discomfort is what makes you delighted that I have arrived?"

"Oh, no, of course not, sir. Why, I have known Miss Addleton for many years and look upon her as a dear friend. I would never do or say anything to cause her any discomfort."

This was spoken so earnestly but Richard knew the truth all too well. "How delighted she must be to have such a friend in you, Miss Heathering." He smiled down at her and she returned his smile and rested her hand on his arm in a familiar manner.

"I would like to think so, sir." Around her, Hanna's friends watched in wonder at the familiarity displayed by the couple. They had been hesitant to believe her connection with Mr Jenson was true until now.

"I was about to find the refreshment stand and take a glass of lemonade. Would you care to join me?" Mr Jenson asked her in a voice that let her know just how much he enjoyed her company.

"I would like that above all else," she told him. She threw an 'I told you so' look at her friends as he led her away. Whispers followed them and she could not help the triumphant smile as she moved through the guests.

Amanda and Millicent watched in surprise as he led Hanna Heathering from the room.

"What do you suppose he is doing?" Amanda asked.

"I have not the slightest idea."

"Why would he want to spend time in her company?"

"I am sure he has his reasons."

"He was meant to put her in her place, not put her on his arm."

Millicent smiled at her jealous friend. "You can be absolutely certain that he has a plan in mind and it does not involve becoming intimate with the likes of Miss Hanna Heathering."

"I hope you are right. That man will have a lot of explaining to do."

Millicent laughed softly and hoped Richard would return soon before Amanda went storming after him.

"People will notice you glaring if you are not careful," Millicent warned her.

"They will believe it is because I am unhappy with his treatment of you."

"Everyone knows he did not treat me in any ill manner."

"Perhaps they should think that!"

Millicent laughed again. "They have returned," she said, inclining her head towards the pair.

"It is about time. Hanna looks very smug," Amanda observed.

"And why would she not? She told all who would listen that she was on very friendly terms with Richard. He is playing on that."

She followed Amanda as she began walking towards them. "What are you doing?" Millicent hissed.

"I don't know," Amanda hissed back.

As they approached Richard and Hanna, he turned towards them with a smile.

"Miss Bladestoke, a pleasure to see you," he greeted. "Miss Addleton," he continued more seriously. "Allow me to thank you for reaffirming your kind invitation to the ball this evening."

"You have no need to thank me, Mr Jenson."

"You are most gracious. I am concerned, however, about the rumours and whispers I have heard since my arrival. It seems that many people here believe it was you who were thrown over."

Millicent glanced at Hanna then looked back at him. "Yes, it seems to be a common belief, I am afraid."

"You may rest easy knowing that I have told several of my acquaintances the true nature of the situation and that it was, in fact, you who put an end to our … let us say, close friendship."

"That was very kind of you," she murmured.

"It was the least I could do after permitting me to still attend this evening. Most ladies would not wish to be seen with a gentleman once she has decided they will not suit."

"It is good that I am not like most ladies, is it not?"

He bowed to her. "It is a very good thing. In fact, I have been telling your very dear friend, Miss Heathering, just how kind hearted you are. But I had no need to tell her anything as she is bound to know that already, being a very dear friend of yours."

Miss Heathering looked startled to be brought into the conversation. "Yes, just so. It is truly horrid how people can believe otherwise and start those terrible rumours." She didn't dare look at the two women standing before her.

"Miss Addleton, I had no idea you and Miss Heathering were on such friendly terms." Richard's eyes twinkled as he looked at her.

Amanda did her best to hide a smile but could not resist making a comment. "Yes, it is most surprising. I had not the slightest idea myself, which is quite remarkable considering you and I are so very close, Millicent."

She turned to look at her friend, the twinkle in her eyes nearly being Millicent's undoing. She looked at all three, her eyes lingering a little longer on Hanna, before speaking directly to

Richard. "Mr Jenson, during our recent … let us say, close friendship, we determined that honesty would always be best and, in doing so, we could remain friends despite what has gone on before. To this end," at which point Miss Heathering began to turn a little pale, "it would be remiss of me not to tell you that Miss Heathering and I are not what you would call close. In fact, it was Miss Heathering who began the rumours about how our relationship, if you will, came to an end. Therefore, you can imagine my great surprise to learn of our apparent friendship." She looked innocently from one to the other.

His brows rose with surprise. "But how is this?" he asked Miss Heathering.

"Mr Jenson, it is not so! Millicent, how could you say something so cruel, after all we have been to each other?" she moaned, brushing away an imagined tear.

"Hanna Heathering, anyone in this room could support Millicent in her statement, as you very well know," Amanda told her scathingly.

"I would ask that you keep out of this conversation," Hanna told her in a cold voice.

"Miss Heathering, do you dare to speak to Miss Bladestoke in such a manner?" Mr Jenson asked her, shocked. He removed her hand from his arm and stepped away.

"Mr Jenson, forgive my rudeness, but Miss Bladestoke has been jealous of my friendship with Miss Addleton for years. It is only natural, given her temperament, that she would react in such a manner."

"No, Miss Heathering, I believe it is you who are jealous. Jealous of not only Miss Bladestoke but also of Miss Addleton," Richard said clearly, moving to stand beside the two ladies. "I also know, Miss Heathering, that is was indeed you who started those cruel rumours about someone I hold in high regard. I believe, Miss Heathering, that I no longer wish to stand in your company." He held out an arm for each of his two friends and they walked away, leaving Hanna looking after them completely stunned.

She became aware of whispers around her and realised, with acute embarrassment, that a large number of guests had overheard the whole thing. Her friends turned their backs on her and laughed at her lies and folly. People stared and their whispers followed her as she hurried from the room.

"Fabulous performance, ladies," Richard congratulated them.

"The same could be said for you, dear Richard," Amanda told him. "I will never forget the look on her face. It was priceless."

"I do wish we did not have to be so cruel. It almost makes us as bad as she is," Millicent said.

"You will never be as bad a person as she is, Millicent, and everyone here knows that," Richard assured her.

Juliette had watched the play unfold from across the room. She and Lord Shelton had been engaged in conversation but her attention had been caught.

"What was that all about?" her brother asked, coming to stand beside them.

Lord Shelton shrugged. "Some young woman causing trouble with Miss Addleton, by the looks of it."

"Millicent has had to deal with some very nasty rumours regarding her ended courtship with Mr Jenson. It appears Miss Heathering was the instigator of them," Juliette explained.

"I see," Jonathon replied.

"Mr Jenson let it be known that it was she who ended the connection but Miss Heathering would tell everyone that it was the opposite, with cruel suggestions as to the reason. I believe she has just been severely put in her place and her words will never be believed again. At least, not by anyone who wishes to remain in the good graces of Mr Jenson."

"Miss Addleton and Mr Jenson appear to be going along just fine at present," he muttered.

Juliette watched, as did many others in the room, as Mr Jenson bowed graciously over Miss Addleton's hand and then led Miss Bladestoke onto the dance floor. It was also quite obvious to everyone that Miss Addleton was very happy to see him dancing with her friend and there could be no whispers from anyone other than that they were all seen to be well mannered, courteous and on friendly terms despite the whole affair.

"Why don't you ask Millicent to dance?" Juliette asked her brother suddenly.

"I think Miss Addleton has more than enough partners."

"Not at this moment. In fact, she is standing quite alone. Lord Shelton, would you excuse me for just one moment?" she asked him and at his nod she took hold of Jonathon's arm. He had no choice but to follow, unless he wanted to cause a stir.

Lord Shelton watched them go with amusement. It appeared this final act would be more interesting than any of them had expected.

"Millicent, I saw the whole thing," Juliette said as she came to her side. "Poor Miss Heathering. I doubt she will be spreading false rumours about anyone for a long time to come."

Millicent laughed softly. "I believe you may be right. I do wish it could have been done in another way but Richard was quite insistent that he deal with her in his own way."

Mr Westercott reached them, having followed at a more sedate pace than his sister, but was unsure if speaking with Miss Addleton was the safest thing for him to do. What he should have done was leave for the country that morning as he had originally planned.

"Good evening, Miss Addleton. It seems your ball is a success."

Millicent's heart skipped a beat at the sound of his voice and she slowly turned to face him. "Good evening, Mr Westercott."

"We saw you standing by yourself and Jonathon felt it was

unthinkable that you be without a partner at your own ball," Juliette informed her, ignoring her brother's look. Instead, she gave him one of her own that he felt he should obey. It was only polite, after all, that he should ask his hostess to dance.

As the musicians prepared to play the next set, he held out his hand. "Miss Addleton, would you do me the honour of this dance?'

"Thank you," she replied in what could barely pass as a whisper. A glance at Juliette showed that young lady looking very pleased with herself. There was a conversation Millicent planned to have with her after the ball.

Mrs Addleton looked on excitedly as Mr Westercott led Millicent onto the dance floor. Two very eligible gentlemen, obviously taken with her daughter. It seemed Millicent would have no trouble securing a match following tonight's ball.

Millicent could hardly breathe. In fact, for an alarming moment she didn't think she could even remember the steps to the dance. She curtseyed as it began and then looked up … and was lost. Mr Westercott was looking directly at her and remained doing so for several steps. Each time he moved close to her she held her breath. As he stepped away, she felt disappointed and looked forward to the turn that would bring him close to her again.

She wanted the dance to go on forever.

She wanted the dance to end.

It was an agonizing dance that left her shaken inside.

He led her from the floor just as the strains of the next dance began. A waltz. Millicent had been given permission to dance the waltz but did not dare look at Mr Westercott. Dancing so close as they had just done was enough to make her feel faint. Twirling in his arms was something she did not think she could survive. Thankfully, he continued to lead her back to Juliette.

"Thank you, Miss Addleton," he said politely. With a glance at Juliette, he left them.

Juliette frowned after him, wondering why he had left so suddenly. One look at Millicent's face gave her even more concern. She hoped nothing upsetting was said. Millicent did not need that after all she had been through recently.

Lord Shelton watched it all with secret amusement. It would not surprise him if several weddings were to take place by the time this season was over. What an interesting visit this was turning out to be.

Jonathon Westercott left the house and did not look back. He cursed himself for attending the ball. He should not have come. He should have gone out of town. He brushed aside his driver, preferring instead to walk for a while. He should not have asked her to dance. Of course, he could have withstood Juliette and not even asked Miss Addleton to dance. But the opportunity to be so close to her was too much to withstand. And now he regretted it. Heaven knows what he would have done if he had given into his urge to ask her to waltz with him. At the rate he was going, he would have shown every person in the room just what his feelings for her were. He could very well have been an engaged man at this very moment! She was bewitching but it was best for everyone if he left town and tried to forget her.

Chapter 26

At the breakfast table the next morning, Mrs Addleton talked almost non-stop of the success of their ball.

"What a wonderful evening," she gushed. "More guests than I could possibly imagine had attended, and Millicent spent quite some time in the arms of both very eligible gentlemen. I am sure a match is mere days away. We must make arrangements for an announcement to be placed in the newspapers."

Millicent made no comment and was more interested in watching Susan. There was an air of excitement about her and, when she forgot to hide it, her eyes grew dreamy and a small smile tugged at her mouth.

Once or twice Susan caught Millicent watching her and looked down at her plate, keeping her expression even.

"Millicent, you must tell me what Mr Farley and Mr Westercott said to you," Mrs Addleton continued. "Just fancy. You may receive two offers! We must make up our mind who to accept. Everyone, simply *everyone*, will envy your good fortune."

"Mother, we cannot be certain either of these gentlemen will make me an offer," she said carefully.

"Of course they will. You should encourage one of them or there will be no other option but to repair the rift between yourself and Mr Jenson."

"Mr Jenson and I have remained friends, mother, but we have agreed that there will be nothing more between us."

Mrs Addleton sat up straighter, a smug expression on her face. "I do believe he may well be convinced otherwise. I have seen the way he attends to you and his attentions to you last night could not go unnoticed. No, my dear, you may well believe me when I say that you will receive an offer within days from any of the three gentlemen in question." She picked up her knife and began spreading jam on her bread. "And if that does not come about, then your father and I will merely choose one for you and convince the gentleman that it would be a beneficial match."

At such a clear and confident announcement, Millicent and, indeed, her sisters, could only stare open-mouthed. Millicent looked to her father but he had his nose buried in the newspaper and was not going to offer any assistance. He tended to agree with their mother in most things stating that she knew what was best for her daughters.

Millicent left the table. She was glad she had agreed to visit Juliette for a few days. She dared not think what her mother would do to bring about an announcement if she stayed at the house.

As she left the room, Pemble was carrying a large arrangement of flowers into the drawing room. Not expecting to receive any for herself, Millicent followed him curiously.

"Who sent these, Pemble?" she enquired, reaching for the card.

"I am not certain, miss."

Millicent was already reading the card and raised her eyebrows in complete surprise. She turned as Susan entered the room and looked at her, full of curiosity at the turn of events. Silently, she handed the card to her sister. She noticed the blush that stole across Susan's cheeks as she read the card.

Trust him to know that her favourite colour was yellow, Susan thought dreamily as she buried her nose in the yellow blooms.

The door closed behind Pemble as he left the room and Millicent turned to her sister. "Are you going to tell me what happened between you and Mr Farley last night?"

"Why would you assume something happened last night?"

Susan asked surprised.

Millicent took the card from her. "It says quite clearly, '....*thank you for a most enjoyable evening. With my love.*' I am quite certain Mr Farley is not referring to me."

Susan glanced at the door to make sure it was fully closed. Then she grabbed hold of Millicent's hand and pulled her down on the settee.

"Millicent, you will hardly believe what I am about to tell you. You know, of course, that I have been attracted to Mr Farley from the first." Millicent gave her a dry look and nodded. Susan laughed softly. "Yes, I have not been very good at hiding my feelings where he is concerned. But, last night the most wonderful thing happened. First, I stole into the ball!"

Millicent gasped. "I did not see you. What did mother say to you!"

"She does not know and I beg of you not to tell her. I did not actually enter the ballroom. I was standing out in the hall trying to gather enough courage to do so when Mr Farley came into the hall. I was so surprised to see him that I was tongue-tied. I thought he would surely think me a silly schoolgirl but he did not. Do you know what he did?" she asked, her eyes glowing.

Millicent shook her head, almost dreading what would come next.

"He asked me to dance, right there in the hallway. And it was simply magical," she breathed. "We waltzed!" she added, rising from the seat and swaying about the room. "We found our way out into the garden, and still now I don't quite know how it happened, but the next moment we were dancing amongst the flowers. Oh, Millicent, it was so perfect. Then we walked and we talked and I felt as if I had known him my entire life. We were standing beneath that large shade tree at the farthest point of the garden and then …" She let out a deep sigh. "And then he kissed me."

"Susan! You did not allow him such intimacies?" Millicent

was horrified at the thought of Susan and Mr Farley being alone in the darkened garden. What if they had been seen?

As if reading her mind, Susan told her, "There was not a single soul around besides Mr Farley and myself. But I must remember to call him Tristan as he has asked me. There is more, my dear sister. Something I had not dared to dream of."

Millicent's mind was already spinning and she wasn't sure she could take any more information.

"Millicent," Susan said as she returned to the seat beside her. "Tristan professed his love for me. We are to be married as soon as possible. Is it not the most wonderful news you have ever heard in your entire life?"

"Married? But has he approached papa for your hand? Have he and mother agreed to this?"

Susan sat back, deflating just the slightest bit. "They do not know. Tristan plans to call on me today and he will speak to papa then. Do you think he will deny us?" she asked worriedly.

"I don't know, Susan. This is all so very sudden. Mother is expecting him to offer for me! Not that I had expected him to do so, so don't look so worried. Mr Farley and I had come to an agreement prior to the ball and it was clear we would not suit. As it seems he is more inclined to spend his life with you, this is a good thing. However, I am not certain how mother will take the news."

"But if I can convince her and especially papa that it is what I wish, they will agree. Won't they?"

"Susan, is this what you truly want? Are you absolutely certain that Mr Farley returns your affection as he says?"

"I have not the slightest doubt in my mind of his love, Millicent. If you had seen his happiness when I told him I returned his affections, you could not doubt it either."

Millicent had never seen her sister look so happy. Being in love obviously agreed with her and, in that moment, she decided she would do whatever it took to make sure her parents agreed to this connection.

A knock sounded on the door and Pemble entered. "Mr Farley to see you, miss."

"Please send him in," Millicent said and soon Mr Farley was walking into the room. After the usual greetings, Millicent gestured towards the flowers. "These are beautiful, Mr Farley."

He glanced between the two women, his expression clearly showing his concern that his offering had not reached the correct Miss Addleton.

"Yes, indeed they are, Mr Farley. Thank you," Susan added quietly. She felt unusually shy, seeing him after their meeting last night. He turned to her and smiled and the tenderness she saw in his eyes removed those last threads of shyness.

"I hope you like the colour? I remembered you said last night …" Realising he had unwittingly revealed their meeting at the ball, he looked at her apologetically.

"It is alright, Tristan. Millicent knows all." Susan went to him and laid her hand on his arm. Millicent saw the way he was looking at her sister and was convinced that there was no deception in his actions towards Susan.

"Our parents will be in shock at the news, I daresay," Millicent said with a touch of amusement.

"No doubt," Tristan agreed. He rested his hand on top of Susan's and looked down at her. "However, I hope it will be a shock they are able to come to terms with and allow our engagement."

Millicent walked towards the door. "I will do all I can to make sure that happens," she informed him. "Now, if you will both excuse me, I have just remembered an errand I must run without delay." With a special look for her sister, Millicent left the room, closing the door firmly behind her.

"I do believe I shall cherish my new sister-in-law," Tristan commented, before pulling his bride-to-be into his arms.

They jumped apart as someone knocked on the door and it opened to reveal Mrs Addleton. "Millicent, I believe we have a visitor. How lovely to see you so soon after the ball, Mr Farley," she greeted. Then she noticed Susan standing far too close to their visitor, her cheeks quite flushed. "Susan, what are you doing in here? Please go and find your sister and tell her that Mr Farley has come calling."

She glanced at Tristan before taking a step towards the door. Now that the moment had arrived, she wasn't sure what she should do.

Tristan's voice stopped her in her tracks. "Mrs Addleton, there is no need. I have not come to call on your eldest daughter. I have come to pay a call on Susan."

"Susan? Why would you want to pay a call on Susan? Please, take a seat and I will have Millicent sent for," she continued.

Susan didn't dare look at him. She could feel all her hopes beginning to fail her. Then she felt Tristan's hand beneath her elbow and he stood proudly beside her. "While your eldest daughter is a lovely young woman, it is Susan who has captured my heart." He looked at her as he said these last words and she couldn't help smiling back at him.

"Susan, what have you done?" Mrs Addleton demanded.

Emboldened by his presence, she said, "I have done nothing, mama, except to fall in love."

"Nonsense! You are barely out of the schoolroom. You must wait until you come out next year and then you may fall in love with whomever you choose. Please come away from Mr Farley and bring your sister here."

Tristan opened his mouth to protest once again but Susan moved away. "It will be best if I bring Millicent," she told him quietly.

She left the room and Tristan had no choice but to listen to

Mrs Addleton's ravings of her ball until she returned. Thankfully, she was only gone a few minutes and both ladies plus a confused Mr Addleton soon returned to the room.

"Farley! Good to see you," he greeted.

"And you, sir," he replied.

"I expect you have come to pay a call on Millicent? You certainly have my permission to do so, which makes me curious as to why everyone seems to have congregated in this room." He looked to his wife and then to his two daughters for answers.

"Sir," began Tristan. "You are correct in your assumption that I have come to pay a call. The confusion seems to be regarding which of your daughters I am calling upon."

"I beg your pardon?"

Tristan reached out for Susan's hand and, after a brief hesitation, she went to his side. "Mr Addleton, I find that I am strongly attached to your lovely daughter, Susan. If you would agree, sir, it would do me the greatest honour if she would accept my hand in marriage."

The parents looked at him in stunned silence. Then Mrs Addleton turned to Millicent. "This is what happens when you delay. You were meant to secure his affections for yourself!"

"Mother, Mr Farley and I have never suited. It was you who wished for the connection, not I. And, apparently, not Mr Farley either," she added, smiling at the couple standing before her.

"You do not wish to marry Millicent?" Mr Addleton put in.

"No, sir, I do not," he said with a glance of apology at Millicent. She readily accepted it.

Mr Addleton looked at his younger daughter. "This is certainly an unusual turn of events." He looked to his wife. "Well, my dear, it seems you have always wanted a union between our two families. I do not see that it matters greatly which of our daughters this young man marries."

Mrs Addleton was still coming to terms with the change of

events and could only look on in silence, giving only a small nod of agreement.

"Then it is settled. Farley, you will come with me while we talk terms," he said firmly.

Susan's joy was clearly evident as she watched both men leave the room. At the last moment, Tristan turned and threw her a wink. Excitement bubbled inside her, knowing for certain that she would very soon be Mrs Tristan Farley.

The rest of the day passed in a blur of excitement and activity. Mr Addleton finalised the marriage agreement with Mr Farley and permitted him to take Susan for a drive. That drive kept her away for most of the day as, equipped with a picnic hamper, they journeyed to the nearer part of the countryside and spent a quiet day together.

Millicent encountered her mother's reproachful stares several times throughout the day. With Mr Farley no longer available and her stubborn refusal of encouraging a change of heart from Mr Jenson, Mrs Addleton felt her daughter had done all in her power to sabotage her prospects for this season. The last remaining gentleman, Mr Westercott, had left town, according to a message received by Millicent from his sister, and Mrs Addleton wondered how a daughter of hers could treat her so poorly. She did not think it was too much to ask that her eldest daughter do all she could to attract an offer. Even an offer from a gentleman less eligible would have been acceptable. But to do all she could to prevent such an event left Mrs Addleton feeling very ill-used indeed.

There was one very upsetting event that stood out from the unbearable day for Millicent. She had retired to her room to read her astronomy book. It was another new one from the library and was more interesting and informative than any she had read thus far. She had hoped hiding away in her room would prevent any encounters with her mother that would be upsetting for everyone. She had not been in her room for very long when a knock interrupted her. She was surprised to see Harry enter.

"What is this I hear about you and Farley?" he began abruptly. "I must say, Milly, it was not good sport to shoot down a friend of mine in such a manner. You know how besotted he was with you, although, why he was is beyond me. I mean to say, you are an attractive girl, I grant you, but who would want to be attached to a woman who spends all day with her nose in a book about planets and the like?" He plonked himself in a chair. "I have not had a chance to speak to Farley about your refusal but I can surely imagine him to be so down in the dumps he will be found wallowing at the club. You mark my words." He jumped to his feet. "How could you do something so thoughtless, Milly?" he demanded.

Millicent watched in silence as her brother raved on. Laying her book carefully on the bed, she rose to her feet. "Harry Addleton, firstly I would ask you how you dare to speak to me in such a demanding manner!" He was startled by her anger. "You have no authority over me and no right to interfere in my business. If I wish to read on a subject of interest to me then it is my right to do so. If I choose not to become besotted with a friend of yours, then that is my right, also!"

"I say, Milly, I didn't mean to upset you," he said placatingly.

"Furthermore," she continued, "it would have been much more useful if you had made yourself available of all the facts in the matter before storming in here and pulling strips off me!"

"I was not – "

"Please do me the courtesy of not interrupting! For your information - although why you should be told I have no idea – but it is very well known by all in this household that Mr Farley and I have agreed that we will not suit and, in fact, I have known this for many weeks past and informed him of my feelings, or lack thereof, some time ago. If you had deigned to find out the truth of the matter before attacking me, you would also know that it is Susan who Mr Farley truly cares for and this very day has gained permission from father to marry her!"

This last piece of news came as a shock to Harry. "Susan?"

"Yes, Susan. Now, I would appreciate it if you removed yourself from my room. I do not wish to see you again, Harry."

"You know you don't mean that, Milly. I am sorry I misunderstood and tore at you like I did." One look at his sister's angry face showed him that his apology was not the least bit welcome.

"I will be going away tomorrow, Harry, and I would prefer not to see you until I return. I thought you, of all people, would understand my feelings and wishes when it came to the idea of marriage but you are just like everyone else."

She turned away from him and Harry knew he was dismissed.

He left the room, feeling like the worst kind of heel for his outburst. It was a habit of his to speak his mind before gaining all the facts but how was he to know that the tables had turned so much since his last visit with Farley? Speaking of which, he had better find him and find out what on earth possessed him to pine away for Susan instead of Millicent. With all her faults, she was far more intelligent and a lot more fun than Susan, who was barely out of the schoolroom. Goodness, she was only … was she really almost seventeen, already? No matter, he would find out what Farley could possibly be thinking!

Millicent snapped her book shut. For the first time that she could remember, the book on astronomy did nothing to ease her mood and she could not summon up even the flimsiest bit of excitement on the subject. To make matters worse, jealousy was niggling inside her at Susan's betrothal. Her sister had longed for this man for so long and now her dream had come true. Millicent knew that her own dream of wedding the man she loved was a fantasy that would never be realised.

She left her room, planning to take a walk before dinner.

Lunch had been a tense affair for her, although her father and siblings didn't seem to be aware of anything out of the ordinary. Millicent knew the evening meal would be the same and needed a fortifying walk before fronting her family again.

Her steps automatically turned in the direction of the library but she stopped and walked in the opposite direction. Books held no relief for her at present and a reminder of that would not be in any way helpful. There was a river not far from where she walked, she remembered. She had not walked along it often as she usually preferred the library or central park. Today would be different.

A small bridge crossed over the river and Millicent stopped halfway across and leaned on the edge of the wall. The water below was murky but ducks swam amongst the weeds and she found herself drawn to their activity. They glided effortlessly across the water, turning this way and that and occasionally dipping beneath the surface. If only life could be so carefree and smooth. Several ducklings lined up behind their mother, making their way to the other side of the water. One dragged quite a way behind but a few sharp quacks from its mother soon had it scurrying to catch up. Millicent watched with amusement as the mother made sure all her little ducklings were accounted for and marched them up the bank.

She turned away and continued walking across the bridge. The sun was beginning to dip in the sky, turning the air cool. She really should make her way back but the thought of facing the looks from her mother did not do anything to hasten her steps home.

Hearing her name called, Millicent looked up to see Amanda hurrying towards her.

"I am surprised to see you here," Amanda greeted.

"I could say the same for you," she replied with a smile, happy to see her friend.

"Yes, I imagine so. Are you heading back home? If so, we

can walk together.”

Millicent decided she could not put off her return any longer and joined Amanda as they walked back the way she had come.

“I have just been to visit an old friend of my mother’s,” Amanda said. “She has not been well and I was asked to take a hamper to her.”

“That was very kind of you.”

“I don’t mind to do it. She was very grateful for the help. So, tell me what happened after the ball. Did your mother realise at any time that Mr Farley was not going to be a match for you?”

Millicent couldn’t help the laugh that escaped her. “If she did not, she soon realised it this morning when he arrived at the house to call upon Susan and promptly asked my father for her hand in marriage.”

Amanda stopped in her tracks. “Surely you are joking.”

“No, unfortunately I am not.” She proceeded to tell Amanda of the meeting between her sister and Mr Farley during the ball and the events that followed. “Papa gave his permission, of course, but now mother is looking daggers at me because I failed to secure him for myself. One would think she would be happy that at least one daughter is to be wed. She tried to convince me to gain back the attentions of Richard and is now cross with me for not doing so.”

“I am stunned,” Amanda told her in a voice that matched her words. “We knew that Mr Farley was interested in Susan but who would have thought it had come to this.”

“I don’t think it occurred to him either until last night. It seems he realised his true affections for her and the rest, as people often say, is history.”

“Well, I am happy for Susan that she has managed to secure the man she loves. Is the wedding to be held soon?”

“It hasn’t been decided as yet but I expect they won’t want to wait too long.”

"You don't seem very happy for them, Millicent. What is troubling you?"

"Oh, but I am. I know Susan has dreamed of this for so long so I am very happy for her that her dream has come true."

"But?"

"There is nothing more."

Amanda threw her a look. "Millicent Addleton, how long have we known each other? I know there is something on your mind." When she remained silent, Amanda filled in the reasons for herself. "You wish it were you getting wed, don't you?"

"Of course not! You know how I feel about marrying," Millicent protested firmly.

"I believe that if a particular gentleman asked you to be his wife, you would think very differently."

Millicent's heart felt heavy but she would not admit to her true wish. Not to Amanda, not even to herself. "I am perfectly content with the choice I have made and, once this is all over and Susan is happily settled, I plan to immerse myself in my study of the stars. I have even thought that I will purchase a telescope which will allow me to see so far. I cannot wait for that day."

However, her excitement was very lack lustre and it did not go unnoticed by her friend. Amanda chose not to push her thoughts on the subject, though, and they walked arm in arm until they reached the turn off to Amanda's home.

"I could call on you tomorrow and we could go for a drive into the countryside. Perhaps we could even visit Aunty Mabel. I know she would love to see you again," suggested Amanda.

"Thank you but I have accepted an invitation from Juliette to spend a few days with her. We thought it would be a good way of avoiding any pressure mother would put on me to secure an offer following the ball. As it is, I do not think I can stay in my house much longer with mother accusing me as she is."

Amanda squeezed her arm. "I can imagine how difficult it

must be for you. Visiting Juliette is the perfect solution." After a short pause, she asked, "Will her brother be at home?"

Trying very hard to keep the disappointment out of her voice, Millicent said, "No, he will be out of town for several days. If he was going to be there, I would not have accepted the invitation."

"Send me a message when you return home and we can arrange an outing."

"You can be certain I will."

They said their farewells and continued to their respective homes. Millicent went directly to her room and had her maid begin packing for her trip. After making sure everything she wished to take would be included, she went downstairs to the drawing room.

Susan had returned and was looking through the latest women's magazine with Catherine. Mrs Addleton sat near the fire working on a piece of embroidery and looked up as Millicent entered.

"I am pleased to see you have returned, Millicent. Your sister wished to share her news with the entire family but, unfortunately, you chose to be absent."

"I did not know she would be making an announcement, mother. I believed she was out driving with Mr Farley and would not return until the afternoon."

Before Mrs Addleton could continue with her blame, Susan cut in with an overview of the day's events. "We had the most wonderful picnic, Millicent. Tristan drove me to a place where we could sit atop the hills beneath a shady tree and view the valley below. It was so peaceful and magical. I had such a pleasant day."

"Milly, isn't Susan's news exciting? Mama allowed her to tell us as soon as she arrived home and we were all filled with excitement for her. Weren't we Susan?" Catherine asked, turning to her sister beside her. "We are looking through the latest fashions to determine which style would best suit Susan. Come and see."

Millicent smiled at her excitement and wandered over to the settee. "Have you found anything that you like?"

Susan screwed up her face. "Not particularly. However, mama is taking me to see Madame Le Cruz tomorrow so that she can make me a wedding gown of the latest fashion. It will be very grand. Will you join us?"

"I am sure you will find just the thing. Unfortunately, I have accepted an invitation to visit Juliette for a few days and leave tomorrow."

"One would have thought your sister's wedding arrangements would come before a visit to a friend," Mrs Addleton put in from the sidelines.

"It is only a day of planning, Millicent, so there is really no need for you to come. I think a visit to Juliette is a much better idea."

It hadn't taken Susan long at all to understand the treatment Millicent was receiving from their mother since her engagement and knew it would do everyone the world of good if Millicent was absent for a few days. Besides, if she were to stay in the same house as Mr Westercott, who knew what news would be forthcoming at the end of her visit.

"It will only be Juliette and her mother at home so I have agreed to keep her company and it will give us the opportunity to have a prolonged visit. I am quite looking forward to it."

"Her brother and sisters will not be at home?" Catherine asked. "I do quite like her sisters."

"No, they will each be visiting various friends." Again that heaviness at the mention of Mr Westercott's absence. Millicent hoped by the end of the visit she would have overcome this unwanted emotion.

Chapter 27

Millicent arrived at the Westercott home late the next morning. As she stepped from the carriage, she was again struck by the beauty of her surroundings. Juliette hurried out to greet her and gave her the now expected hug in greeting.

"I am so pleased you came. I wasn't certain how things would be for you following the ball and was worried your mother might have convinced you to stay home in order to pursue a match."

Millicent rolled her eyes. "Juliette, there is so much to tell you!"

Intrigued, Juliette gave instructions for Millicent's bags to be taken to the rose guest room and then led her to her own room. Here she knew they would not be disturbed.

"Tell me what has happened," she said intently.

Millicent told her everything that had happened since the night of the ball. Juliette let out gasps throughout and stared wide-eyed at parts. When Millicent came to an end, Juliette let out a huge breath.

"You most certainly need to be away from your house at the moment. Imagine. Susan betrothed to Mr Farley! Forgive me for saying so, but I think it is most unfair of your mother to blame you as she has done. It has been clear to anyone who knows you well that you did not wish for a match during this season. While I can understand your dear parents' wish that you obtain one, I do think it unfair to blame you when one of the gentlemen offers for someone else."

"I completely agree but I think it will take some time before she forgives me for not trying harder. We both know I did not try at all."

"Does Amanda know that your mother urged you to reunite with Mr Jenson?"

Millicent nodded. "Yes but she also knows that I would never do so. Not that my mother was convinced so easily," she added ruefully.

"You poor dear," Juliette uttered, giving her friend a big hug. "Well, while you are here we will only speak of interesting things that do not involve unfair families or weddings."

Millicent let out a soft laugh and did feel better for having unburdened herself on her friend. They went to Millicent's room where Juliette helped her to unpack.

"Did your maid accompany you?" Juliette asked. In the excitement of finding out the news, she had completely forgotten about any additional staff.

"No, I chose not to bring her. There is too much risk of her reporting to mother on my activities here. Not that there will be anything much to report on but I do not want mother to be in any way involved in my visit. Does that make sense?"

"I understand completely and there was no need for her to come with you, in any case. I had already decided that Clara, my own maid, will be able to assist you with anything you need. She is a treasure and nothing is ever a problem for her. I am sure she will be quite happy to assist the both of us for a few days."

Both young ladies made their way downstairs where lunch was soon to be served. Following the meal, Juliette informed Millicent that they would spend a good part of the afternoon in her new garden. It was such a lovely day, Millicent was quite looking forward to being out of doors in this wonderful place.

By mid-afternoon, Millicent felt more like her old self. Working in the garden had been fun and both ladies had spent a large amount of their time laughing. Millicent had never planted anything in her life and her attempts had Juliette in tears much of the time. However, by the end of the afternoon, they had planted several bushes and arranged stone borders, and enjoyed a picnic of afternoon refreshments amongst the blooms.

"Thank you, Juliette," Millicent said as they were packing up to return to the house.

"For what?"

"For today. I was feeling a bit down in the dumps when I arrived but feel much better now."

"I am so pleased. It is surprising what digging around in the dirt can do for one's mood."

"Well, I don't know that I did much digging rather than making a huge mess, but I thoroughly enjoyed myself. Oh, I just realised I have not asked you about your Lord Shelton! How thoughtless of me."

"It is not at all thoughtless. You have had a lot of things on your mind."

"Well, now I have you and Lord Shelton on my mind. I saw you both, of course, at the ball."

"Yes, we danced several times. Edith teased me about it to the point where I was very glad when she left the house." She added shyly, "I think mother is expecting that he will make me an offer."

"Considering his high regard for you and his constant attention, she may be right."

Juliette smile and her cheeks turned very pink. "I don't like to raise my hopes but he did give me a hint that his feelings were very strong for me."

"My dear Juliette, how could he not love you? From my conversation with him that day I spent in his company, he only needs encouragement of your interest and affections. Once he is sure of this, I believe you will be swept off your feet."

Juliette smiled and hoped her friend's words were true. He had left to undertake business on his country estate that would keep him away for two weeks but, after that time, she felt certain she would know just where this relationship was headed. And she suspected very strongly it would involve wedding bells.

They continued to chatter and laugh all the way back to the house.

"My goodness, girls, look at the state of you both," said Mrs Westercott as they entered the house. "I will instruct the maids to bring bathtubs to both your rooms so you can clean up before dinner. Don't chatter for too long, now. We would hate to miss you at dinner."

"Yes, mother," Juliette said cheerily and led Millicent upstairs.

"Your mother is such a lovely lady," Millicent told her. "If I had walked into my home looking like this, I think mother would nearly faint."

Juliette laughed. "As children we often ventured into the house in a worse state that we are in today. Why, even mother has been known to get her hands dirty playing with us as children."

Millicent was amazed and was again glad she had come to the Westercott home.

Dinner was a quiet but friendly affair. Millicent was made to feel very welcome by Mrs Westercott.

"Millicent, I heard that your ball was a great success."

"Yes, I believe it was, Mrs Westercott. It was a very enjoyable evening."

"I was sorry I could not attend but Juliette told me so much that I felt as though I had been there. I was quite surprised when Jonathon offered to escort Juliette and very relieved. He is the most darling son and I can always rely on him when I cannot take Juliette to events as I should."

Millicent swallowed. "You are lucky to have a son who cares so much for you," she said politely.

"Oh, yes. I am truly blessed. Why, if it had not been for his kindness and thoughtfulness, well I don't know what would have become of us."

"I am sure we would have managed. Mother is very resourceful," Juliette said proudly. "However, Jonathon's assistance means so much to us all."

Millicent listened politely as they continued to talk of Jonathon Westercott but inside she was aching.

"I believe you shared a dance with Jonathon at the ball." Mrs Westercott's words almost had Millicent choking.

"Yes, we did," she managed to get out. She hoped her cheeks weren't as pink as they felt.

"He does not dance as often as I would like. He is an excellent dancer, though, did you not think?"

"Yes, very good."

"I am hopeful he finds a young lady who will inspire him to dance more often. It does everyone much good to twirl to the music." After a small silence, she startled Millicent by saying, "You have danced with Jonathon several times over the past weeks, from what I hear."

Millicent's eyes flicked between Mrs Westercott and Juliette. "I don't know if I would say it was several times. We have danced a few times, perhaps."

Mrs Westercott gave a satisfied nod and cut into her dessert.

Millicent's heart was racing. Was Mrs Westercott hinting at a relationship between herself and Jonathon because he danced with her more than once over the past several weeks? Or was she merely making conversation? Millicent glanced at Juliette and surprised a knowing look on her friend's face.

Thankfully, the servants came in at that moment to remove the plates and place fruit platters on the table, causing a lull in the conversation and hopefully a change of topic.

Following dinner, Juliette read from a novel that she and her mother were obviously part way through. It was one of those that Millicent's own sisters liked and, even though she was not partial to these stories, she enjoyed the evening. Mrs Westercott's obvious delight in the story drew Millicent in to the atmosphere. Juliette was a very good reader and was able to put just the right amount of feeling into the adventures and emotions of the heroine.

Later that night, Millicent left the curtains pulled back so she could gaze at the night sky as she lay in bed. The stars appeared brighter and no buildings hindered her view. Feeling more relaxed than she had in a while, she drifted off into a dreamless sleep.

*

The next day, Juliette arranged a ride with a picnic lunch to follow. Millicent was thankful her maid had thought to pack her riding habit and both ladies were soon cantering around the pond and across the hills. The Westercott grounds were more extensive than Millicent had thought and she enjoyed herself as they made their way across grassy land, through a small forest of trees, ending up at a small stream that trickled over boulders on the edge of the woods.

The setting was peaceful and Millicent fell in love with the spot instantly. If she lived here, she would come to this stream every day. Tying their horses to low hanging branches, they strolled beside the water inspecting every little wayward pool.

"Are you enjoying your visit, Millicent?" Juliette asked.

"Very much. You have such a beautiful home, Juliette, and such wonderful places to visit."

Juliette beamed. "I am so glad you like it here. I hoped you would."

"How could anyone not like it?"

They returned to where the horses were tied up and collected the small picnic basket and blanket. Finding a shady spot, they spread the blanket and began unpacking the food. They were both ravenous after riding for so long and made short work of the meal.

Relaxing afterwards, Juliette looked across at Millicent. "May I ask you a personal question, Millicent?"

"Of course."

"Are you in love with my brother?"

Millicent almost fell over, she was so startled. "Whatever makes you think such a thing?"

Juliette shrugged. "I see the way you look at him and your reaction to the mention of his name."

"Juliette, I think you are reading far too much into my reactions. I don't react in any way out of the ordinary and I certainly don't look at him in any special way." She turned away from Juliette, not wanting her to see her flushed cheeks.

"I don't mind if you do love him. In fact, I would be quite delighted to have you as a sister," Juliette said quietly.

"Juliette, that is such a lovely thing to say."

After a pause, she said. "You didn't answer my question, though."

Millicent flicked a glance at her and took a deep breath. "I cannot love any man."

Juliette picked up on her choice of words. "That does not mean that you do not love a man."

Millicent looked away again. Suddenly, there seemed to be a huge lump in her throat that she couldn't seem to move. She stood abruptly and walked a few steps away. Juliette was by her side moments later.

"I am sorry if I upset you, Millicent. I didn't mean to."

"No, you didn't upset me. Sometimes life just does not turn out how we expect. Or hope."

Juliette looped her arm through Millicent's as they strolled along. "If you did decide that you loved him, I think he would like to know of your feelings."

Millicent's breath seemed to catch in her throat. "What do you mean?"

"Just that I do not think he would be averse to a match."

For a brief moment, Millicent's hopes rose but she pushed them down. Regardless of their feelings, she had to stay true to her plan. If she was to continue her love of the stars and planets and spend her time studying them, then she could not become attached to any man. She would not lose her freedom to star gaze for anyone.

"Do you think we should make our way back?" Millicent asked, changing the subject.

Juliette followed her back to the horses. They packed up the picnic remains in silence and began their journey back home.

Despite her denials, Juliette knew how Millicent felt about her brother and was determined to bring about her happiness. A happiness that would not remove her friend's freedom that she clung to so tightly.

Chapter 28

Millicent had spent several relaxing and pleasant days at the Westercott home. Each day, she and Juliette had undertaken some activity whether it was riding or gardening or investigating the true extent of the property. Millicent had also spent more time at the little stream where she and Juliette had picnicked.

Susan had sent a message letting her know that mama had grown more accustomed to her engagement with Mr Farley and was now professing to any who would listen that she had known from the start that they would make a match of it. Mr Farley visited the house almost every day and Mrs Farley had called to welcome her to the family. Millicent breathed a sigh of relief. At least life should be somewhat easier when she returned home.

"Millicent, dear, are you ready?"

She put away the message and hurried down the stairs. "Yes, Mrs Westercott."

"Very good. Juliette will join us shortly. We can wait for her at the carriage."

Millicent followed her outside and climbed into the smart barouche. Juliette joined them moments later and they were on their way. One of the homes nearby was holding an open invitation to view their magnificent gardens and Mrs Westercott had not missed such a day since she had moved to the area. The artistry of the landscaping, she had told the girls, was so exquisite as to take one's breath away.

Ten minutes later, they were rolling to a stop at the designated entrance to the gardens. The three alighted and Mrs Westercott led them down the first of several paths. Millicent had to agree that the gardens were certainly exquisite. Ornately shaped hedges lined some pathways and colourful blooms created patterns in the open spaces. Mrs Westercott was breathless at the sight of some of the newer pieces of sculpture and took the girls on a meandering walk across the large lawn that displayed several life sized pieces.

Millicent was not overly fond of sculptures but Mrs Westercott's enthusiasm was hard to resist. She was passionate about most things that she was interested in and Millicent could understand that feeling. It was how she felt about the planets. Looking at the information sheet they had received on arrival, Mrs Westercott determined they would continue with a look at the newest exhibit.

"I believe this will be of great interest to you, Millicent," she said as she led them to an enclosed area. Hedges rose around them to a height of fifteen feet. Millicent was amazed at that fact alone. Moving further into the enclosure, it was soon possible to make out a pattern in the shrubbery and ivy was trained to create leads attaching different bushes. A raised platform was set aside in order to view the display from above and they climbed onto this and looked down.

Millicent caught her breath. Shrubbery and plants had been aligned in such a way as to depict the very planets in the heavens above them. It was just as she had seen in the books.

"I can see that you like it," Mrs Westercott said, smiling at her.

"It is beautiful," Millicent agreed.

"I knew you would think so which is why I especially wanted to bring you here. Juliette told me of your interest in the planets."

Millicent looked quickly at her friend.

"I knew mother would understand," Juliette told her quickly. "Forgive me for not asking you first."

"Yes, it is something we have known of for I don't know how many years," confirmed Mrs Westercott.

"You have?" Millicent asked surprised.

"Of course."

That was all that was said and Millicent didn't like to pry, though she was sorely tempted. To think there might be another woman with the same interest was more than she had ever hoped for. She would find a way to bring up the subject another time.

Nothing else they looked at during their visit could in any way compare to that one exhibit. Millicent was so pleased she had been able to attend the gardens and thanked Mrs Westercott as they made their way home.

"No thanks are needed, dear. I am pleased you found as much enjoyment in the gardens as I did."

Once back home, they freshened up and gathered in the small drawing room for afternoon tea. The maid brought in a pot of hot tea and a plate of biscuits.

"What part of the exhibition did you like best, Juliette?" Millicent asked her.

"The new seedling garden, of course. I felt somewhat superior as my seedlings are already much larger."

The laughter that this comment brought on continued for most of the afternoon. Mrs Westercott was a delight, as Millicent had already found out, and she felt a closer bond to Juliette than she had before. Her visit had been extended for another three days but then she must return home. Millicent would be sorry to say goodbye.

During dinner, Mrs Westercott made mention of a message she had received from Edith and Lilian. They were enjoying their visit and expected to return home by the week's end. Apparently, Lilian had caused quite a stir when she ventured to the kitchens and requested the cook show her how to make scones.

"Where does she come up with these things?" Mrs Westercott queried and Juliette told her of their recent visit to the tea shop where Lilian decided she needed to learn the art of scone making.

Mrs Westercott merely shook her head at the unusual interest of her young daughter.

"Millicent, if you wish to write a message to your mother, there is paper and ink in the study across the hall. You may feel free to make use of anything you wish. Consider yourself quite at home," Mrs Westercott invited.

"Thank you, Mrs Westercott. That is very kind of you." Millicent was touched by her kindness and open acceptance.

In her room later that night, Millicent expressed her thoughts to Juliette. "You are so lucky to have such a woman as your mother."

"Yes, she is very kind-hearted and giving. After the death of papa, she retreated within herself for a long time and we began to fear she would never be herself again. However, after a year of grieving she began to return to her usual high spirits and now enjoys every day. She often comments that one never knows when one's time will come to an end so we should make the most of every day."

"That sounds like a very good philosophy."

"It is one we should all make note of, I think."

Millicent didn't miss the hint contained in her words but chose to ignore it. She had made her choice and she had chosen the heavens.

"What would you like to do tomorrow?" Juliette asked.

"I had not thought of anything in particular. Although, I might write a letter to my mother. Susan wrote to tell me that mother has quite forgiven me and believes the match between her and Mr Farley was ordained."

"She probably believes the match was her own doing."

Millicent laughed. "You already know mother too well."

*

The next morning, Juliette had to run a few errands and so Millicent took advantage of Mrs Westercott's offer to write a letter home. First, a stroll in the gardens would be the thing. As she walked out of the front door, she stood for a few moments on the top step gazing over the view. It never ceased to move her. She had never felt such a connection to a property before.

She continued on to the garden and smiled when she walked past the newly planted section that she and Juliette had worked on. Her planting could easily be identified by the poorly placed seedlings and the few crooked sprouts. She was thankful that none of this would be noticeable once the plants grew to size. The gardens continued past the shade trees, around box hedges, and opened into a central court filled with dozens of blooms laid out in elegant patterns. Seats were spaced around the garden and Millicent lowered herself onto one.

Gazing at the flowers, her thoughts drifted over the events of the past months. She had not entered this season with much enthusiasm and, while her plan to remain single had worked, she was also happy in the fact that she had made new and treasured friendships. More recent times had been eventful with the soon-to-be announced match between her dear friend Amanda and Richard Jenson, and, of course, the match between her sister and Mr Farley. She had dealt with play acting, gossip and heartache and yet, in spite of it all, it had been a very interesting season so far. Soon it would be over and she would return to her books and daydreaming without any pressure from her mother. In fact, it seemed her mother had quite given up on the prospect of her gaining a match at all, if Susan's message was to be believed. Millicent could plan her future without any regret.

She stood and walked back towards the house. Juliette would return soon so it was time to write the letter home. She entered the house and stood looking down the hall, trying to remember which room was the study. She knew it was opposite the small drawing room but there was more than one room fitting this description.

A door stood slightly ajar so Millicent made her way to this room first. As she approached, she knocked incase the room was in use. Receiving no response, she slowly swung the door open. An object caught her eye and she moved in to take a closer look. It was a carving of an image she had seen in one of the library books of a planet with a ring extending around it. She let her gaze wander around the room and stared in amazement at what she saw. On the wall above her was a picture containing all of the planets she knew, and more. Various carvings and ornaments of different sizes were set about the room, all of which depicted one or several planets. The bookcase on her left was filled with scientific books, many of which held information on the galaxies and stars. She reached out instinctively to run her hands over them. Sitting in pride of place on top of the shelf was a gold telescope.

A sound had her turning around and she was startled to see Jonathon Westercott standing in the doorway.

"Mr Westercott. I did not expect to see you here," she stammered.

"Good morning, Miss Addleton. My business was completed sooner than expected. I did not expect to find you here, either."

"Mrs Westercott kindly invited me to stay a few more days. She has been the most charming hostess."

"Yes, she does like to entertain," he agreed, his voice taking on a warmer tinge at the mention of his mother.

"I am sorry if I am intruding. I was looking for the study and the door was open ..."

"You have found the study. Is there something I can assist you with?"

"No. I was merely going to write a letter but it can wait until another time." She hesitated for a few seconds and then walked towards the door.

"Aren't you interested in what you see?" he asked.

She looked at him, startled. "Excuse me?"

He gestured to the room. "I know you are interested in what lies above the heavens. This room must hold great interest for you."

"I don't know what gave you that impression but I assure you it is of little interest to me."

"A pity. I find it very intriguing myself and had hoped to show you some of my collection, as you are in the room."

She looked around, her eyes wide. "This is all yours?"

"It is."

She turned back into the room and looked more closely at the contents. "Your book collection on the subject is much better than the library's," she commented, looking longingly at the shelves.

"You are welcome to borrow any of the books you see," he offered.

"Thank you but that won't be necessary. As I said, the subject holds little interest for me. I will leave you to your business," she said and went to move past him.

He reached out to stop her without actually touching her. "Why do you deny your interest? I have twice found you reading books on the subject and even helped you to borrow one. I would think you would be glad to admit to such an interest."

Millicent let out a short laugh. "Admit such a thing? Do you know what society thinks of women who show an interest in anything other than fashion, housekeeping or gardening?"

"I don't care what society thinks. Personally, I find it intriguing. I have never met a woman with such an interest before. I am curious to know how you came to find a passion for the stars."

One look at his face and she knew she could not continue denying it. She turned and walked towards the desk. As she turned back to face him, she looked into a corner of the room not yet noticed. Her eyes opened wide when she saw the large telescope standing on the floor. When tilted upright, it must have stood over six feet tall.

Jonathon followed her gaze and walked towards it. "This is my prize possession. I set it up outside on a clear night and I can see several planets quite clearly."

"You can?" she asked, eager to hear more.

"Yes. It is the most amazing thing. I have even watched a falling star. It is a sight I will never forget. If the weather is clear tonight, would you care to join me in some star gazing?"

Her eyes glowed at the prospect. How she would love such an opportunity. But spending an evening alone beneath the stars with Jonathon Westercott was not something she should even contemplate so she thanked him but declined the invitation.

"Suit yourself but if you change your mind you will know where to find me," he said, ignoring his disappointment.

She nodded and with one last look of longing at the large telescope, she moved towards the door.

"Wait," he called. He strode to the bookshelf and then held out a book for her. "If you do not wish to see the stars tonight, you might like to read about them. I know the library does not stock this volume. It is a new publication and one I think you will enjoy."

She hesitated but the prospect of a new volume on the subject was too tempting to turn down. She reached out to take the offered book. "Thank you."

He caught her hand in his. "Remember, if you change your mind and wish to see the real thing, meet me in the garden at ten o'clock this evening."

Millicent found it difficult to breathe while her hand was held firmly in his. She raised her eyes to his and felt the same turmoil inside that she had during their dance at the ball.

"Will you?"

Her confusion showed in her face.

"Join me tonight, I wonder," he continued. When she made no answer, he said softly, "I hope so." Then he placed the book in her hand and stepped back.

Millicent looked at the book, feeling somewhat dazed. With a slight shake of her head, she turned and hurried from the room.

Chapter 29

"Millicent, dear, did you venture into the study today?" asked Mrs Westercott during lunch.

"Yes, I did," she replied, wondering if the lady knew of her encounter with her son.

"I can imagine your surprise when you saw Jonathon's collection. I knew you would enjoy the room. I, myself, do not have a great interest in the subject but it pleases me to know that there is a woman who can join him in his passion."

Millicent didn't know what to say to that.

"I did offer to show Miss Addleton the stars tonight through the telescope but she has declined," came a voice from the doorway. They all turned as Jonathon entered the room.

"Jonathon! I did not expect to see you so soon," cried Mrs Westercott, rising to kiss his cheek. It was clear how much she cared for her son.

"I was able to finish my business early. The skies are meant to be completely clear tonight so I could not pass up such an opportunity to set up the telescope. I hurried home as quickly as I could."

Mrs Westercott laughed softly. "You and your stars. I was just saying to Miss Addleton how lovely it is to have found a young lady who can share your interest."

Jonathon glanced at her and Millicent felt her cheeks grow pink. She was beginning to suspect that Mrs Westercott had a hobby she was previously unaware of. Matchmaking!

"I was as surprised as you, mother. The first time I met Miss Addleton, she was reading a book on planets."

"How wonderful. I can imagine you talked for quite some time on the subject."

"No. We have not talked at all on the subject. At the time, Miss Addleton did her best to hide the book from my notice."

Mrs Westercott looked at Millicent. "Oh, my dear, why would you not discuss it with Jonathon? He is very knowledgeable on the subject and would have been delighted to share such a special interest."

Millicent felt she should say something but was finding it hard to think clearly. "I am sure he is, Mrs Westercott," she began, although she had no idea of the extent of his knowledge. "However, at the time I did not know of Mr Westercott's interest in the subject. Not many people are, you know."

"There are more than you would think," Jonathon told her.

"Perhaps amongst the male population but I have not found another woman who studies the planets. Not in this area, in any case."

"That is likely true," he agreed. "Perhaps now that we are all aware of your interest in the subject and there is no reason to hide it from us, you will find it possible to have discussions on the matter. I would be pleased to show you my collection and hear your thoughts."

Millicent glanced at Juliette. She smiled at Millicent, obviously happy at the way the conversation was turning.

"Yes, dear, how could you miss such an opportunity!" exclaimed Mrs Westercott. "When lunch is finished, why don't you show her around, Jonathon? I have some things to discuss with Juliette so Millicent will have some free time." She turned to Millicent. "I am so excited for you. I can imagine you did not think when you accepted Juliette's invitation that you would find such a prize in our home."

Millicent could only murmur her agreement to the comment. Inside she was a mess. She didn't know quite how it had happened but in a few short minutes she had been manoeuvred into spending time alone with Jonathon Westercott in his study.

Lunch was almost over when Mrs Westercott struck again. "Millicent, dear, make sure you take a warm cloak with you when you join Jonathon tonight with the telescope. It does get quite cool in the evening."

"But I am not joining him," she said quickly.

"Of course you are, dear. To miss such an opportunity is unthinkable! I have looked through it myself and if I found it exciting, without being very much interested in the subject, then you, my dear, will be beside yourself with joy. See if I am not right."

Millicent had fallen neatly into the trap. Not only was she to spend an hour or so in the study with Jonathon, the thought of which was already making her pulse race, she was also to spend who knew how long in the gardens with him that evening. Both Westercott women looked very pleased with themselves and Millicent excused herself from the table with a murmured excuse. She needed to get herself under control before she entered the study.

From her room, she had a view across green pastures and the woods in the distance. Millicent had stood there for the past hour trying to decide what to do. She had contemplated packing her bags and returning home but that would be hard to explain. It would also appear rude to her hostess and she could not do that. But the thought of spending time in the company of Jonathon had her nerves jittering. Realising she could not put it off any longer, she turned from the window and went to the study.

The door was open as she approached and she saw him standing by the desk. He turned when she entered and looked at her for a few moments before speaking.

"I wasn't certain you would come."

"It seemed expected."

"My mother has a way of making things happen," he mused.

Millicent stood quietly by the door. This was more uncomfortable than she had imagined. And, surprisingly, he seemed to feel it as well. She glanced around the room, wondering if she should turn around and leave.

He became brisk and motioned for her to join him near a set of shelves. She hadn't noticed them on her previous visit to the room and soon found herself immersed in the subject and forgot all about her discomfort. Lined up in a neat order were painted ornaments of all known planets in their correct order. Beneath each one was a small plaque which noted the name of the planet and a few points of information. Millicent made her way along the shelf, spending several minutes admiring the detail of each one.

By the time that collection had been viewed, they were both more at ease and focused on the subject in more detail.

Jonathon became excited as he showed Millicent around his collection. He had never before shown it to someone with as much interest as himself. To finally share his passion with someone who fully understood was more uplifting than he could have imagined.

He pulled out book after book and showed her earlier drawings and then more detailed ones as scientific knowledge progressed. Millicent was amazed at the difference that a short amount of time could make to the detail depicted.

Millicent realised she had enjoyed every minute of her time in the study – apart from the initial discomfort. The time had flown and she was surprised to learn they had been in there for two hours.

"Thank you for sharing your collection with me," she said.

"It was my pleasure. It certainly makes a difference when the person being shown is genuinely interested." He smiled down at her. "There is one more thing I would like to show you." He walked behind the desk and reached into the large bottom drawer. When he returned to her, he was holding a box in his hands. Millicent recognised it instantly. "Last time I gave this to you, it was returned. I am hoping it will not be this time," he said, holding the box towards her.

Millicent began to shake her head. "Mr Westercott ..."

"It is yours. You may leave it here if you wish but it will stay hidden in the bottom of the drawer. I would much prefer to know you are using it and enjoying the gift."

She was sorely tempted to take it but it was not right to accept such a gift from him. After seeing his collection, she could understand why he was so eager for her to take it. She didn't know what she should do.

"Might I make a suggestion?"

She nodded.

"You will be here for another few days. You could take this and use it while you are here and then, when it is time for you to return home, you can decide whether to take it with you."

That sounded like a compromise Millicent could live with. Of course, she could not take it home with her but there was no reason she could not use it even once while she was here. She took the box and removed the lid. The telescope sat neatly on its cushion as she had last seen it. A piece of paper sat on top and she realised it was the note she had sent along with it. She replaced the lid and looked at him. "Thank you."

"You are welcome."

She stood looking at him, feeling as if she should say more but not sure what to say.

"Goodbye," she finally said and left the room.

Mrs Westercott entered the room, glancing curiously at her son.

"I just saw Millicent running up the stairs. What was it you gave her?" she asked.

"A telescope."

"Oh, Jonathon, what a thoughtful gift. Was it from your collection?"

"No, I purchased it some time ago but she would not accept it. I suggested she use it while she is here and then decide if she wishes to accept it and keep it."

He spoke in a matter-of-fact manner, walking about the room as he put away parts of his collection. He didn't fool his mother one bit.

"You really feel she is the one?" she asked gently.

He smiled briefly. His mother was far too observant. "I have never known a woman who is as passionate about the planets as I am."

"Yes, that information caught my attention. Apart from her interest, are her other qualities to your liking?"

"Mother, I do not think this is a conversation a man usually has with his mother."

"Perhaps not but I know more than you think, dear." She reached out and patted his cheek. "I am sure she will come to feel the same way about you. If she hasn't already," she added knowingly.

Then she left the room and Jonathon watched her go with a thoughtful expression on his face.

Juliette found Millicent in her room a short time later.

"Millicent, would you like to go riding?"

She nodded absently. "That sounds nice."

"What are you holding?" Millicent showed her the telescope. "Did Jonathon give you that?" At Millicent's nod, Juliette sat down beside her. "He has never given anyone such a gift before," she said quietly.

"That you are aware of."

"No, I know he has not. He knows very few people who are as interested in the stars as he is and he always says he would not waste such a gift on anyone. For you he has changed his thinking."

"It is more a loan than a gift," Millicent told her. "I will return it when I leave here."

"You won't accept his gift?"

Millicent looked at her. "Juliette, it is not right to accept such a gift from a man. I could not possibly."

Juliette did not miss the wistfulness in her voice.

The box lay discarded on the bed and Juliette noticed a piece of paper resting inside. She picked it up and began to read. Then she looked at Millicent. "When did he give you this telescope?"

"Not long ago, in the study."

Juliette held out the note. "I mean, when did he first give you this gift."

Millicent looked at the note and turned away. "It doesn't matter. I could not accept it then and I cannot accept it now."

Juliette carefully folded the note and placed it back in the box. "Do you really think you can leave it behind when you return home?"

"I must. Now, I believe you said something about riding," she said, changing the subject.

"I thought we could take a picnic lunch and ride to the stream. I know how much you like it there."

"That sounds perfect."

Half an hour later, the two young ladies rode off, blanket and hamper in hand.

"They are going to the stream," Mrs Westercott told her son as he stood on the top step watching them ride into the distance.

"I am sure they will have a nice time," he said.

"Did you know that out of all the places Millicent has been to since her arrival, the stream is her most favourite place?"

Jonathon looked at her. "How do you know?"

"She has said so many times. If she were able, she would visit it every day." She watched his face as he turned back towards the riders. "It seems the planets are not the only interest you both have in common."

Jonathon went inside and closed the door behind him in the study. Ever since he had first discovered the stream, it had been his favourite spot to visit. He often went there just for the sheer peace and beauty of the place. Sitting next to the trickling waters helped to clear his head and work through any problems or decisions he needed to make. It seemed trivial but he felt a swell of pleasure to think that Millicent felt the same about his special place.

"Edith and Lilian arrive home tomorrow. They will be so pleased that they did not miss seeing you," Juliette said as they rode slowly back to the house.

"I will be happy to see them, also. I wonder if Lilian has been terrorising the cook any further?" Millicent laughed.

"No doubt. I do know that mother has instructed our own cook to teach Lilian anything she wishes to know."

Millicent looked at her in surprise. "What will people think when they hear that?"

"Mother doesn't care what people think. She cares more for her children and making them happy and if mingling with the staff and learning culinary skills is what will make Lilian happy, then so be it."

"She is a remarkable woman."

"She told me that you are welcome to visit here any time you like. I think she is quite excited at the fact that you have a strong interest in the stars."

"She doesn't, though, so that should not have any bearing on my visits," Millicent said carefully.

"No, but it means that Jonathon will have someone to talk to about it and, therefore, she won't have to listen to things that are over her head. Mother loves her children dearly and encourages Jonathon in his passion but, as you can imagine, sometimes it is hard to remain focused when someone is talking about a subject that is hard to understand. So, in you she has a saviour on many levels."

"Juliette, if I visit it will be to see you, not to spend time with Jona ... with Mr Westercott."

"I don't know why you don't just call him Jonathon, especially while you are here. We don't stand on ceremony. You may have noticed we are quite informal."

"I am quite happy to call him Mr Westercott, as I should. The fact remains, my visits are not designed to spend time in his company. I hope your mother does not expect that of me."

"Oh, I am sure she understands this but on the off chance he is home and wishes to discuss it, and you are here, then it will be helpful to her," Juliette said airily. "We are almost home. I wonder what cook can put together for afternoon tea. I am quite starved!"

Millicent felt a touch of concern as they rode towards the stables. She felt the matchmaking fingers of Mrs Westercott again at work.

They were enjoying a cup of hot tea when Mrs Westercott joined them in the drawing room. "Did you girls have a nice time at the stream?"

"Yes," they replied in unison.

"Wonderful. It is such a lovely spot. I know Jonathon goes there almost every day." Millicent almost choked on her tea. "I don't know if I ever told you that it is his favourite place?" she asked Millicent.

"No, I don't believe you mentioned it."

"You have such similar interests. It's difficult to find."

Millicent looked to Juliette for help. "Mother, how was your day?" she asked, trying to steer the conversation away from Millicent.

"Oh, I had a lovely day. Jonathon showed me a new addition to his collection. He most likely showed it to you, Millicent, and you would have understood all he said but I did find myself quite out of my depth. But we had a lovely chat. I believe he gave you a telescope, dear. It is not often he passes on something like that to anyone so I do hope you treasure it as much as he would. Which I am sure you would."

Millicent had placed her cup back on the table. She didn't dare risk taking a sip of the tea or she would surely choke on it. Mrs Westercott was barely hiding her hopes now and Millicent was feeling a little closed in. Juliette had tried to help but there was no stopping this woman when she was set on securing her children's happiness. Why she thought she would be a means to that, Millicent did not know, but she was beginning to think it was time she returned home.

"Juliette," she began. "I have had the most wonderful time here with you but I will be returning home this afternoon."

"Millicent, so soon? But you are meant to stay another two days yet. Has something happened at home?" Juliette was obviously disappointed.

"No, everything is well at home as far as I know. They did expect me home yesterday and, as I haven't had a chance to send off a letter to my mother, she may be worried."

It sounded like a poor excuse and it was clear Juliette thought the same. "Please stay," she urged quietly. "I promise I will make her stop."

"What are you girls whispering about? Now, Millicent, I am sure your dear mother will be more than happy for you to continue here a little longer. Besides, you are star gazing tonight. Such a terrible shame to miss such an opportunity."

Millicent looked helplessly at Juliette. At the same time, the thought of being able to see the stars and planets for real gave her a lift of excitement. "I will stay to see the stars," she agreed. Then softly to Juliette, she added, "But please speak to your mother. I know she means well but she must be told that your brother and I will never be a couple."

"If you say so."

"Juliette!" she hissed.

"Alright. Alright. I will tell her but I don't know that she will believe me."

"I cannot hear what you are saying, girls. Please speak up when I am in the room, I beg of you. Millicent, I am pleased to know you will stay for the viewing. You may even see a shooting star! I hear that is most exciting."

Chapter 30

Dinner was tense. Millicent had to force the food down her throat and pretend everything was normal but all she could think of was the appointment she had with Jonathon later that evening. He sat at the head of the table and she barely heard any of the conversation. Thankfully, Mrs Westercott had not said anything even hinting at a connection between them both so Juliette must have been able to make her understand.

Finding out that Jonathon had the same passion for the heavens that she did had affected her deeply. In all this time, she had decided to remain single because she knew that there was no man who would allow her to continue her study of the stars once married. Now, to find she had been wrong and that such a man did exist made her question her decision. Not to mention, that particular man just happened to be the one she had fallen hopelessly in love with! It was the perfect solution, except she was fairly certain he did not return her affection. Oh, he liked her well enough if their time in the study was any indication. Had even hinted at more, if she really thought about it. But love? No, she didn't believe he felt nearly as strongly for her as she did for him and that was the problem.

For so long she had planned never to marry and now that she was changing her mind, she realised that if she did marry it would have to be with a man who loved her in return. Marrying someone just because he shared her passion in the stars was not conducive to a happy life.

Life had become far more confusing than she had ever imagined.

"Millicent?"

She looked up to find them all looking at her and realised she had missed part of a conversation. "I am sorry. What was the question?"

"I was merely wondering if you were looking forward to your viewing tonight," Mrs Westercott repeated with a smile.

"Oh. Yes. Of course."

"Wonderful. The weather looks like it will be perfect for the event. Juliette has a warm coat you can borrow so you don't get chilled."

"Thank you," she murmured. She glanced at Jonathon and he was looking at her with a glint that she could not interpret.

She was dreading this evening.

She was excited about this evening.

She wished the evening was already over.

*

Several lanterns stood at the front door along with blankets and a small hamper. Millicent looked at it in surprise.

"We cannot sit on the dew wet grass and the lanterns will help us to find our way. Supper to quieten my grumbling stomach," he added, holding up the hamper.

She smiled briefly and then followed him and the servants from the house. The servants set out the blankets and placed the lanterns at intervals along the ground. The telescope was already in place and directed at the sky. Millicent felt the stirrings of excitement replace her apprehension. She looked up to see the stars winking clearly in the night sky. Very soon she would see them up close.

The servants returned to the house and Jonathon wasted no time in chit chat. He was looking through the telescope and turning knobs before they had even reached the house. With a sound of satisfaction, he lifted his head from the viewing piece and smiled at her.

"It is time for your first viewing, Miss Addleton."

She stepped forward, her heart beating with excitement. He gave her instructions for looking into the telescope and making any adjustments and then she was looking in amazement at the heavens above. It was more beautiful than she had ever imagined. Even more beautiful than the pictures she had seen in the new volume she had read earlier that day.

She let out her breath in a long sigh. "It is beautiful," she breathed.

"Move it this way," he said and gently guided the telescope to aim further to the right. Before her eyes was the moon as clear as day. She could see more detail than she could have ever imagined. It glowed down at her and she was mesmerised. She lifted her head from the telescope and looked at the moon with her naked eye. Then she looked at it through the lens to gauge the full effect of the magnification.

"I can hardly believe what I am seeing," she whispered. She stood suddenly and turned to him. "Thank you. Thank you so much. I never hoped to see anything like this. I dreamed, of course, but never thought it would happen."

He smiled at her excitement, filled with pleasure at giving her this gift. "There is more," he told her intriguingly.

Millicent didn't think anything could surpass what she had just seen. She was wrong. When she next looked through the telescope, she was looking at a large planet tinged with shadows of colour and light. She felt as though if she reached out she could touch it.

She looked at Jonathon. Words failed her. In a rush of what she later referred to as insanity, Millicent threw her arms around him and hugged. "I don't know how I can ever thank you."

Jonathon was completely surprised by her actions but not at all unhappy. He took advantage of this opportunity and wrapped his arms around her. For so long he had dreamed of holding her in such a way. All too short, the moment was over.

Millicent came to her senses and blushed scarlet as she realised what she had done. She jumped back several feet and looked at him, horrified by her actions. "Please forgive me. I don't know what came over me. I am terribly sorry."

"There is no need to apologise."

"Oh, but there is. What must you think of me!"

What he thought was that he wanted her back in his arms and what he thought was that he did not want to hear any more apologies for what, to him, had been a very pleasant experience. He turned back to the telescope.

"Take a closer look," he said. "I have adjusted the sight to give you an even clearer view."

Millicent hesitated. How could he be so calm when her pulse was beating a mile a minute? He stepped back to allow her clear access to the view piece. She stepped towards it but her excitement had lessened considerably. She was so mortified by her actions it was hard to focus on the view in front of her. The change of focus on the planet did bring it into clearer view, though, and she could not help but appreciate it.

She sat on the blanket and left Jonathon to view the heavens for himself. She was quite content for the moment to look at the stars from the ground. It was so much clearer than the view she had from her room at home. She was startled when he suddenly called for her to look quickly through the telescope.

"Hurry, you will miss it," he urged.

She scrambled to her feet and allowed him to help her adjust the view. She gasped as she watched a shooting star trail across the sky. It was so clear she could see the trail of what looked like fire. The books had come nowhere near to describing the true beauty of this event.

"I had no idea that is what a shooting star truly looked like," she said in awe.

"It is not often one occurs at just the right time. You are privileged tonight."

"Oh, you missed it," she exclaimed, feeling bad for taking up the telescope.

"I have seen them before. It is said they show only for special moments. I am glad one showed itself tonight just for you."

"So am I," she replied, unable to hide her smile of pleasure.

"Would you care for something to eat?" he suggested and opened the hamper.

Millicent lowered herself to the blanket and took a piece of cheese. "How often do you do this?"

"Look at the stars? As often as I can. Sometimes several times a week."

"You are very lucky. I envy you."

"Now that you have experienced this for yourself, I hope you reconsider keeping the gift I gave you."

She longed to keep it, especially now, but how would she explain such a gift to her parents? "I am not sure…" she began.

"I wish you would. I purchased it especially for you. There is nobody else who will use it."

She looked at him. He was looking at her in such a way that made it almost impossible for her to breathe.

"Mr Westercott," she began, not really knowing what she wanted to say. Not even sure if she could utter more than a few words.

"Miss Addleton."

She opened her mouth to speak but nothing came out. She had to get away. She had to go back inside. This was madness, being alone out here with him. She rose to her feet and turned away. "I must go," she murmured.

"Wait." He was beside her in seconds. "Must you leave? We have not even viewed half the treasures that lay above us."

"I have seen so much. I don't know how anything more can compare," she said softly, not knowing if she believed her own words.

"I would enjoy showing you the rest of it."

"Mr Westercott," she said, turning to face him.

"Jonathon."

"Pardon?"

"I would be pleased if you would call me Jonathon," he told her.

"I could not," she uttered, shaking her head.

"I am sure you could. It is quite an easy name to say," he said lightly.

She looked down at her hands. This had been a mistake. She should not have come here tonight. Because, now that she was here, in truth she did not want to leave him. But she had to.

His hands reached out to hold hers. "Millicent."

And it sounded so wonderful to hear her name on his lips. She looked at him, knowing that she was not going anywhere. He took a step closer.

"Millicent," he said again and it sounded like a caress to her ears.

"I should … We shouldn't …" She had no idea what it was she was trying to say.

"You must know how I feel about you," he said softly. Her eyes opened wide. He smiled at her surprise. "Perhaps you don't." He brushed a dark curl from her face. "Do you know what I thought when I first saw you in the park? There you were sitting alone beneath a tree reading a book on astronomy. I was surprised and very intrigued. I thought now here was a woman after my own heart. You took a piece of it with you that very day," he admitted.

Millicent could hardly believe what she was hearing. "I did?"

He nodded. "It took me quite by surprise. From that day, I took every opportunity to see you. Things took a turn that I didn't quite expect," he said ruefully, "but, despite it all, I never stopped caring about you. I had hoped my gift would have shown you how I felt. But you returned it."

"I am sorry," she whispered. And she was sorry that her actions had seemed to cause him sorrow.

"You have no need to apologise to me," he told her gently. He took a deep breath. "Do you think that there is a chance that you will come to care for me? I know this is a shock for you and perhaps my timing could be better but I have never shared a night like this with a woman before. There is no other woman like you. I could see myself spending every night gazing at the stars with you by my side."

Millicent couldn't breathe. She was certain her hearing was impaired. He could not possibly be asking her what she thought he was about to ask her. She shook her head.

He took that as her answer. "I see." He let his arms slowly drop to his sides. "It was a false hope. I am sorry if I made you uncomfortable."

His voice was quiet in the stillness of the night and Millicent tried to focus on what he was saying. She shook her head again. "You misunderstand," she managed to get out.

"I do?"

"Are you saying … Am I to understand …" She swallowed. "Mr Westercott."

"Jonathon," he urged softly.

She swallowed again. "Jonathon. Are you asking me …?" She couldn't finish the sentence. If she had misunderstood him it would make things extremely awkward. She had never felt quite so not in control of herself before.

"Millicent. Do you care for me?" he asked, not daring to raise his hopes. She looked at him and nodded. He took her hands in his. "Do you think there will ever be a time that you could love me as I do you?"

A lump formed in her throat. "You love me?"

He let out a soft laugh. "Have I not been telling you that for these past minutes and more?"

"You didn't use those words precisely."

"What a fool I am. Here I have been rambling without getting to the point. Millicent Addleton, I love you with all my heart. More than even the stars above. Will you do me the great honour of becoming my wife?"

Millicent didn't think she could ever be happier than this very moment. Everything she had dared to dream was coming true. She had found the perfect man for her who shared her passion for the stars and loved her as much as she did him. Her life was complete.

"Millicent?"

"Yes?"

"Dearest, you have not answered me."

"Oh. I was lost in my thoughts, wondering how I could have become so lucky in so short a time. My answer, dearest Jonathon, is yes. Most definitely, yes."

"And do you love me?" he murmured, gathering her close.

She smiled tenderly. "More than the heavens above."

As his lips met hers, she forgot all about the stars, finding heaven in his arms instead.

Neither of them noticed the second shooting star streaking across the sky just for them.

Epilogue

To say Mrs Addleton was overjoyed at the news would have been the understatement of the year.

When Millicent had arrived home under the escort of Jonathon Westercott, she never imagined the reasons why. When Mr Westercott immediately requested a meeting with Mr Addleton, her hopes grew. When the two men emerged from their meeting and the announcement was made, Mrs Addleton was almost faint with joy.

Of course, to all who asked she told them that she had known, simply *known*, that the two would make a match of it from the very start!

Mrs Westercott, in contrast, had been quietly delighted when at breakfast the morning after the star gazing Jonathon and Millicent had stood before her and announced their engagement. It had been what she had hoped for since learning of their shared passion for the stars. She had hugged them both and wished them the best of happiness before ordering a special luncheon for that day. Juliette had been thrilled, as had her sisters when they returned home and heard the news.

Millicent stood on the top step of her new home looking at the view that had called to her so long ago. So much had happened in the past month. She was now Mrs Jonathon Westercott. Susan was engaged to be married to Mr Tristan Farley. Amanda and Richard had announced their engagement, much to the surprise of many unsuspecting people. And the wonderful Lord Shelton had proposed to Juliette not two nights ago. It was truly a wonderful and happy season for all.

As for Millicent, she was so filled with happiness she could barely take in anything that anyone said or did. Her thoughts were filled with Jonathon and their future together. It surpassed all her dreams. And to add more excitement, her dearest man had informed her that he had commissioned the purchase of a very large telescope which he would be installing in the new building that was underway, all especially for her!

She turned as her new husband wrapped his arms around her. She had wished upon the stars and her dreams had all come true.

The End

ABOUT THE AUTHOR

Elizabeth Jayne lives north of Sydney, Australia, close to tranquil lakes and sandy beaches. She began writing after raising her family and has since written several historical romance novels. She loves immersing herself in her characters' lives and hopes you enjoy reading their stories as much as she enjoys writing them.

OTHER BOOKS BY THIS AUTHOR

Threads of Time
Love across the centuries - When Julianna finds herself transported two hundred years into the past, she must learn how to live in this strange new world while trying to find her way back home to the present. But William has her questioning where her heart truly lies – a decision that could change her life forever.

Rogue
Love and betrayal on the high seas - Samantha despises arrogant men. Jake is adamant no woman belongs on his ship. When they are thrown together for several weeks, it's not just the weather that turns stormy.

Bertie
Waiting for a sign - Bertie will barely consider an outing with a gentleman or to a ball without a sign to confirm it is the right move. Signs put her in the path of one man, but her heart is drawn to another. Which sign should she follow?

Jocelyn
Danger and forbidden romance – Jocelyn tries to save her friend from a disastrous betrothal. Things take an unexpected turn and she is drawn into the dangerous mission of Sir Gaden as he fends off threats to overthrow the king. Everything is at risk – her life, her reputation and, above all, her heart.

*

Website: www.elizabethjayneauthor.com/books
Facebook: facebook.com/ElizabethJayne.Author